"I was pregnant. I couldn't find the father,"

Kendra said in a stark, unemotional tone.

The stranger on her doorstep seemed to absorb the accusation behind her words before saying, "If I'd known— You should have told me you were pregnant."

"Told you? I should have *told you?* Just whom would I have told? Some anonymous stranger on Santa Estella?"

"No. Daniel Benton Delligatti," he said, properly introducing himself three years too late.

"And who the hell is Daniel Delligatti? I know nothing about you."

"You know the most important things about me, like I know the most important things about you, Kendra. You learned them during that hurricane. You learned—"

"Mommy?"

The small, sleepy voice stopped them on identical indrawn breaths. Their eyes met.

Then Daniel Delligatti turned to see his son for the very first time.

Dear Reader,

Welcome back to Special Edition, where a month of spellbinding reading awaits you with a wonderful lineup of sophisticated, compelling August romances!

In bestselling author Jodi O'Donnell's memorable THAT'S MY BABY! story, *When Baby Was Born,* a pregnant woman with amnesia meets a cowboy she'll never forget! Beloved author Ginna Gray sweeps us away with another installment of her miniseries, A FAMILY BOND. In her emotional book *In Search of Dreams,* a woman with a scandalous past tries to say no to the man who vows to be in her future. Do you think a reunion that takes seventeen years to happen is worth waiting for? We're sure you'll say yes when you read *When Love Walks In,* Suzanne Carey's poignant story about a long-ago teenage passion that is rekindled—then a secret is exposed. When the hero of Carole Halston's *Because of the Twins...* needs help caring for his instant brood, the last thing he expects is a woman who turns his thoughts to matrimonial matters, too! Also this month is Jean Brashear's *Texas Royalty,* in which a tough, once-burned P.I. seeks revenge on the society girl who had betrayed him—until she manages to rekindle his desires *again!* And finally, Patricia McLinn kicks off her compelling new miniseries, A PLACE CALLED HOME, with *Lost-And-Found Groom,* about a treacherous hurricane that brings two people together for one passionate live-or-die night—then that remembered passion threatens to storm their emotional fortresses once and for all....

We hope you enjoy this book and the other unforgettable stories Special Edition is happy to bring you this month and all year long during Silhouette's 20th Anniversary celebration!

All the best,

Karen Taylor Richman
Senior Editor

Please address questions and book requests to:
Silhouette Reader Service
U.S.: 3010 Walden Ave., P.O. Box 1325, Buffalo, NY 14269
Canadian: P.O. Box 609, Fort Erie, Ont. L2A 5X3

PATRICIA McLINN
LOST-AND-FOUND GROOM

Silhouette®

SPECIAL EDITION®

Published by Silhouette Books
America's Publisher of Contemporary Romance

To Celeste Hamilton and J.P., who have the wisdom
to know the right words to say at the right time,
and the unfailing generosity to always share those words.

The author is very grateful to pilots Abbie Fridell and
Tom Buckman for their generosity and insights in answering
her many questions. They truly helped this story take off.

And many thanks to Jenni Sapp for her winning contest entry
that gave this book a name.

 SILHOUETTE BOOKS

ISBN 0-373-24344-8

LOST-AND-FOUND GROOM

Copyright © 2000 by Patricia McLaughlin

PATRICIA McLINN

says she has been spinning stories in her head since childhood, when her mother insisted she stop reading at the dinner table. As the time came for her to earn a living, Patricia shifted her stories from fiction to fact—she became a sportswriter and editor for newspapers in Illinois, North Carolina and the District of Columbia. Now living outside Washington, D.C., she enjoys traveling, history and sports but is happiest indulging her passion for storytelling.

**SILHOUETTE SPECIAL EDITION
IS PROUD TO PRESENT
A BRAND-NEW MINISERIES BY
PATRICIA McLINN**

A PLACE CALLED HOME:
Where Wyoming hearts beat true...
Three couples find love in each others' arms
when coming home to Wyoming.

**On sale in August 2000—
LOST-AND-FOUND GROOM (SE #1344)**

Kendra Jenner reunites with the one man
she ever lost control with—and who gave her a
child—when Daniel Delligatti unexpectedly arrives
on her doorstep.

**On sale in September 2000—
AT THE HEART'S COMMAND (SE #1350)**

Faced with the chance to win over the woman of his
dreams, Colonel John "Grif" Griffin must first learn
to follow his heart in order to woo beautiful single
mom Ellyn Sinclair.

**On sale in October 2000—
HIDDEN IN A HEARTBEAT (SE #1355)**

Luke Chandler refuses to believe he can be tamed...
until he meets the proper Miss Rebecca Dahlgren
who turns his world upside down.

Prologue

Twenty years ago,
Far Hills Ranch, Wyoming

"Tell us the Far Hills legend, Aunt Marti," urged eleven-year-old Kendra Jenner.

Before Marti Susland could respond, Dale Sinclair, who wasn't even part of the family, scoffed with all the disdain of a thirteen-year-old, "We don't want to hear that old story again."

"Yes, we do," Amy asserted staunchly. Although Marti's half sister was a few months older than Kendra, she always followed Kendra's lead.

Twelve-year-old Ellyn Neal backed their vote up with a nod.

"Aw, only girls and babies want to hear that story, right, Grif?" Dale appealed to the oldest, consigning to babyhood the youngest of the gathered youngsters, Luke Chandler, son of the Far Hills foreman.

At fourteen John Griffin was noticeably more serious and silent than in previous summers. He looked at each of the faces around the campfire until he came to her. Marti looked back at the only child of her oldest sister and felt a renewed ache of loss at Nancy's death three years ago.

"I'd like to hear it, too. One last time."

Marti's breath hitched. It was as if the boy had read her mind. Or shared her premonition. *Was* this last campfire of the summer also the last for this gathering? Could she truly feel the ties that bound them to this place and these summers unraveling?

All these children had spent summers at Far Hills all their lives. Even after Father remarried and had Amy, Marti's older sisters, Nancy and Wendy, had returned to the ranch with their husbands and children. At least for a while.

First, Father and his second wife, Cindy, were killed in that hotel fire, leaving Marti, at twenty, to take over Far Hills and raise her infant half sister.

Then Wendy's pilot husband, Ken Jenner, became an MIA in Vietnam. Soon the strain in Nancy's marriage to Lieutenant Colonel John Griffin Sr. became too obvious to miss, followed by her diagnosis and long, losing fight.

But even with the adults scattered, Marti had begged, cajoled and badgered them into sending their children— Nancy's son, Grif, and Wendy's daughter, Kendra—each summer to the ranch that was their heritage.

Each summer, with Kendra and Grif joining Amy and Luke in living here, along with Dale Sinclair and Ellyn Neal spending more time here than at their homes in town, Far Hills Ranch was nearly what Marti had always dreamed it could be. Unclouded by the past.

A past embedded in the legend these innocents considered a thrilling story heard around a campfire. No, she wouldn't tell it this time, because if she did—

"Please, Marti," whispered Amy.

Marti looked at her half sister and relented. As always.

"It happened right here, in 1878," she began, using the familiar words she first heard from her grandmother. Every face turned toward her. "The campfire burned for four days and four nights on that outcropping on Crooked Mountain that lets you see all over Far Hills, until Charles Susland— your great-great-grandfather, Kendra and Grif," she broke off to explain, as if they hadn't heard this too many times to count.

"And our great-grandfather," supplied Amy.

"That's right. That fire burned for four days and four nights after Charles Susland turned Leaping Star away from the house, until, finally, he rode up the mountainside. He only did it then to still his new wife Annalee. If she hadn't been expecting a baby he'd have ignored her blathering and vapors. She'd given him one son already, but he wanted many sons.

"The Crow woman rose slowly when he rode into her camp and spoke to her."

From long custom, Marti automatically dropped her voice to gruffly speak her ancestor's part.

"'I told you when you came to the house—you have no place here.'

"'This is my place, my only place, my people's place,' Leaping Star told him. 'They brought you to it when you took me as wife. They helped you. And you took our place.'

"'Far Hills is mine. I built it. Your people didn't make anything of this land, I did. And now your place is the reservation. Go back, Leaping Star.'

"'Your children die there. White Deer and Yellow Sky died at the full moon. Runs At Dawn is very weak.'"

Amy drew in an audible breath of sympathy.

"'Then go take care of her.'

"'There is nothing left in me. Only enough to come to you, Charles Susland. Care for our daughter or she will die.'

"'I can't go running off leaving Far Hills. And I have a son now. A white son. He'll learn to build something on this land instead of roaming like a pack of animals.' He pivoted his horse.

"'Charles Susland.'

"He would have kept riding if he could have, but Leaping Star's will was too strong.

"'You turn away from your children, so your blood will be alone. You turn away from my people, so your blood will have no home. You turn away from me, so your blood will be lost. Only when someone loves enough to undo your wrongs will the laughter of children live beyond its echo in Far Hills.' One more night the fire burned on the outcropping. And then it went out."

At Marti's final hushed words, a log shifted on their small fire and dimmed the flames.

Dale emitted a ghostly laugh. "And so you're all doomed—*cursed!* Just like everybody in town says—the Far Hills Curse, that's why all those Suslands die like flies."

"Shut up, Dale," ordered Amy. "You don't know anything about it—you're not a Susland."

"So what. Neither's Luke!"

Luke calmly watched Dale and Amy, but contributed nothing to the dispute his name had been dragged into.

"He's a lot closer than you'll ever be, because he's part of Far Hills Ranch."

"Big deal. Who—"

"How could he not go back to his children?" Kendra's voice trembled, but it seemed to be with outrage, not imminent tears.

"Maybe he didn't know how to be a father." Grif stared into the fire as he spoke. "Some men just don't."

Marti licked her dry lips, tasting the whisper of winter's coming cold. "There's one more part I've never told you before."

All eyes turned to her.

"But now...now I think I have to tell you. In case there's not another time...in case we're not all together again."

Marti swallowed and resumed her story-telling voice. "Leaping Star said one more thing to Charles Susland. 'If these wrongs are not righted in five generations of your blood, then they will never be undone, and Far Hills will be ever silent.'"

Amy's wide eyes stared at her. "What does that mean?"

"It means somebody who had Charles Susland as an ancestor needs to make right all those things he did wrong," said Kendra. "But there are others besides us, aren't there?"

Grif shook his head. "I remember Mom showing me a family tree. Lots of people died off young and—"

"Just like I said!" crowed Dale.

"—that means the group of us sitting here's the last of Charles Susland's descendants. But even if you believe in this sort of thing, Aunt Marti, how could folks living now make right something that happened a hundred years ago?"

"If I knew, Grif, I'd do it, no matter what."

By his widening eyes, she could see her nephew recognized her words gave away that she *did* believe.

"All I know is Amy and I are the last to carry the Susland name, but it will be our children, if we have any, and you, Grif, and you, Kendra, who must make sure the curse is lifted. Because you're the fifth generation of Charles Susland's blood.

"You're the last hope of Far Hills."

Chapter One

"I am *not* cursed."

Kendra Jenner set the mug on the wooden table with an emphatic *clunk*. The gesture lost a good deal of its effectiveness because the mug resembled the head of a cartoon duck, complete with blue bill. It was her son's favorite.

"First of all, the entire idea of that legend is absurd," Kendra declared. "And second—"

"Oh, I don't know—" started her friend and neighbor, Ellyn Sinclair.

"And second," Kendra repeated, "I'm not a Susland."

"Not by name, but Charles was your ancestor, right?"

Kendra opened her mouth to reply, but a more pressing matter intruded.

"Mo' doose."

Kendra looked at her son seated beside her at their kitchen table. Despite the familiar swell of love that always twinned with an ache of loss, she kept her voice light.

"Only if you'll drink it this time instead of using it as hair mousse."

Matthew, his thick, dark hair displaying new and interesting spikes, ignored that caveat and returned to the heart of the matter, hands opening and closing as he reached for the mug. "Mo' doose."

"Single-minded child you have there," Ellyn said with a smile from across the table. She had arrived early for their meeting, catching Matthew in the midst of a lunch where more food went on than in. Although Meg and Ben Sinclair were school-age now, as a widowed mother of two, Ellyn had taken in the situation—including, no doubt, Kendra's frazzled state—served herself coffee and taken a chair at a safe distance. "Must take after his mother."

You wouldn't think so if you met his father.

The thought came before Kendra could stop it, and so did the ache. She pushed both away.

"Determination is a good quality," she said as she gave her son the mug. "Both hands, Matthew."

"Doose." He drank loudly then raised his head to beam her a smile. "Dank you."

Matthew's smile eased some of her tiredness. "You're welcome, sweetheart."

"Hello, sorry we're late." The back door opened to Marti Susland and her three-and-a-half-year-old adopted daughter Emily.

"Come on in, Marti."

Kendra had stopped calling Marti Susland "aunt" so long before she had come back to Far Hills to live that she couldn't remember exactly when she'd started viewing the older woman as an equal. Since Kendra's return to Far Hills, she and Marti and Ellyn had formed a support system built on friendship and all being single parents.

"I'd like to blame it on traffic—" Kendra and Ellyn chuckled, since Marti lived just up the private road at the Far Hills home ranch. She shook her head, sending her mixed brown-and-gray chin-length hair swishing. "But I fear I'm getting slower and slower. Sometimes keeping up with Emily makes me feel like I'm a relic from history, instead of researching it."

They were meeting today to organize their work on a freelance local history supplement to the *Far Hills Banner,* where both Ellyn and Kendra worked part-time. Using Marti's research, Kendra would do the writing and Ellyn the graphics and layout. Kendra already had the extra income earmarked for her son's college fund.

Matthew's interest was riveted on Marti's daughter, a dark-haired, dark-eyed sprite. He craned his head around the side of the high chair to call hello, then whipped his head back to his mother.

"Down. Down," he ordered, already trying to undo the tray.

"First you need to be cleaned up, young man, or the first time you touch Emily the two of you will be permanently bonded." Wiping the worst of the damage from Matthew's scrunched-up face and squirming arms, hands and neck, Kendra added to Marti, "You're not late at all. We'll get the kids situated and then get to work."

"Down, p'ease. Down."

Kendra lifted Matthew's sturdy body and swung him down to the floor. He made a beeline for his friend.

Emily eyed him askance. "You dirty?"

"No dirty," Matthew denied. He raised his small hands palms up in a gesture of reassurance. A memory blindsided Kendra. *His father had made that exact gesture to her.*

"Kendra?"

She blinked back to the present to find Marti and Ellyn staring, clearly waiting for a response to something she hadn't heard.

"Sorry. What did you say?"

"Not much," Marti said, "The truck battery is truly dead,

so I hooked a ride with Luke when he came to start fixing that fence so you won't have cattle in your yard anymore.''

Luke Chandler was foreman of the Far Hills Ranch, but all three women's households relied on his skill and generosity as general fix-it man.

''Do you need a ride to the baby-sitting co-op meeting tonight?''

''No, that's okay, Luke's going to run me in to town later this afternoon to get a new battery. He said he could get it in time for me to meet Fran for supper before the meeting. So, Kendra, do you want to set the kids up in the den? I brought a couple of Emily's favorite videotapes.''

''Sure. That's fine.''

She joined Marti in arranging their children in the small den off the kitchen with Matthew still thrilled enough to see Emily to accede to her demand to watch *The Little Mermaid.*

''This is quiet time, Matthew and Emily,'' Marti instructed as the adults returned to the kitchen. ''If you can't be quiet together, it will be nap time. Understand? Emily? Matthew?''

Already lured into the movie, they responded with absent nods.

''Go sit down, Marti, and I'll get your coffee,'' Kendra offered.

''Thanks. I finally got those prints you each asked for from Matthew's birthday party. I figured I better do it fast or his next birthday would be on top of us.'' She placed two packets of pictures on the table. ''So, how far have you gotten?''

''We haven't even started.''

''Except to talk about the curse.'' A glint of mischief lit Ellyn's eyes as she tucked curling strands of rich brown hair back into a loose knot at her nape. Kendra was glad to see Ellyn's humor returning after Dale Sinclair's death, she just wished Ellyn had found a different topic.

''It's not a curse, it's a legend. And I wish you'd never

badgered me into telling you about it,'' Kendra grumbled as she wiped remnants of Matthew's lunch from the table and high chair.

''I just wanted a few details filled in. You forget—I heard it all long ago during our summers together. But it wasn't until you moved back that I started thinking part of the Susland curse fell on you.''

Kendra snorted as she placed the coffee in front of Marti.

''Why do you think Kendra is cursed?'' Marti asked with a seriousness that caused Kendra to try to catch Ellyn's eye to warn her off.

Ellyn missed the signal. ''Being cursed would explain things about her that are hard to figure out otherwise.''

''Like what?''

''Like why a woman with Kendra's talent is reporting for the *Far Hills Banner* instead of the network like she used to and—''

''A life-style choice makes—''

''And,'' Ellyn overrode her, ''like why a woman like Kendra is alone and—''

''I'm not alone. I have Matthew and all my friends here, including you two. Unless,'' she added darkly, ''you keep talking about this ridiculous legend, and then I'll have one less friend.''

Kendra's protest didn't stop Ellyn from adding. ''And it explains why you look like hell.''

Kendra pushed her hair back from her forehead with both hands, then propped her elbows on the table. ''Thanks a lot, Ellyn. Compliments are not going to get you out of your share of work on this supplement.''

''I mean it—you look like hell. Or at least as much like hell as you ever look. You have that annoying habit of looking pulled together and cool even when you're not.''

''You *do* look washed-out, Kendra,'' Marti contributed.

''I'm tired, I suppose. Now, about the section—''

''Ah-hah!' said Ellyn. ''You had the dream again, didn't you?''

''What dream?'' Marti asked.

The dream. The dream that whispered into Kendra's not-quite asleep mind like the softest breeze fluttering silk against her skin.

The first year she'd fought both the dream and the memories. Now she knew fighting did no good, especially not against the dream.

It lifted her out of herself, carried her against her will from her orderly, practical life in Far Hills, Wyoming, taking her back…back to Santa Estella…back to those fear-drenched hours…back to *him.*

She opened the packet of pictures in front of her with a show of examining them.

''I didn't sleep very well.''

Ellyn shook her head, dismissing that excuse. ''I remember that look from when the kids and I stayed with you.''

''What dream?'' Marti repeated.

Ellyn turned to her. ''The one that made her cry out during the night and look like this in the morning. It happened a couple times in the week we stayed here during the work on Ridge House.''

With troubled eyes, Marti stared at Kendra. ''A nightmare?''

Kendra put her hand over the older woman's. ''Not really.''

During her childhood visits to Far Hills, Kendra had seen Marti as a distant figure, as remote from her as her mother. Kendra had known Marti through Amy's eyes then—how Marti had taken over the ranch and raised Amy when their father and Amy's mother had died. Amy had later been Kendra's college roommate and closest friend. When a car accident killed Amy, grief brought Marti and Kendra together in a bond that endured even as the grief eased.

When Kendra's life shifted irrevocably three years ago, it had seemed right to turn to Marti.

Their new relationship was cemented when Kendra helped Marti adopt Emily from an orphanage on Santa Estella, a small island off the coast of South America, shortly before Matthew's birth.

Since she'd returned to Far Hills, Kendra had come to an even greater appreciation of Marti's strength, generosity—

"So what is this not-exactly-a-nightmare about?"

—and tenacity.

Kendra sighed. "It's...the hurricane."

"That's all?" Ellyn said. "The hurricane?"

"Don't you think that's enough? I could have been killed. It was the most frightened I've been in my life." Her laugh grated on her own ears. "And it was the stupidest I've been in my life. I should have left with my crew instead of hanging around trying to get a scoop on Taumaturgio."

"Taumaturgio?" Ellyn stumbled over the pronunciation.

"It means miracle worker. A legend on Santa Estella. Sort of a cross between the Scarlet Pimpernel and Robin Hood. Some authorities there were incredibly corrupt, lining their pockets with proceeds from aid meant for the island's children. Taumaturgio 'liberated' supplies before the officials could sell them, and he took them to the children. He also flew kids who desperately needed specialized medical care into the United States—highly illegal. But the doctors who treated the kids weren't about to turn him in."

"Sounds like someone worth knowing," Ellyn said.

"Certainly someone worth doing a story on," Kendra said dryly. "Oh, how I wanted to do the story.... But that's a pretty weak excuse for being stupid."

"Some stupid things have good results." Ellyn glanced toward the spread of snapshots taken at Matthew's birthday.

"Yes." Kendra looked at the laughing face of her son, caught by the camera as he stood on a chair contemplating the possibility he could defy nature and fly. He was a miracle in every minute of her life. She would never—could never—regret having him.

That didn't change her stupidity. Barely two days of madness had turned her practical life upside down.

"So, what are you going to do about it?" Ellyn asked.

"About what?"

"The dream."

"Not sleep?" Kendra suggested.

"Looks like you've tried that. I should have said about making the dream stop."

"Believe me, I tried. I've given up. So I lose some sleep. I'll survive. I was tired when Matthew was a newborn and when he was teething and God knows I've been tired since he started walking—"

"I told you to enjoy the peace when he was crawling," said Ellyn. "Wait until he goes to school and comes home with his first bloody nose."

"Hellfire, wait until he goes on his first date," added Marti, who'd gone through that phase as surrogate mother to Amy.

Kendra groaned, then they all shared a grin.

"But I suspect that doesn't have anything to do with this dream," Marti said. Oh, yes, she had tenacity to spare.

"It's not—"

"You should go after him."

Ellyn's pronouncement surprised Kendra into an unguarded "What?"

"You should go after Paulo."

"Who's Paulo?" Marti asked.

"I don't know," Ellyn admitted. "But I've got some ideas."

They both turned to Kendra, who said, "He's no one."

"Okay," Ellyn said. "You have no reason to tell me who Paulo is, but I know he's not no one, because that's the name you call out like your heart's breaking right before you wake up. But I do understand if you don't want to talk abo—''

"No, Ellyn, you *don't* understand. He's really no one. He doesn't exist. I mean, the man exists. Or he did. The man who... Let's just say Hurricane Aretha brought us together, and when it passed, there was no reason to stay together.''

"Wasn't there?'' Ellyn asked with a significant look toward the den doorway where Matthew and Emily were visible.

"You're right. He was Matthew's father. But *Paulo* doesn't exist.''

"I don't understand,'' Marti said.

"I'm not sure I understand myself,'' Kendra admitted. "He rescued me, he kept me safe—'' *He gave me Matthew.* "And afterward, he took me back to the American consulate and disappeared.''

"He just disappeared?'' Marti's voice was harsh.

"I asked at the consulate—but no one knew him. I was evacuated from the island as soon as they repaired the runways. When I got back to the States I tried to forget. It should have been easy, because the ironic thing is my reports on the hurricane did for my career what I'd hoped the Taumaturgio story could do. Then, I found out I was pregnant....''

She remembered shaking as she'd dialed Marti's phone number. Marti had laid no blame, asked no questions— she'd simply said to come home to Far Hills.

"I tried to contact him. I advertised he had a reward coming. I called the consulate and asked for help finding a man named Paulo Ayudor. The storm kill a thousand people, and more died afterward, and I wondered... But he wasn't on any of the lists. Nothing.''

"You mean you told the consulate you were expecting the man's child, and they didn't help?''

"I didn't tell the consulate official. It was none of his business, besides...''

"You weren't sure if Paulo would run even farther," Ellyn filled in softly.

Kendra didn't answer. She didn't have to. So many times she'd wondered if Paulo had seen her efforts to contact him...

"You feared he would turn his back on his child."

Marti's voice sounded a little odd to Kendra, but Ellyn didn't seem to notice, asking, "What happened?"

"The man at the consulate shunted me off to local officials. One told me Paulo Ayudor was the name of a character in island folklore. Santa Estella's Johnny Appleseed. Only he planted miracles—helping people in their direst hour of need. A close relation," she said with a twist to her mouth, "of Taumaturgio."

Ellyn's eyes widened. "Oh, my... You mean Paulo was—"

"I don't know. I've wondered. From the little description I got of Taumaturgio, it could have been. How would that be for irony? The man I'd sought all over Santa Estella was the one who ended up—"

Sound erupted from the small room off the kitchen.

"Mermaid!" declared Emily.

"No!" responded Matthew with his new favorite word. "No Mermay! No. No!"

Kendra and Marti swooped in and efficiently settled the dispute with the Solomon-like option of putting both children down for naps in Matthew's room. They had sat down again when the front door bell rang.

"Who on earth...?" Locals used the kitchen door.

"Must be somebody who got lost," Marti suggested.

"Or a salesman. I'll get rid of him." Kendra started to rise, but Ellyn put her hand on her shoulder as she passed behind her.

"I'll do it. I can use the practice," she added with a smile. "Remember me? No more Ms. Nice Guy."

They heard the squeak of the front door hinges, unaccustomed to being opened, then a male voice.

"Is this the home of Kendra Jenner?"

"Yes."

"Never answer their questions," Marti murmured.

But the overheard exchange absorbed all of Kendra's attention.

"May I speak with her, please."

Kendra's heartbeat stuttered. That voice… She'd heard it before, hadn't she?

"I'll ask if she can see you. What's your name?"

"Daniel Delligatti."

The name meant nothing. But the voice nagged at her. Familiar, but not quite…right. She had stood when Ellyn appeared.

"Who is he?" Marti asked.

"I don't know, but…there's something about him."

"There's something about serial killers, too," Kendra said grimly. "I know, I know. My cynicism is showing. I'll see him."

Aware Ellyn and Marti followed her closely, she turned the corner from the kitchen, staring down the short hallway created between the back of the couch and the wall, toward the man who stood at her front door.

Late August sunlight from the small windows across the top of the door backlit the figure. But she could see more than enough.

The clothes were vastly different—a soft blue oxford cloth shirt tucked into faded jeans instead of near rags. The hair was different, too, shorter, and the waves mostly tamed by a precise cut. But the features were unchanged. She knew the strong jawline and penetrating dark eyes in less than a heartbeat.

She should know them. She saw them every day. They were the features of her son.

And she saw them many nights in her dreams.

"Paulo."

Chapter Two

Three years ago, Santa Estella

The damned hurricane was half a day early.

Wind rushed at Kendra Jenner like a mad bull. She barely saved herself from falling by bracing herself with a hand against the rain-slickened adobe of Senora Valeria's house.

Her cameraman and sound guy, surely safe in Miami by now and probably enjoying a drink in a hotel bar, would laugh at her being proved wrong. She could have taken the last plane out with them. They'd wanted her to. So had that American consulate official with the shaggy dark hair, thick glasses and baggy suit.

But she couldn't give up on finding Taumaturgio—"Miracle Worker"—the benefactor to Santa Estella's children whose daring so outraged the island's officials. This story she had to tell.

So, she'd hired Esteban to guide her through narrow

streets twisting between shanties, squat adobe buildings and pockets of partially completed construction abandoned under the weight of local corruption. She'd felt like a human pinball, bumped by every one of the hurrying crowd carrying bulging string bags of bottled water and canned goods. Like a pinball, she'd gone ever downward, from the hilltop where the consulate sat amid hotels and estates, down, down toward the water. Deeper into La Baja.

Senora Valeria was the seventh of Esteban's promised sources—not one had anything to tell her of Taumaturgio. After he'd led her inside the old woman's tiny adobe house, he'd stepped outside for a smoke. He'd never returned.

So Kendra would have to get herself back to the protection of the American consulate. She slung the strap of her shoulder bag across her body and started climbing the narrow street.

Rivulets of cold water, mud and stones tumbled down the rough stone surface under her feet. Rain beat into her face. Soon, her numbed feet no longer felt the stinging blows. But they couldn't feel the street, either, and walking required faith and guesswork. In unpredictable bursts, wind drove the rain at her like pellets. Her clothes became a sodden weight. A hunk of green wood that might have been a shutter cartwheeled in front of her.

From behind her, the surf seemed to grow louder each second. She didn't look back. She kept climbing.

The water was ankle deep, and coming faster. Fighting up another twenty yards, her feet slid on the slick stones. She came down hard on her palms, but saved herself from going all the way down. The wind eased, and she straightened, dragging in air.

A few more yards and she stumbled again. The water pulled at her, but she resisted. Against water streaming past her mid-calf, she pushed on.

The third time she went down, she knew she'd never make it. Not like this. Not all the way to the consulate.

Fear crested over her. She pushed it back. *Think,* Jenner. *Think. Panic's the worst thing to do. Think, damn it!*

First, she had to find shelter. That was the only practical thing to do.

Squinting against the rain, she caught a flash of movement. Someone else trying to find shelter? She pushed her hair back, but saw no sign of humanity. Not a person. Not a light. To her left, blue fabric that had once been an awning whipped and twisted in its death throes. The far side of the narrow street was a blur.

To her right, a narrow indentation cut into the street. Movement. A door, swinging wide on its hinges. Perhaps it covered only another, sturdier door that would be locked, but maybe...

She pushed off the wall and started toward the swinging door. Reaching it, she barely absorbed the fact that it opened into a dark space enclosed by plywood before she launched herself inside, then stood, hands on thighs, and gulped in air. Slowly she became aware of her shivering. Of the smell of mud. Of abandonment. And then of...a presence. A faint sense of something else breathing in the space...

Her head jerked up. Someone stood on the bottom step of a steep, rickety stairway.

A man. Tall, with broad shoulders. That much she saw despite the shadowy gloom.

He said something she didn't understand, and spread his arms, palms out in an apparent gesture that he meant her no harm. She backed up. He stepped forward. She pivoted and bolted out the door. A gust of wind-driven rain slashed into her like innumerable knives.

The next moment unfolded in slow motion.

The man coming behind her, a glimpse of something above and to her left. The man diving at her, crushing her against a wooden wall. Seeing, around his shoulder, a huge earthenware urn with bits of flowers clinging to it, fly past and shatter in a spray of dirt and pottery on the spot where she had stood. Almost silently. The crash swallowed by the blast of wind that had propelled it off a rooftop garden.

Then they were inside.

The man released her and stepped back, but she felt the force of his grasp like an imprint on her skin.

He spoke again, his breathing slightly labored. It sounded like the same thing he'd said before. Again with his hands open and in sight.

"Yo no habla español." She hoped that much translated to the island's mutation of Spanish.

"Ah," he said. His hands dropped. She watched them every inch, but they hung there, innocently. Then a spate she didn't understand, until, finally, "American?"

Some places were anti-American, but not Santa Estella. She nodded. "Yes. American."

He nodded back, and water dripped from a hunk of black hair over his forehead. His head and the bottom of his worn pants were nearly as wet as she was, but a dark green slicker protected the rest of him.

"There you go."

Her spirits rose. "Oh. You speak English."

His rapid words flowed past her nearly as fast as the water in the street, ending with "There you go."

"There you go?" she repeated.

He nodded. "There you go."

He didn't speak English. He spoke "there you go."

He jerked his head toward the top of the stairs, retreated two steps, and gestured to her to follow.

She shook her head. He might have saved her, he might not seem threatening, but she'd done her share of stories about murderers who looked like choirboys.

With his hands out straight, he slowly raised them, then nodded to the door behind her. Glancing over her shoulder, she saw water seeping over the sill and across the mud-packed floor. He was right. The water was going to rise.

"On the other hand," she muttered to herself, "sometimes a choirboy is really a choirboy."

She followed him up the stairs.

During the next, awkward half hour the man prowled the cavernous second story of the unfinished building gathering items he apparently thought could be of use. He brought them back to where a pair of shoulder-high walls, one about ten feet long and the other six feet, met to form a protective corner. He indicated a closetlike structure to one side could be used as a sort of toilet, with his and hers chamber pots.

Finally, they sat in the walled corner and shared their resources, hers from her bag, his from a backpack.

Her bottle of water. His lantern flashlight. Her two cheese-and-crackers packets. His string bag of oranges. Her Swiss Army knife. His matches.

All the while, the wind howled louder and the light grew dimmer.

She shivered so hard her teeth clicked audibly. He interrupted his efforts to start a small fire in the bowl of a hubcap he'd found, using torn sheets from her notebook, scraps of wood and his damp matches, to give her a sharp look. With emphatic gestures he instructed her to change into the dry shirt and socks he drew from his backpack along with the flannel lining he detached from his slicker. She didn't argue.

Slipping behind the wall to change, she realized the ferocious wind drove the rain through the outer wall, creating a fine mist. But their refuge had the benefit of steel posts that apparently rose from the ground level and extended beyond where she could see.

Wrapping the slicker lining around her waist as a sarong to complete her outfit, she grabbed her wet things and returned to the protection of their corner.

"Gracias."

He nodded. He'd taken off his holey shoes and laid them near the small fire, with the slicker spread nearby. She started to do the same with her clothes, when he said something in the island language and shook his head.

"What? I don't understand."

He stood, and took her slacks from her as she automatically backed away. He was tall, especially for an islander—some four inches taller than her five-seven—and broad-shouldered enough to block the light from the fire. He ignored her retreat and wrapped powerful hands around the fabric, then twisted. The water wrung out splashed on the wooden floor between them.

"Oh, I see. Yes." She followed his example with her blouse.

With her clothes at last laid out, the man gestured for her to go first through the narrow opening between the hubcap fire and the corner where he had set flattened cardboard boxes atop a long narrow cushion. She sat with her back to one wall and he rested against the other, with the fire at their feet.

"I'm Kendra Jenner," she told him.

He looked at her, but said nothing. The firelight shifted shadow and stark brightness across a strongly boned face. Pronounced cheekbones, sharp jaw, high forehead, all beneath thick, dark hair that waved despite being slicked straight back.

"Kendra," she repeated with a hand to her chest.

"Kendra." He rolled the "r" and lingered over the final "a." His extended fingers brushed the back of her hand. The unexpected contact fizzed at her tautly strung nerve endings. "Kendra."

"Yes."

His large hand spread across the faded red cotton of his shirt. "Paulo Ayudor."

"How do you do, Paulo?" Not surprisingly, he didn't answer. His eyes remained on her face. His eyes were dark, so dark their only color seemed to come from the tiny reflection of firelight. "I wonder what you were doing out on the streets of La Baja when Hurricane Aretha came to call?"

"La Baja," he repeated. Then words she didn't understand. But she sensed in them a faintly disapproving question, and a tilt of his head made her think he'd asked what she'd been doing there herself. He continued another stream of words in the island language. But one word caught her ear. It sounded like *impetuoso*.

"I suppose it could appear impetuous. But I'd call it a calculated risk. Though, I'll admit I don't usually take chances like this." She wasn't sure if she meant chasing the story, pushing her luck with the storm or trusting him.

He rubbed his hand twice across his eyes, then dropped it.

She reached for her hairbrush from among the second pile of items she'd pulled from her purse. This larger pile of items her companion—Paulo—apparently didn't think would aid them. Maybe a hairbrush wouldn't help them survive, but it sure made her feel more human as she pulled it through her dripping hair.

"I can't shake this story. There's something about this Taumaturgio. A man who comes out of nowhere to help the children. No one knows when he's coming. No one knows who he is.... Not that I'm starry-eyed about an unknown hero the way my cameraman kept saying. A breakthrough story could move me up a notch on the ladder. That would be another step toward financial security. Not having to ever rely on—" She bit off the words and set the brush down. "I don't know why I'm telling you this, since you don't understand what I'm saying."

As she said the words, she knew that was precisely why she was telling him.

A second reason for talking scratched along her nerves as the wind cried louder and something above them creaked a protest. One of her profs had drummed into her that a reporter who was talking wasn't listening. For the first time, she realized breaking that rule might provide a benefit.

"Anyway," she went on, talking louder, "Taumaturgio's the perfect breakthrough story. Sexy, daring, mysterious. I could get great play—fantastic play—if I could find Taumaturgio."

Paulo watched her with concentrated interest.

"What is it? What did I say?"

He blinked, and his expression shifted to mild confusion. Maybe it had been a trick of the firelight.

He rubbed his eyes again.

"Taumaturgio? Do you know Taumaturgio?"

His strong-boned face stayed blank. He shrugged.

The movement reminded her of the power in his broad shoulders when he'd pushed her out of the way of the falling urn. She should remember that and keep her guard up. But it was hard when he'd helped her, she wore his clothes, they might share a fate—

A crash shuddered in the distance, adding eerie emphasis to that thought.

They had both instinctively looked in the direction of the noise. As she turned back, she met his eyes. Slashes of dark brows and those strong bones gave his face a strength softened only by the long, dark lashes framing his deep-set eyes.

"I trust you." The wind's moaning nearly drowned her words. She tried to laugh. It came out rusty. "Lord, I sound like my mother. And I haven't done that often."

A guttural groan of wind-tortured wood came from above them. She jerked her head back and stared up. But beyond the sphere of their tiny fire stretched a void. A swirling, damp, dark void spattered with moans instead of stars.

Was it night? She didn't know. She checked her wrist. Her watch had stopped at 4:38—minutes after leaving Senora Valeria's.

She masked a shiver by shifting position on the cardboard-covered mattress.

"Mother," he said, condensing the "th" into a harder sound.

Kendra wasn't sure if he meant to remind her of what she'd been saying or was trying to make sense of the word. "Mother. *Madre*," she translated.

"Ah, sí. Madre." His pronunciation gave it a twist she couldn't describe, but she recognized the word. He smiled. He had straight, white teeth, unlike so many islanders. He also had a smile that shifted sharp planes into lines of warm pleasure.

"Yes. *Mi madre*." She sighed. "She would have loved you—she loved most men. Looked up at them with her big blue eyes and trusted every man she met after my father died to take care of her the way he had. And man after man took advantage of her, while she thought she could hide behind their broad shoulders."

Broad shoulders... She *had* hidden behind broad shoulders. His. From a hurricane she'd walked right into.

Aretha. The banshee clawing at their shelter with breath and voice. This time Kendra didn't hide her shiver.

She pushed herself to keep talking, so she wouldn't listen. "But these are unusual circumstances."

His dark eyes held so much intelligence that for a moment she wished he could understand her. Only then she wouldn't have told him any of this.

She extended her hand. "Friends?"

His gaze slowly shifted to her hand. He repeated her word, then said another resembling *amigo*.

"Amigos." She nodded. "Friends."

He stretched his arm across the space between them and put his palm to hers for an instant before curling his long fingers around her hand. She hadn't known how cold her hand was until the warmth of his surrounded it. A hand to hold on to while the dark world screamed around them.

She shook his hand more emphatically than she'd intended, while trying not to feel too grateful for the warmth.

When she tried to withdraw her hand, he held on. Not tightly, but securely. She glanced up as she again exerted a slight pressure to withdraw her hand. They were still looking at each other and he was still holding her hand when the roof fell in.

He used his hold on her hand to jerk her toward him, and underneath him. Crammed into the corner of the two interior walls, his body sheltered her. She knew she screamed. His shoulder muffled the sound. The impact of debris pounding against his back transferred to her, echoing in her bones.

Waiting for the final, crushing blow.

Would they die?

She might have passed out. Time slid sideways into uncertain territory. When time righted itself, she became aware of a difference. A change.

Silence.

Silence.

No moaning wind. No howling rain. No screaming storm.

But also no movement from Paulo.

Oh, God. Please. Oh, God.

She worked one hand free from between their bodies, but couldn't get her fingers to where she thought there would be a pulse. She shifted more strongly, spreading her hand wide, reaching for a reassuring flutter.

"Kendra."

Paulo had said her name. He was alive. She could feel his heartbeat, pushing his blood through his veins.

He murmured something else, which sounded almost as if he asked if she was okay. But he couldn't have asked it in words she would understand.

"Paulo."

He raised his head. She couldn't see his face; the fire must have been smothered, the lantern destroyed. But now she could hear his voice, and knew he spoke in the island tongue, rising at the end in interrogation.

"I'm okay. Are you hurt?"

He said something else that sounded somehow reassuring.

He carefully raised his upper body, balancing on one arm above her while he started to clear debris with a cautious hand. Their lower bodies were pressed together, their legs entwined.

She should have been embarrassed, uneasy. She wasn't. She lay there, aware only of a lung-filling gratefulness for the reality of his weight and warmth against her.

They were alive.

When he had cleared enough space to lift off her, she forced herself to sit up, to take in their situation.

She brushed bits of wood, mud, shingles and jagged hunks of wallboard off the cushion while Paulo patiently restarted the fire.

The quiet pressed around them like a heavy blanket, cutting off the world as completely as the noise had. The eye of the storm. With the second half soon to start battering at them as harshly as the first half. And that would bring the storm surge, a hurricane's deadly swell of water.

But for this moment, they were alive.

"Well, at least we have plenty of kindling," Kendra muttered, tossing a piece of wood onto the meager flame.

Paulo turned then, his mouth starting to lift in a smile. His expression froze at the same instant she gasped. A jagged fragment of wood, as long as a pen but three times as big around jutted from the skin in front of his ear. Amid all the other stings and blows his body had taken, he must not have felt it until he started to smile, shifting those muscles.

"No." She grabbed the hand he started toward it. "You might drive it deeper. I'll do it. Here—"

She knelt in front of him, gesturing for him to turn toward her. He slid one long leg past her and bent the other, bringing his knee by her hip.

"Tip your head so I can see better."

He stared at her. She put her fingertips to either side of

his stubbled jaw to turn and tip his head toward the firelight. As his head moved, his eyes never left her face.

In the flickering light she saw the spine of wood running under the skin for two inches. If she could slide it out, carefully, without leaving fragments... But that would mean doing it slowly and that would hurt more.

"This is going to hurt." Her eyes met his for an instant, then skidded away. She put one hand along his jaw below the wound, thinking to hold him still if he jerked.

"Kendra."

Her name was followed by a flow of soft words. She met his eyes again and knew he reassured her. Her breath came out in a rush. He touched the back of her bracing hand lightly, and she knew he'd sworn to hold still.

Drawing in a steadier breath, she shifted her hand to feel the point of the shard, just under his skin. Biting her lip hard enough that the moisture in her eyes might have been from pain, she started drawing the wood up and out.

The first inch she feared her hands would shake. The second inch she feared she would pass out.

He never moved, never made a sound.

Her legs trembled as she shifted her hold on the slick, narrowing shaft of the shard, pinching it hard. Her guiding finger felt the tip finally give up its hold on his flesh.

She gasped and dropped back on her heels, throwing the wood fragment out of their circle of light.

"*Gracias,* Kendra."

Paler, Paulo still gave her a small smile and reached again toward his wound. His fingers came away red.

"You need a bandage. The blood—"

Even as she came up to her knees to look at the blood-oozing wound, she searched for a makeshift bandage, but saw nothing.

She needed something—anything. She grabbed the tail of the shirt she wore—his shirt—and drew it up to his cheek, pressing it against his wound. That corner soaked through, so she unbuttoned one, then two buttons from the bottom to free more material.

"It won't stop bleeding. It won't stop—" Her voice broke, and she realized she was crying.

"Shh, shh. Kendra." Paulo's arms were around her, his hands stroking down her back. "There you go... Kendra."

She threw her arms around his neck and held on as tight as she could while his shoulder absorbed her brief, violent tears.

She shifted, realizing he'd drawn her into his lap. She could smell the damp heat of his skin, a faint whiff of soap mixed with the earthy, watery scent of hurricane. And something deeper.

She'd known his kindness. His gentleness, even. Now, where her body touched his, she felt his heat. His humanity. His maleness.

They were alive...alive.

"Paulo."

He went still at her whisper against his neck. She tipped her head back to see his eyes. They were on hers. Then they shifted to her mouth. She moved or he moved or they both moved. It didn't matter. They were kissing. No testing of lips, no teasing of tongues. But hard, hungry kisses that made her gasp. Long, stroking, driving kisses.

She arched against him, he laid her back, following her down, pressing against her.

No subtlety slowed frantic fingers against straining bodies. No thought tempered urgent cries.

They met, hard and fast. He entered her, she took him in. The rhythm already set, already sprinting. The finish brought her off the cushion, her head flung back. She heard him groan out a word, then felt his taut body tighten even more. A great warmth spilled into her, and then his body blanketed her completely.

How long had their frenzy lasted? How long had they laid like this, still joined? She didn't know. She didn't care.

She heard the storm raising its voice, first sighing then moaning. But it didn't reach inside her the way it had before.

Paulo kissed her before shifting away, covering her with the clothes they'd discarded. He rigged the slicker over them, narrowing to a cavelike opening to the small fire. Their world had condensed to this tiny space, this flickering light, these moments.

He wrapped her inside the slicker liner, then cocooned her in the warmth of his body. They sat that way for some time she couldn't measure, hearing the wind beyond them, watching it bat at the struggling fire.

"It's starting again. Past the eye. Into the trailing half of the storm. If it sits over us like the first half..."

Paulo slid his hands up and down her arms, the friction and warmth of his touch pulsing into her newly chilled skin. He kissed the side of her neck, and she rested her head on his shoulder. He stroked slowly across her breast, finding her hardened nipple.

This is different from before. This is more...

She pushed all thought away and absorbed his touch.

The storm grew beyond them, howling and dashing water at their covering. But the one inside her was stronger. He laid back, carrying her and turning her with him so she was above him. With him. Taking him inside her.

She fell asleep at times, for minutes or hours, she didn't know, but each time she awoke, his arms were around her and she felt the steady pulse of his heart.

She talked. Of growing up with her mother and without her father, and then of her mother's death last year. Of Amy and childhood summers at Far Hills, and then Amy's death five years ago. Of her job. Of her dreams. Of her fears.

And he listened.

Sometimes he sang to her, in a low voice that rumbled

in his chest. Snatches of a tune she didn't recognize, words she couldn't understand. But it soothed her.

When she woke to see narrow strips of brightening sky high above them, he peeled two oranges and they shared them. Then he licked the juice from her fingers, and she did the same for his, and they made love again.

The next time she awoke thoroughly, she could tell the sun was waning. From outside, she heard gunshots, and knew that's what had awakened her.

Paulo sat up, drawing her with him, still inside the circle of his arms. He faced her and spoke in a steady voice, while the gunshots and a low roar of shouts came from a distance.

At the end, she could only shake her head. "I don't understand, Paulo."

He kept his eyes on hers for a long moment, before he released her to stand and start dressing. Then she understood.

He was leaving.

But he would come back. She understood that promise from his eyes. He slipped into the murkiness beyond their small fire for a moment, then returned with a stout length of wood he handed to her with a nod. She understood that, too. Protection. Nature had done its damage and now humanity added to it with looting and other crimes.

Paulo looked at her for a moment, then took one step away.

She lurched up. "No!" *Don't go.* She wanted to scream it out, but didn't.

He caught her when her unsteady legs might have given way, his arms around her warm and familiar. He kissed her forehead and set her away from him.

"I understand." No dignity had come harder. "I'll wait for you here."

He raised her hand, dirty, scratched and cold, to his lips and kissed her scraped knuckles.

When he disappeared, she dressed in her still-damp

clothes, gathered what she could of her belongings, kept the fire going at a low, steady burn. And waited.

A corner of her mind knew she should question if he would return, but she never did.

When he returned—she didn't know after how long—she stood outside the fire's light in case the footsteps belonged to someone other than Paulo. She could see his face a moment before he saw her, could see his fear for her.

"Paulo."

She dropped the wood and stepped into his arms. He wrapped her tightly to him and kissed her temple, her cheekbone, then her mouth. Their tongues delved in the rhythm their bodies ached to follow. But they broke apart.

"I know," she said. "There's no time."

He took her hand and led her into predawn darkness of a day that promised clear skies over the storm-devastated island. They slipped through ruined streets, following twists and alleys, ducking into a deserted building and out of an empty doorway to a courtyard that spilled into another alley, over barricades formed of broken dressers, battered bicycles, shredded roofs, always edging higher.

Finally, Paulo drew her in front of him as a darker mass rose out of the shadows. Only when he reached over her shoulder and she heard a staccato knock on wood did she realize he'd brought her to a gate. The wooden surface opened, she blinked into the brightness of battery-operated lights and knew they'd reached the U.S. Consulate.

"Ms. Jenner! What a relief to see you!" She blinked fast, trying to adjust to the light, and recognized a female consulate employee. "Are you all right? We were so worried—"

"I'm fine. Thanks to Paulo."

"Paulo? Who's Paulo?"

She turned, but Paulo Ayudor was nowhere to be found.

Nowhere to be found until he arrived at her front door in Far Hills, Wyoming, three years later.

"Paulo?" Ellyn and Marti echoed the name, then moved closer to Kendra, closing ranks.

She reached out, needing to touch him. Below the rolled-back sleeve of his shirt, his forearm was warm and firm, the hair crisp beneath her fingertips. Real. He was real.

"You're alive. You're really alive…. Oh, God." She put her hand to her mouth, but a sob still escaped.

He reached to her, wrapping his large, warm hands around her upper arms, his eyes looking directly into hers. "It's okay, Kendra. Everything's going to be okay."

"But…but Paulo Ayudor doesn't exist."

"I've used that name, and others. But I'm Daniel Delligatti."

She stepped back abruptly, breaking the connection. His hands dropped to his side.

"What are you doing here?"

"I came for you—and our son."

Chapter Three

"You...you know..."

The death of a fragile hope staggered Kendra. How many times in the lonely, uncertain nights had she pitted her common sense, her realism against the stubborn, foolish hope that if he was alive and knew she'd had their son he would have found her somehow? But the hope had persisted. Until this moment, when his own words revealed he had known, and he hadn't come.

She sank back to support her hips against the top of the couch's back. Ellyn took her arm, but Marti turned on her heel and headed for the kitchen.

The man remained standing before her, hands loosely fisted at his side, eyes intent on her, expression solemn.

"Now I do. I didn't for a long time. I couldn't look for you. Not until recently. And then—you weren't easy to find. The network wouldn't tell me anything. Official channels weren't much help, not even the consulate. But I heard you were pregnant when you left the network. Eventually I found out you'd had a son—and when he was born.''

The heat of his dark eyes threatened to kindle memories from nine months before Matthew's birth. She doused them by an act of will.

His shoulders shifted as if he'd wanted to take a step toward her, then thought better of it. ''I knew... I'm his father, aren't I, Kendra?''

But her mind had snagged on one phrase. One phrase clicked a thousand shards of memory into a mosaic that made sense for the first time.

''The...consulate...'' She had to form the word twice to get it to come out. ''My God, you were there. That day. The day of the hurricane, before I went to La Baja. Before I found the guide. Before... You tried to talk me out of going. Tried to send me to the airport with the others. The baggy suit. The hair. And the bad posture...Tompkins.''

''Yes.''

''That was you. And afterward, after the hurricane, you're the one I talked to—the one I talked to when I called to try to find—that's why the voice nagged at me. It seemed so familiar, but... My God, I talked to *you* when I called the consulate asking for help finding Paulo. How's that for irony?'' The strangled sound from her throat could hardly be called laughter ''When you—Paulo—had walked away from me, from *us*.'' Her hands spread over her abdomen, an instinctive gesture to protect the child she'd carried from his father's desertion. ''You must have had a good laugh over that.''

''You know I didn't.''

''*I know?* How can I? I know nothing about you!''

Memories streamed through her mind now, driven by a different kind of hurricane. Altered by the storm of her emotions. Shock. Relief. Joy. Pain.

She'd known Paulo, the Paulo she'd made love with, didn't truly exist. She'd accepted that...hadn't she? But to be faced now with how completely and thoroughly she'd been deceived—

"Kendra, let me explain."

"I don't think you can."

"I couldn't tell you before. I'm still not... They wanted absolute secrecy, but I never agreed."

"Secrecy? Having secrets seems to be your strong suit."

"Kendra—"

"I'm glad you survived—or Paulo did—or the man from the consulate or whoever the hell you really are. But I don't..." She put a hand to her forehead, as if that would slow the spinning thoughts. Then she forced herself to straighten. "I don't know that I have anything to say to Daniel Delligatti."

"Then listen. Because I have things to say to you." Now he took that single step forward. She stiffened, and felt Ellyn's supporting hand tighten on her arm. "And things to ask."

"I don't—"

"The boy—Matthew, that's what you named him, right?—he's my son, isn't he, Kendra?"

Matthew.

A new fear roared into her head. She'd worried and mourned for so long that his father wasn't part of Matthew's life that she'd never considered this other possibility. How stupid of her. How careless and unthinking.

He'd said he'd tracked them down, once he knew he had a son.

"Kendra."

He said it the way he had during those hours of the hurricane, stretching and rolling it like a caress. Her eyes met his for the first time without darting away. Did she see something of Paulo Ayudor in them? More likely a reflection of her own pathetic hopes.

She shook her head, mostly at herself, but he responded to it.

"I want to know my son. I want to be in his life. I need..." Something flickered in the darkness of his eyes, something more complex than anything she'd seen there in those hours on Santa Estella. "I would never try to separate you. I would never do anything to keep my son from being with his mother. I swear to you."

"Because I was fool enough to have trusted you before doesn't mean I would trust you—"

"You weren't a fool."

"Right. To trust a total stranger?" she scoffed. "It was idiotic. I know better—I *knew* better. My God, someone I'd never met, didn't know."

"You knew me, Kendra." His voice was deep, sure.

"Knew you? Of course I didn't know you."

His certainty didn't waver. "You knew me. And I knew you. The real people."

"That's absurd. A tall tale, like *Paulo Ayudor*. It's a—"

She hadn't heard the back door open, but the rap of boot heels on the kitchen floor caught her attention. Boot heels in a hurry.

Luke Chandler, foreman of Far Hills Ranch, rounded the corner.

"Everything okay, Kendra? Marti thought you might want some help." He spoke to her, but pinned a warning glare from under the brim of his hat on Daniel Delligatti. Luke planted himself beside her, half a step in front, so his left shoulder provided a partial barrier between her and Daniel.

But she could see enough to know the two men were exchanging a long stare. And to sense something in Daniel.

Relief? Was that what he felt? A sense that if Luke did take a swing at him he'd know how to deal with it. And it would be an escape from the talking, from trying to explain....

"It's okay, Luke," Ellyn offered when Kendra didn't answer.

Luke broke off the stare-down to shoot a look at Kendra. She nodded, agreeing with Ellyn's assessment.

Maybe getting rid of this man as fast as possible wasn't the best response. She deserved an explanation. If that made him uncomfortable, too bad. She'd get the explanation. Then she'd send him on his way.

She hadn't yet sorted out words to express this new determination when Marti came around the corner.

"He's still here." The older woman looked from Daniel to Kendra. "Luke can make him leave."

"Marti, I don't think Kendra wants..." Conflicting doubts crowded into Ellyn's voice. "I mean, they have a lot to talk over."

"Not unless Kendra wants to talk to him." Marti's flat statement rang with unqualified support.

Four pairs of eyes came to Kendra.

Luke broke the silence. "Kendra, you want this guy outta here?"

She didn't doubt Luke would try his damnedest to remove Daniel Delligatti from her house, from Far Hills and from her life, if that's what she said she wanted. Did she want him to? She wasn't sure.

She looked at the man who'd returned so unexpectedly to her life, and knew—with the same certainty she'd felt in the aftermath of a hurricane that Paulo Ayudor would return and lead her to safety—if she said she wanted him to leave now, he would go.

But he'd be back.

And he'd keep coming back.

She released a breath so deep she might have been holding it for three years.

"No. No, thank you, Luke. It's okay. Ellyn's right. We...we need to talk." She glanced at each of her friends. "Alone. I'm sorry about our meeting on the supplement. We can reschedule—"

"Don't worry about that." Ellyn gave her a quick hug. "Give me a call when you can."

"Kendra, are you sure…" Marti's frown shifted from her to Daniel and back. "As long as Emily's asleep, I might as well stay."

"No, Marti. If you don't want to wake Emily, I'll bring her up later."

Still the older woman didn't budge.

"I'll get Emily," Luke volunteered.

"Second door on the left," Kendra told him.

"Are you sure—"

"I'm sure, Marti."

"C'mon, Marti," urged Ellyn. "Let's get our stuff from the kitchen. About tonight, Kendra, if you don't think you'll make the meeting for the babysitting cooperative—"

"No, no I'm still going."

"Okay, then come by at seven, so we can settle the kids. See you then." Ellyn left after a quick, reassuring smile at Kendra.

With a final hard look toward Daniel, Marti followed Ellyn. Luke emerged from the hallway carrying the still-sleeping Emily snuggled against his broad chest. With a nod toward Kendra, he headed out.

Daniel stared toward the hallway, and Kendra tensed, waiting for him to ask to see Matthew. What would she say? She'd cried silent tears so many nights that Matthew didn't have a father, knowing the pain that would bring him as he grew older. And, yes, she'd cried worried tears for Paulo Ayudor.

But now Matthew's father was here, now *Paulo* stood in front of her alive and well and as another man…. She could never have anticipated so many emotions churning in her.

Staring blindly at the off-white wall that showed signs of close encounters with grubby toddler hands, Kendra stood stock-still and listened to Ellyn and Marti's whispered conversation accompanied by the rustlings of them gathering their things. Only the sound of the back door closing released her from her stupor.

She met Daniel's gaze.

"Would you..." She swallowed, licked her lips and started again. "We can sit in the kitchen."

Before he followed, he paused, as if he might be looking toward the hallway again. She gestured to a chair at the table and continued on to the counter.

"Would you like coffee?"

"Yes, thank you."

She'd set out sugar earlier, knowing Marti liked her coffee sweet and Ellyn took hers black. But how did he take it? She didn't have a clue. The father of her son. A man she'd done the most intimate act with—not only making love but creating a life—and she didn't even know how he took his coffee.

She jerked her shoulders straight, forcing calm into her words. "I don't have cream. But there's milk or—"

"Black, thanks."

She poured two cups and brought them to the table, taking her usual seat, with one chair safely between them.

"I suppose it's easier that way. Not needing sugar or cream in your coffee, I mean, when you're on the run."

His finger stroked slowly across the surface of the cup. His touch had been that light on her skin sometimes, yet she'd felt each contact of his roughened fingers— She dropped her gaze abruptly, wishing she could discipline her thoughts as well.

"I have never been a criminal, Kendra. Some have called me an outlaw, but I don't speak well of them, either." From the corner of her eye, she saw his hands still.

She looked up to find his dark eyes intently focused on her.

"You're Taumaturgio, aren't you."

"Yes."

She'd suspected. Maybe at some level she'd known from the start. Yet his answer raised a thousand more questions.

But before she could say anything, he added, "I was, anyway. Taumaturgio won't be helping the Santa Estellans anymore."

Behind those words lay a bleakness that surprised her almost as much as the surge of sympathy it provoked in her.

"What happened?"

He rubbed his hand across his eyes twice, before dropping it to the table. A flash of memory showed her Paulo Ayudor making the identical gesture.

She pressed the side of her knee against the table leg, hard enough to hurt. She needed that reality. She needed to hold on to it while she tried to absorb that sitting across her kitchen table was a man she'd known so briefly, but so intimately, then dreamt about so often. She knew his gestures and—an unstoppable heat seeped into her—she knew his body. Yet he remained a virtual stranger. No, a *total* stranger.

That was what she had to remember.

"The chain of command pulled the plug a couple months ago."

Her reporter's instincts hummed—the distraction she craved.

"Taumaturgio was an official mission?"

"Not precisely."

"What precisely, then?"

He shook his head, apparently more at himself than her. "When I left Santa Estella, I took a leave of absence from my job in, uh, government. I started looking for you."

He stared out the window. She'd nurtured grass in the front, but here the yard consisted of bare spots, rock, sage and the occasional head of cattle that had found the openings in the fence. But beyond a windbreak of evergreens, the view to the north and west showed rolling hills rising to ranks of mountains, topped by sky so blue that some days it seemed to vibrate.

He smiled slightly, his teeth white against the sun-deepened tint of his skin. She remembered thinking how good Paulo's teeth were for an islander. What an idiot she'd been.

"I'd have found you faster if you hadn't come to such a distant corner. Finally got the address through your college alumni roster."

"They gave you my address?"

"Not pre—"

"Not precisely," she said, finishing with him.

"You'd talked about a ranch, about coming to a ranch as a kid, but you were so intent on your career.... I didn't expect to find you in Far Hills, Wyoming."

"I was pregnant. I couldn't find the father," she said in stark, unemotional words. "I couldn't see raising a child alone with my network job—not with the long hours and travel and unpredictable schedule. So I worked as long as I could, then I came here. It's quiet, I have a share in the ranch and I knew Marti would help out."

He seemed to absorb the accusation behind her words for a moment before saying, "If I'd known—"

"You did know." Her sharp voice gave away more than she'd intended. "You knew it all, while I knew nothing. You knew who I was. You knew who you were—and who you weren't. You even knew I was looking for Paulo Ayudor."

"If I'd known," he repeated steadily, "you were pregnant. You should have told me. If I'd known why you wanted to find Paulo when you called the consulate—"

"Told you? I should have *told you?* I talked to some anonymous bureaucrat named Tompkins whom I'd barely exchanged a half-dozen sentences with when I was on Santa Estella."

A flicker of something crossed his dark eyes at her accusation, but he didn't flinch. And he didn't back down.

"I had a right to know you were pregnant."

"*You* had a right? *Which* you? Daniel Delligatti? He didn't have a right—I never heard of him until a few minutes ago. Taumaturgio? I'd never met him, for all I knew. Tompkins certainly didn't have any right. Only Paulo Ayudor had the right. Someone who didn't exist except for in your imagination. And mine, I suppose." This attempt at a laugh was no more successful than her previous try. "Good Lord, it's like getting pregnant by a character in a play."

For the first time his calm cracked.

"I'm a man—not a damned character in a play."

Her words had struck a blow. Too bad. His ego, or whatever she'd wounded, wasn't her concern. *He* wasn't her concern.

"Really? Which man are you? The hero Taumaturgio? That rumpled bureaucrat Tompkins? The kindly, simple Paulo Ayudor?"

"Daniel Benton Delligatti."

"And who the hell is he?"

"He's all those men. *I'm* all those men. They're—" the words jerked out of him, so unlike the smooth flow of Santa Estellan Spanish she remembered "—part of me."

"I know nothing about you."

He leaned forward, the crack in his calm repaired, but a new intensity showing. "You know the most important things about me, like I know the most important things about you, Kendra. You learned them during that hurricane. You learned—"

"Like your name? Or who you really were?"

"You know—"

"I *don't* know—"

"Mommy?"

The small, sleepy voice stopped them on twin indrawn breaths.

Their eyes met. She caught a whirl of emotions in his. Maybe with enough time she could have sorted them all out and identified them. But maybe no amount of time would have been enough.

Then he twisted in his chair to see his son for the first time.

Chapter Four

"Hello, sweetheart." Kendra held out her arms, trying to make her concentration on her son block out her awareness of the man who'd gone absolutely still. It was hard when the boy carried such an imprint of the man.

She scooped up Matthew and sat him sideways on her lap. "Did you have a nice nap?"

As usual, her son ignored such unimportant matters and cut to the core of his interest. "Em'ly?"

"Emily went home with her mommy. You'll see her later. Remember? You and Emily will visit with Ben and Meg for a while?"

"Now?"

"No. Later. After supper."

Matthew frowned, preferring "now" as the answer for everything except bedtime. He pointed a chubby fist at the newcomer. "Who?"

At her hesitation, Daniel's eyes lifted from Matthew's face to hers. Wary, faintly questioning, he waited.

Did he expect her to drop him into Matthew's life the way he'd dropped into hers? Did he expect *Daddy?*

"This is…Daniel."

"Hello, Matthew." Despite her efforts not to watch him, she saw Daniel's throat work on a hard swallow. "It's good to meet you."

"Hi, Uke."

"No, sweetheart. His name is Daniel."

Matthew nodded emphatically. "Uke, Uke, Uke."

She thought Daniel winced, but couldn't be sure.

She should have expected this. With Luke Chandler the only man Matthew saw daily, he'd taken to calling all men by that name. But any misconceptions Daniel had about Matthew's use of the name were his problem.

She watched him from the corner of her eye while she rubbed her chin on the soft, dark waves at the top of Matthew's head.

So like dark waves she'd once felt against her skin, under her hands came the traitorous memory.

Leaning forward with his forearms across his thighs and his hands hanging loose between them, Daniel's face was set, intense, while his eyes followed Matthew's every flicker of movement. He'd probably want to hold his son, take him in his arms….

Unconsciously Kendra's arms tightened around her son.

"No, Mommy. Down! Down!" He arched his back and squirmed toward the floor, and Kendra complied with the demand. Slightly off balance, Matthew reached out to steady himself on the nearest object—which happened to be his father's thigh.

For an instant she thought Daniel would reach for the toddler. Instead, he clenched his hands between his knees, and he remained utterly still as Matthew, unaffected, marched off toward his toy chest by the hallway to the bedrooms. By habit, Kendra watched to make sure he didn't indulge in one of his favorite activities—Empty the Toy

Chest. This time, Matthew took out only three other toys before finding the pull train he wanted.

When she looked back at Daniel, he had his head down, studying his still tightly clasped hands.

As if he sensed her watching him, he spoke almost immediately. "I know this has been a shock, Kendra. My showing up out of the blue. And we've got a lot to talk about. But I should go now. Let it sink in. Let you...get used to it."

Get used to Paulo not being dead? Get used to Paulo being Daniel Delligatti? Get used to Daniel Delligatti also being Taumaturgio and a bureaucrat named Tompkins and who knew what else? Get used to Matthew having a father? Get used to this man moving from her dreams to her kitchen?

She had a lot to get used to.

But she wondered if he, too, didn't have things to get used to. The reality of having a son, for starters.

"Yes, I...I have to fix dinner and—" phone calls to make "—I have plans this evening."

"Yes. I understand." He lifted his head, turning his gaze toward Matthew, and leaving it there as he stood. "I'm staying at the motel out by the highway, beyond the garden center—"

"I know where it is—there's only one in Far Hills."

"Okay. I'll give you some time, but if I don't hear from you—" This time the brown eyes she met were the dark, intense brown of the man who'd kept her safe from a hurricane, the man whose eyes had sworn he'd return. "I'll come back on my own. Soon."

Daniel pulled into the spot in front of his motel room and turned off the car. He should get out, take his suitcase in and unpack. Now that he knew he'd found them and he'd be staying here.

He should have touched the boy. Matthew. His son.

From the instant that cameraman who'd worked with Kendra had so casually mentioned she'd been pregnant when she left the network—with a baby due nine months after Hurricane Aretha—Daniel had known he'd move heaven and earth to protect his child.

At the moment he'd turned and seen the two-and-a-half feet of humanity with the bright intelligence of Kendra in his eyes, the straight-as-an-arrow line of her nose and a miniature version of her independence, he'd have welcomed the task of moving a hunk of hell in addition to heaven and earth.

But simply touching the boy? That had defeated him.

What did you do with a child that perfect?

Not what he'd done, that was for sure.

And Kendra? He'd made even bigger mistakes with Kendra.

Maybe because seeing her left him feeling like a depressurized plane—all the oxygen sucked out of him, with no oxygen mask in sight.

She'd looked so different from the way he remembered her best. When he closed his eyes and saw her chestnut hair tangled under his hands, saw her shadow-spattered body warmed by their lovemaking, saw her eyes on his mouth and her lips parting to his coming kiss.

She'd looked sleek and sure today. A little pale. A faint shadowing under cool gray eyes lacking the blazing flecks of green he recalled. But beautiful still.

And…he searched for the right word…*fortified.*

Fortified by her anger. Fortified by her friends. Fortified by the years.

From that moment when her long, slender hand had rested on his arm, his body had responded like it had been three hours instead of nearly three years since he'd touched her. Outside the consulate. Saying goodbye, though she hadn't known it was goodbye. Guiding her inside the gate, then merging back into the familiar shadows.

It's like getting pregnant by a character in a play.

He'd focused so absolutely on finding her. He'd never wondered if he might be a fool to think those hours during Hurricane Aretha were the most real of his life. Had he held on to a mirage?

No, dammit. He knew what was real and what wasn't.

And he knew what he meant to do about it.

He'd come here to claim his son and his son's mother.

Period. End of story.

But learning to read people had kept him alive—as Taumaturgio and long before. Today he'd seen that the woman who'd emerged during Aretha had retreated behind her personal wall, her *fortified* wall. He'd seen that wall firsthand as the bureaucrat Tompkins watching reporter Kendra Jenner chase Taumaturgio.

It had only dropped for Paulo. When the hurricane had clawed at them. When she'd thought he couldn't understand what she shared with him. And when they'd shared with each other a need deeper than words.

Now that wall was between them again.

A wall of brick and mortar might be easier to dismantle than the one she'd constructed, but he'd faced worse in his life. Much worse.

"So, how did the talk go?" Ellyn asked as soon as they pulled from the Sinclairs' driveway into the ranch road. They had left Matthew and Emily being entertained by ten-year-old Meg and eight-year-old Ben, with Luke Chandler close at hand as he tried to patch together Ellyn's old clothes dryer one more time.

Kendra shrugged. "How can I tell? I have nothing to compare it to."

"Sure you do—the time with him in Santa Estella."

"That was a different person."

"I see. Well, then, let's start with what you talked about?"

"Mostly about..." With a sideways glance she extracted a pledge she knew was unnecessary. "You can't repeat any of this."

"Who would I have to tell except you and Marti?" Under Ellyn's good-natured realism, Kendra thought loneliness peaked through.

"All the news networks. I'm surprised he admitted it to me."

Ellyn's eyes widened. "You were right—he *is* Taumaturgio."

Kendra looked both ways before turning onto the highway more from habit than necessity. Traffic rarely posed a problem.

"Yes. But he says Taumaturgio has been retired now."

"That couldn't have happened too long ago. There've been stories about him on the news, haven't there?"

"Yes. It happened recently."

"Oh, really?"

"What does that mean?"

"What does what mean?"

"That *oh, really,* like you're reading a lot into something—" for instance, his making finding her a priority as soon as his reign as Taumaturgio ended, or so he said "—when, in fact, there is *nothing* to be read into *anything.*"

"Me? I'm not reading anything into anything. So he quits being Taumaturgio, and the first thing he does is come to Far Hills, Wyoming—that makes sense."

Kendra didn't buy her show of innocence, but let it pass. "He's on a sort of leave of absence."

"From what?" Ellyn's voice skidded up in surprise. "Being a masked crusader? I didn't know they gave leaves of absence. Does he get benefits, too?"

For the first time since her doorbell rang five hours ago, Kendra laughed. "I don't know about Taumaturgio, but apparently Daniel Benton Delligatti works for the government."

"Daniel Benton Delligatti, huh? That's got a nice sound to it. For what it's worth, he seems like a nice guy."

Kendra gave a skeptical snort.

"Yeah, I know. I only saw him for a few minutes, but you've got to admit those few minutes were under trying circumstances, and that *does* tell you something about a man—about a person."

"Now you sound like him." It was an accusation.

"Maybe he's right—at least partially."

They'd reached the first stoplight at the edge of town, and with the red bringing them to a stop, Kendra turned to her.

"Oh, come on, Ellyn. It takes time to truly know someone. Not a couple days in the middle of a hurricane. He's a stranger. I don't know him. He doesn't know me. What happened on Santa Estella—it was no more than a one-night stand."

"Give yourself a break, Kendra. It wasn't a one-night stand."

"What would you call it? Not knowing who he was. Having only a name—not even his real name. Not speaking the same language. What possible outcome could a responsible person have expected? No matter what, I would have been asking how he took his coffee and—"

Kendra bit off the rest of the sentence, concentrating on driving precisely the speed limit on the residential street that led to Far Hills Community Church.

Ellyn stared at her for half a block. "I'm tempted to say the simple solution would be to make him fix his own coffee, but somehow I don't think that's what's bothering you."

Kendra blurted out the truth. "I made love with him. I trusted him with my life. I got pregnant by him and had his child and I didn't know the simplest things about him—his name or how he takes his coffee. What sort of person lets that happen?"

One like her mother. One hoping for love so desperately she'd close her eyes to reality.

"One who's caught in a hurricane and thinks she could very well die!"

Without answering that defense of her actions Kendra pulled into the church parking lot and found an empty space.

"Besides," Ellyn continued, "now you have an opportunity to get to know him, to find out all about each other. And you can take that as slow as you want—as slow as you need to."

"I'm going to find out all about him, all right," Kendra said grimly, "but not slowly."

"Good grief—you're investigating him!"

"You bet I am. I made phone calls after he left. I already found out some, and by tomorrow morning I should know a lot more."

Kendra turned off the engine and slid the keys into her jacket pocket. She reached for the door handle, but didn't open it when she noticed how still Ellyn had gone.

"You know, Kendra, I knew exactly how Dale took his coffee." Ellyn faced the passenger window, muffling her voice. "I knew every job he'd held and every grade he'd made. I knew his favorite color and how long he took in the shower and when he'd lose his temper over bikes in the driveway. But..."

"Knowing all those other things didn't help." Ellyn turned, and Kendra saw hurt and sorrow and confusion in her friend's eyes, but also an acceptance that hadn't been there even two months ago. "Sometimes something much more important than anything you can know with your brain is missing...and sometimes it's there. Either way, there's no explaining it away."

Ellyn leaned forward to make her point.

"Don't try to explain it away, Kendra. Certainly not yet. You found out this afternoon that the father of your child is alive, *and* he's not the man he told you he was—that's a

lot to deal with. You're relieved and angry and confused.
Give yourself time. And in the meantime, talk to him—
really talk to him.''

"We talked—"

"Right, about Taumaturgio," Ellyn scoffed. "That's a lot
easier than talking about what happened between you—or
what's going to happen next. And I just bet you latched
onto the topic."

"It's the reason I went to Santa Estella in the first place,"
she defended herself.

"Right. To find a man who showed up against all odds—
in an airplane, by the way—to help children in need of
rescuing. Haven't you ever wondered about that?"

Ellyn obviously thought she was making a point, but
she'd lost Kendra. "It's a great story."

Ellyn stared at her a moment, then waved it off. "No
matter why you went to Santa Estella, your *great story* is
not the reason you dream about it now. It's not the reason
you dream about *him*. And I'll bet you didn't talk to him
about *that!*"

Kendra shrugged as she opened the car door. "It doesn't
matter. After all, this isn't about him. Or me. The important
person in all this is Matthew."

Whose father hadn't even touched him. And whose
mother didn't know whether to be relieved or heartbroken
over that fact.

Marti had saved Kendra and Ellyn seats up front for the
standing-room-only turnout for the proposed child-care cooperative at the community church. With her usual no-
nonsense authority, Fran Sinclair led the meeting in the
basement room where the cooperative would be housed.

Far Hills had experienced its own baby boomlet. The
need for child care formed a recurring topic in encounters
Kendra had in the grocery store, the bank or pumping gas,
since the station owner was the harried father of twins.

The only one who'd done anything about it was Fran Sinclair, an organizer from way back and as the stepmother of the late Dale Sinclair, now the step grandmother of Ellyn's kids. Fran supported Ellyn and the kids in a hundred ways. As Marti's lifelong friend, she was also a frequent visitor to Far Hills Ranch.

Kendra liked and respected Fran. She just couldn't keep her mind on her words tonight.

When a question was asked about the proposed after-school program to start in a few weeks, Kendra twisted around to look at the asker, hoping that would focus her attention.

And there, against the back wall, leaned the dark-haired, broad-shouldered form of the man named Daniel Delligatti.

He'd said he'd give her time to absorb his reappearance in her life. What right did he have to come here, throwing her even more off balance than she already was?

She'd clamped her lips shut when she spotted him, but she must have made a sound, because Ellyn, on her left, asked, "What?"

"Nothing."

"You don't look like *nothing*." Ellyn twisted farther around, then added a significant, surprised "Oh!"

Kendra faced forward. "What on earth is he doing here?"

"This was the best he could do for nightlife in Far Hills?"

Kendra glared at her friend.

"Ellyn, that's—"

"Did you have a question, Kendra and Ellyn?" Fran asked from behind the lectern.

Exchanging a look like first-graders caught talking in class, they muttered no in unison and remained quiet—and facing forward—for the rest of the meeting. As soon as people started filing out, however, Ellyn turned to the back of the room.

"He's still there," she reported in a low voice. "Go talk to him."

"I'm not—"

"I'll wait in the car. Take your time."

Without waiting for a response, Ellyn corralled Marti and Fran, easing them toward the door along with the handful of people who'd lingered to ask Fran questions.

Then she closed the door behind them, leaving Kendra alone in the room with Daniel.

He hadn't budged, arms folded over his broad chest, leaning against the wall. Only his eyes moved as she walked toward him.

"You followed me? I didn't know Taumaturgio indulged in spying."

He grinned, swift and short. "No, I didn't follow you— this time. You and your friends talked about a meeting for a baby-sitting cooperative. A copy of the *Far Hills Banner* did the rest."

He'd listened very closely if he'd picked up all that.

"Why bother?"

"I have a son who'll be coming here, don't I?"

"Matthew will be coming, yes."

"There you go, Kendra." He said it the way he used to— Paulo used to. She held off a flood of memories as he continued, "So, shouldn't I know what it's about? Shouldn't I expect to be putting in my share of time, too?"

She felt a jolt in her chest—surprise or fear?

He meant to stick around long enough to get involved in that sort of commitment?

"Fran doesn't want people dropping in and out of the program."

"I heard."

"Why so interested now, Daniel?"

"I've been interested from the moment I knew I had a child."

"Really?" she challenged him. "Then I would have

thought you might have touched him, held him this afternoon.''

Daniel didn't look away from her, didn't change his posture, but Kendra had a sudden impression of withdrawal. His strong bones appeared harsher, his dark eyes colder. And yet, for no reason she could fathom, it made her think him more vulnerable.

In the unforgiving overhead light she noticed for the first time the jagged scar on his cheek from the wood fragment she'd removed from his flesh. She had to clench her hands to keep from tracing it with her fingertips, to assure herself it had healed.

''Guys don't have the same advantage women do—we're not born knowing how to deal with kids.'' From lightly mocking, his voice sank to almost a growl. ''I don't know how.''

Jerked back from her thoughts, she stumbled out a ''What?''

He didn't answer, as if he regretted his words.

''You can't be serious.'' She studied his face, which gave away nothing. The same sort of expression she'd gotten from Paulo when he hadn't understood—when he'd *pretended* to not understand—her English. ''You hold him the way your father held you. Besides, you can't tell me you're not comfortable with kids—you of all people. All the tales I heard about Taumaturgio and children? How children loved him. How he could get children to trust him, so they weren't frightened, even when he put them in an airplane and flew them far away where strangers with a strange language treated them in hospitals. This should be a snap after that.''

''Those children had nothing.'' The words came out in low, uneven spurts. ''Food, clothing, the hope of health— Taumaturgio brought them those things. I understood those kids. But Matthew…he's perfect. He's strong and well fed and clean and…loved. I can't give him anything he needs. He has everything.''

Her reaction came immediately and from somewhere deeper than thought.

''He doesn't have a father.''

He looked at her, his dark eyes fierce, as if her words had pushed aside the doubts of a moment ago. ''He *does* have a father. What he doesn't have is a family. That's what I want to give him. That's what I want us to be.''

''Visitation and—''

''No. Not visitation.'' He straightened away from the wall and took her hand in both of his. The motion brought him close enough that she felt the temperature around her rise and she drew in a scent her pulse recognized as his. Until this instant, she hadn't realized she'd carried that scent with her these past three years, that it had lived in her memory or her senses or her heart.

The deep murmur of his voice captured her attention.

''Marry me, Kendra.''

''Wh-what?''

''Marry me.'' He cupped her cheek with his palm. ''We'll be a family with our son.''

He'd touched her this way during the hurricane. The gentle strokes of sensation against her skin. The comforting, stirring touch that had opened the flood of desire in her. At first the need to celebrate, to validate that they still lived. But even at the time she'd known the other times they'd made love could not be so readily defined or limited.

There'd been something deeper, wider—

No… Whatever had happened on Santa Estella had been with Paulo, a man who'd never existed. Daniel Delligatti, the man who stood before her now, was not the same man…even if her body reacted as if he were. She knew nothing about him.

''No… *No!* Marry you? That's the craziest thing I've ever heard.''

She moved away from that heat and temptation. But stepping back resembled retreat. She pivoted and took a seat in the end chair. Her knees might have been a bit unsteady.

"Do you remember the hurricane, Kendra? Do you remember when the roof collapsed?"

Yes, she remembered.

"We made a pledge, Kendra."

"A pledge?" She tried a laugh that rasped against her throat. "We didn't make any pledge. We didn't even speak the same language."

Without releasing her gaze, he advanced the two steps to her chair. He took her hand again and, before she could resist, he brought it to his chest, and opened it, so her palm absorbed the rhythm of his heart. Her pulse remembered that rhythm, adapting to it, amplifying it, until it drummed in her ears.

"It's a pledge I intend to keep, Kendra."

"That storm—that storm wasn't real life." She pulled her hand free, and he dropped his hands to his side, still standing in front of her. "That person wasn't really me. I was in an altered state. It wasn't reality."

"Is that what you think?"

Why should she sense danger in that quiet question? Why should those soft words make the hair on her arms stir?

She defied him and her reaction.

"Yes."   .

He tipped his head back, letting the light from the ceiling fixture stream down on him, highlighting his strong nose and sharp bones, dropping shadows into the lines around his mouth and at the corners of his eyes. Lines born of squinting into the sun, of laughing, of concentrating. On life and death.

He nodded once, as if agreeing with his own thought, then slowly leveled his gaze on her. She didn't shrink back. She sat there, solid and steady, ignoring the stirring of fine hairs not only on her arms but up the back of her neck.

He leaned over her, close now, but his face less readable because the angle of his head shadowed them both from the light. Closer. Ever closer, his hands resting on the back of her chair. Close enough that he could kiss her if he wanted, his lips brushing against hers or taking her mouth deeper, taking it completely, and she would have nowhere to go to evade him. Nowhere…

"The storm drugged you?"

How could such a question feel seductive? How could it fire images and sensations into her mind and body? She swallowed, but she stayed still.

"Yes."

"Ah." His soft breath stirred the hair at her temple. His gaze locked with hers. "All over the world, people are drugged to make them give up a truth they would give up no other way. That is what the storm did to you, Kendra. To us."

He didn't wait for a response, but straightened and pivoted away in one easy motion, his triumph complete. He'd outtalked her and outmaneuvered her and outreasoned her.

Only as the sound of the door closing informed her he'd left, did Kendra realize it had not been triumph she'd seen in his eyes.

Not triumph at all, but pain.

The phone in his motel room rang, pulling Daniel from sleep to alertness before the first ring finished. Only one person he knew would call him here—Kendra.

He'd pushed too hard, too fast last night. Acting, when waiting might have been wiser.

He intended to give Matthew the family he deserved, but it had been much too soon to tell Kendra. He'd already seen how she'd retreated that afternoon—so what had he been thinking?

Obvious answer—he wasn't thinking.

The phone rang a second time.

If she was calling him—he checked the clock—before eight-thirty, maybe he hadn't blundered after all.

"Hello."

"Daniel? This is Robert. Your brother."

Robert invariably identified himself that way. Daniel wondered if Robert doubted Daniel would recognize his voice from one infrequent phone conversation to the next, or if Robert needed to remind himself of their relationship.

"Hello, Robert. Everything okay?"

Robert had been in college when his staid parents had adopted a nameless scrawny kid from the streets of South America. At first they'd tolerated each other for the sake of Robert Senior and Annette. Over the years of sporadic contact their suspicions had eased. More was unlikely.

"Yes, yes, everything's fine. I saw Mother and Father last week for dinner in Florida. Both appear to be enjoying excellent health. They told me you'd stopped over on your way back from Sa—um, after your latest assignment."

Now, that was interesting. Daniel had never mentioned where he'd been, so they couldn't have told Robert about Santa Estella. *He'd* certainly never told Robert. Nor to his knowledge would Robert have any reason for knowing his assignment.

Although…he'd wondered what Robert did in Washington. Robert Senior's advances in the foreign service had been straightforward and public. Robert Junior operated in the shadows. Daniel had his suspicions, but no certain knowledge.

For one thing, Robert had an uncanny knack for knowing how to contact Daniel even when the number of people who knew where he'd be could be counted on one hand.

"Yeah, I hadn't gotten loose for a visit in a while—" an understatement; during his years as Taumaturgio, trips back to the States had been sporadic and brief "—so I stayed longer."

"Father mentioned that you'd received a number of phone calls while you were there."

"Yes." Some from contacts working on Kendra's whereabouts and some from his bosses.

"I understand you're taking a leave of absence."

"You didn't hear that from Mother and Father." Because he hadn't told them.

"No, no I didn't."

Daniel had little patience for fencing—besides he'd never beat the master at it.

"Robert, what's this about? I visited in Florida. I made phone calls. I took a leave. Is that a problem for you?"

"For me?" The older man sounded genuinely surprised. "Not at all. However, Daniel, it has come to my attention that some people have been making inquiries about you with certain sources here in Washington."

Kendra.

"That so?" He wondered if Robert would hear the grin in his voice, or understand it if he could.

Why was he not surprised?

Because the fact of her being a resourceful, skeptical and tenacious reporter had worried him when he'd first encountered her on Santa Estella. It was the reason he'd followed her when she'd refused to leave the island with her crew and instead headed out on the trail of Taumaturgio—*his* trail. It was the reason, once the hurricane hit and she'd been fighting her way up the street, that he'd made sure she heard that banging door so she'd take shelter where he could keep an eye on her.

Well, part of the reason.

But it was the *only* reason he'd stayed away after Hurricane Aretha. Reporter Kendra Jenner had been too dangerous to Taumaturgio.

She'd have dug and dug until she knew exactly who he was. As Taumaturgio he couldn't afford that. Now, if it helped her feel about Daniel Delligatti what she'd once felt for Paulo Ayudor...

"Yes. It also came to my attention that a certain university's alumni roster was accessed on your behalf shortly before you left for Wyoming."

Daniel's grin evaporated. Came to Robert's attention, his ass. "Are you tracking me, Robert?"

"No." He said it with convincing simplicity. "However, a number of people know of our connection. In addition, I have had occasion to talk with the people who have supervised you while you dealt with certain, uh, issues, and they have expressed their concern about this abrupt move to take an extended leave and their eagerness to have you return to your former status."

"I'm not ready to go back."

"Will you be soon?"

"I don't know."

"Is there a problem, Daniel? Something... Well, with these questions being asked..."

"The questions have nothing to do with my job, Robert. Tell anyone who asks it's fine with me to answer anything that doesn't breach security. And don't worry, I won't breach it, either, if that's why you called."

"I never thought you would." Robert's calm answer both irked and pleased Daniel. The guy just didn't get riled, but his underlying certainty about Daniel's trustworthiness also stirred a kernel of warmth in Daniel. "I called because I thought you should be aware of these inquiries, and..."

When Robert uncharacteristically allowed that to dangle, Daniel prompted, "And?"

"If you're having a personal problem that I can help with..." Robert cleared his throat and paused.

Well, I'll be damned.

That was all Daniel could think, too surprised to say anything.

"I hope you know you could call on me, Daniel."

"Thank you," he managed to say. His voice sounded rusty, unused. "I...I appreciate that. But it's not anything anyone can, uh, help with."

"I understand. Would you prefer that I not indicate to Mother and Father where you are at the moment?"

"No—I'll call them soon myself."

"Very well, I'll leave that to you, then. Goodbye, Daniel."

"Goodbye, Robert."

Daniel still had a hand on the phone when it rang a second time. He jerked it up and barked out a hello.

This time it was Kendra.

"Do you have time to come by this morning?"

It was not the voice of a woman who'd reconsidered a man's proposal and decided to say yes. It was clipped and businesslike.

"I have nothing but time."

"Around nine. My house. We have to talk."

Chapter Five

"Morning, Kendra."

Silently, she stepped back and let him pass. He hadn't wasted any time. Nine-o-two.

His eyes searched the room as he came in.

"Matthew's at Marti's, playing with Emily this morning."

He nodded. "I suppose that's good."

"It can get difficult carrying on a conversation when he's in top gear."

She gestured for him to take the same chair he'd occupied yesterday. Had it only been yesterday? She'd experienced so many emotions—

She cut off that thought with a dose of the mundane.

"Would you like a cup of coffee?"

"No, thanks."

She'd already been moving toward the coffeemaker, expecting to have the excuse to fiddle with it for a while. She poured herself a cup she didn't particularly want.

"If you're going to stay around Far Hills awhile—"

"I am," he interjected.

"—you might as well come to the back door. That's what folks do around here. Especially if we ever get the rain we've been needing and it's muddy."

"I'll remember. What do you want to talk about?"

His directness made her foray into a weather report stand out all the more. What was her problem?

She'd thought this out last night. *All* of last night.

From that first moment of joy at seeing him, of knowing he was alive and safe, her feelings had jumbled contradictions on top of contradictions. She wouldn't have thought it possible to feel so many conflicting emotions at once.

In the end, the rational and understandable point remained that she'd always wanted Matthew to have a father who loved him and was involved in his life. She had to pursue any possibility of that wish coming true for Matthew.

Daniel Delligatti pulled on different identities without a blink. How could someone like him be a good father? But she had to give it a chance—any failure to give Matthew his father must be on Daniel Delligatti's plate, not hers.

Still, she had to guard Matthew against being hurt if— *when?*—his father dropped out of his life.

She took a swallow of coffee before finally answering, "I want to talk about Matthew. He's the important issue."

"Yes, he is."

"I might have given you the wrong impression yesterday. With the shock and…" She watched her hand lower the cup, as if fitting it into the depression of the saucer constituted a tricky maneuver. "I won't stand between my son and his father. We'll work it out so you can see him."

"Thank you." His intense eyes studied her for what felt like an hour. "And you?"

"And me what?"

"Will I see you?"

"I'm not about to hand over Matthew and leave you to

your own devices, if that's what you mean. I'm going to be around as much as it takes to make sure he's okay—and you can be trusted."

"I would never let any harm come to him."

Despite their history, despite his lies, despite her good sense, she believed him. And that roused her anger.

"You won't get a chance to harm him. I'll see to that. So, yes, you're going to be seeing me. As often as you see Matthew. There won't be unsupervised visits until I'm totally satisfied."

"I understand. But that's not what I meant about seeing you."

"Then I have no idea what you meant."

"Yes, you do, Kendra."

His brown eyes regarded her steadily. They were Paulo Ayudor's eyes. The eyes of a man who hadn't existed.

Except… In this light they weren't as dark as they'd been in the murkiness of their shelter from Aretha. There they'd seemed as black as his pupils. But now she saw the warmer tones of chocolate brown and even flecks of green and gold.

Paulo's eyes had accepted whatever she'd told him. These eyes challenged her to admit the truth—at least to herself.

She *did* know what he meant. And that part of her that had hesitated over his outrageous marriage proposal last night wanted to agree. That made her even angrier.

"You can't disappear into the night as a Santa Estellan named Paulo Ayudor, go back to being the legendary Taumaturgio for three years, pop up as Tompkins, then stroll in as someone named Daniel Delligatti and think things will be the same."

"What was there between us *is* the same. Unless… You're not married—are you involved with someone?"

"That has noth—"

"This Luke?"

"Luke's a friend." She'd meant to *get* answers, not *give* them. "And that isn't the issue. You and I—we're strangers.

Strangers in the uncomfortable position of having a child together. We don't—''

''We're not strangers. We're the same people who spent those hours together we thought might be our last on earth. The hours when we made Matthew.''

She ignored his final words, and the frisson they set loose along her backbone.

''No, we're not the same. You're certainly not—that was all fiction, for God's sake.'' She hurried on before he could object. ''And I'm not the same. From the time I found out I was pregnant, from the time I knew I would be raising my son alone, I became a different person.''

''Not deep inside, Kendra. There you're the same person. So am I. And you know that person. But if you think you don't know me, I'll give you the opportunity to fill in blanks you think need filling in, like some form. Go ahead, ask me whatever you want. And—'' he slanted a faintly amused look at her ''—whatever your sources haven't already told you.''

This wasn't going at all the way she'd planned. Pushing back the uncomfortable sensation of being caught off guard, she snapped, ''You're surprised I wanted to check out your story?''

''Not surprised. A little disappointed. But you shouldn't be surprised I knew about it, either. You have your sources, I have mine.''

''Disappointed? That I don't take you at your word… again…and let myself be lied to…again? Let me tell you, Daniel Benton Delligatti, when it comes to my son, I'm not taking any chances.''

''I know.'' His words were not the least contrite. ''That's why I told people to tell your sources anything they want to know that doesn't compromise security.''

''And you shouldn't mind answering my questions directly, either,'' she challenged, glaring into his eyes. Almost immediately, the danger of locking looks announced itself in a new warmth under her skin. She blinked, then studied his shoulder as she added, "Starting with how you became Taumaturgio."

He said nothing. As the silence continued, she realized he would wait as long as necessary—until she met his eyes. She jerked her chin up and met his gaze.

"This is off the record, Kendra."

"I doubt the *Far Hills Banner* would be interested in secret missions in Santa Estella. Organizational meetings for child-care cooperatives are more its style."

"It's not the *Far Hills Banner* I'm talking to. It's Kendra Jenner, and I know what kind of reporter she is—wherever she's working. Off the record."

She was tempted to tell him she didn't let sources dictate to her. But she'd never report this story. Not only because her job had changed, but because of Matthew. A spotlight aimed on Taumaturgio would almost certainly reach Matthew. And, to be honest with herself, she would never report the story because of *him*—Taumaturgio, Paulo, Daniel, whatever name he used. It would feel too much like betrayal.

"Off the record," she agreed.

"People at the consulate knew what was happening in Santa Estella, with some officials selling off aid and getting rich, and they didn't like it. Trouble is, when a country's government is swearing up and down that the aid is getting to where it belongs, it's hard to push in and make things right. Causes nasty talk about Yankee imperialism and such. So our hands were tied...officially."

"You already worked at the consulate?"

"No. I was brought in."

"The consulate staff knew?"

He shook his head. "Only one contact."

"But you're career foreign service?"

"Not exactly, though I do get a government paycheck."

"CIA?"

He grinned, a sudden, vibrant flash of white teeth against deeply tanned skin. Just like he had— *No.* She would *not* let memories of a man who hadn't truly existed affect her. That had been excusable yesterday, with the shock of seeing him. But she'd thought this through, and she couldn't afford that. The volatile compound of memories could blow up in her face.

"Bite your tongue. CIA's too public. Too many people know what it's doing, it's too big a bureaucracy and generally too unimaginative to handle that kind of job."

"I didn't mean to insult your professional dignity," she said tartly, and his grin widened. "But I've always heard about the CIA having people at embassies."

"Some embassies and consulates have CIA types around, but they aren't the only, uh, specialists. Some specialists are officially in the foreign service. Some aren't. I wasn't. But I had the background to pass muster and they needed someone who could fly."

She'd heard pieces of that background from her sources. As the younger son of a career foreign service officer, Daniel Delligatti had been brought up in consulates around the world. His older brother had continued in the same business and was working his way up the ladder, though the titles were vague. Daniel's work history was even more difficult to pin down.

"Then exactly who do you work for?" she asked. Her sources hadn't come up with that yet.

He shook his head ruefully. "That's one of the things I can't tell you. It wouldn't mean anything to you even if I did tell you the name, but— No, maybe *you* would have heard of it. But I still can't tell you. It's part of the deal when you sign on with the outfit."

He said it simply, but it had the ring of a man who stood by his pledges.

Pledges.

We made a pledge, Kendra.... It's a pledge I intend to keep.

She shook off the echo of his words and reminded herself that his convincing delivery could also be the hallmark of a consummate liar.

She had to remember how many times he'd fooled her already. Had to hold on to that knowledge for her peace of mind and to safeguard Matthew's heart.

"So, you're not with the CIA, but you *are* a spy."

"Kendra—"

"You must have had special training."

"Some, but—"

"Like how to kill? Have you killed people?"

"No."

The stark way he said it not only convinced her, but reminded her that what he'd done in Santa Estella had been about saving people—children—not killing. But his next words returned a hint of self-mockery.

"I'll tell you this, mostly what I do—did before Santa Estella—was fly for this government outfit when...well, let's say in the sort of situations when our people couldn't go standby on the next available commercial flight, if commercial flights went to those spots. So they had me and a few other pilots available. I had training in case things didn't go exactly according to plan, but I'm a pilot, not a spy."

On her answering machine last night, one of her sources had left the information that he'd had a pilot's license since about the same time he'd acquired a driver's license. If she'd had any doubts before about how she would respond to his ridiculous proposal to make them a family, that had ended them.

"I remember hearing tales about Taumaturgio's flying—no instruments, no lights, in planes held together by chewing gum."

"Sometimes old chewing gum," he said wryly.

"A daredevil."

He frowned. "Not when I didn't have to be. The idea was to make sure aid got through to the people who needed it—especially the kids. A crashed daredevil didn't do them any good."

"So what happened?"

He shifted, resting his forearms against the edge of the table, with his spread fingers meeting tip to tip.

"Nine months ago, I got called to Washington. The kind of invitation you don't refuse. On a mission like this they allow latitude, they said, but not as much as they felt I'd taken. They said to retire Taumaturgio."

"Nine months ago? You mean when that story broke about a second planeload of kids you'd flown to the hospital in Miami."

"Yeah." He shook his head. "I'd hoped to keep it quiet, but no hurricane saved me from a nosy reporter that time."

She ignored the hint of teasing. "It was a good story."

A story she'd followed with so many conflicting emotions. Was that when the suspicion that Paulo and Taumaturgio were linked first surfaced to her conscious mind?

She'd spent hours taping the reports. There'd been a lot about the plight of the children and much praise for Taumaturgio—from the children, the medical personnel and the people of Santa Estella, but no reporter had caught up with him. Gradually, the story died out. She'd put the videotapes in a box, and hadn't taken them out since.

"I'll take your word for what makes a good story."

"It got a lot of attention for Santa Estella."

He shrugged. "So did Hurricane Aretha. The gain wasn't worth that price, either. Unfortunately that story brought a lot of attention to Taumaturgio bringing in kids illegally. The chain of command didn't care for that. I suppose they'd known before, but they hadn't had it out in public. The Santa Estellan officials raised a stink, and Washington said Taumaturgio had to disappear."

"Disappear? But the stories didn't end nine months ago. Only two months ago—"

She stopped, recognizing what her words revealed—a woman who'd tracked all mentions of Santa Estella and Taumaturgio. But he took her statement matter-of-factly.

"I held out. Kept running supplies in, while I tried to get some big relief groups to put Santa Estella on their list."

"But you had orders."

"Call it a differing interpretation of exactly how much latitude I had."

She raised her eyebrows. "I don't suppose that went over too well."

"Not particularly. When the date to cease operations came and they realized I hadn't closed down, they took measures to enforce their orders. But they had to find me first."

She shook her head. Daniel Delligatti or Taumaturgio, he certainly had nerve. "And after that you still have a job?"

"Yeah. They had me in Washington for a couple weeks for debriefings that ended up being mostly telling me how many rules I'd broken. They encouraged me to *consider my future* during this leave. But I've got a job to go back to."

From what she'd read between the lines earlier, a job that would mean unscheduled departures to dangerous spots for unknown amounts of time. His life wasn't his own.

"How does Matthew fit into this?"

"Whatever I do, Matthew will be part of it. As for specifics…" He spread his long fingers flat on the table. "During the four months of this leave, I intend to be around as much as you'll let me, and let my son know he has a father who loves him."

She didn't know which part of that to respond to first, so she focused on the most practical part.

"*Four months?* You're staying here four *months?*"

She had a sudden vision of Daniel Delligatti sitting at her kitchen table day in and day out for four months, and her trying to ignore him with about as much success as ignoring the proverbial elephant in the living room.

She'd go nuts.

"Yeah."

For a second she was unclear if he'd answered her spoken question or agreed with her unspoken assessment. She *would* go nuts.

"What would you do in Far Hills for four months?"

His hesitation was more telling than any words. *He'd* go nuts sitting at her table day in and day out. After all, up until a couple months ago, he had been living two, three or who knew how many lives.

"I can take care of Matthew on the days you work."

"Daniel, you haven't considered the practicalities of this. You're not comfortable with Matthew and—"

"That's going to change."

"—I have child-care arrangements. Besides, I work three days a week, so you'd still have four days a week to fill even if you took care of Daniel every minute I worked. I know the rates at the motel aren't on a par with the Ritz, but even so, four months of staying there and eating out, and—"

"I'll find a place."

"Daniel—"

"I'm staying, Kendra."

When she saw that stubborn expression on her son's face she expected a true battle. And this time it was backed by the brawn and experience of one very determined adult male.

"You should think this through. Decide what you want to do—"

"I know what I want to do. I want to see this ranch you talked so much about during Aretha. I want to see Far Hills."

"You can't leap into this—"

"C'mon. You seem to be out of questions, so let's—"

"I'm *not* out of questions. I have plenty of questions. I just think—"

"Fine. Ask them while you show me around."

But she didn't ask questions, and he didn't get much of a tour. Instead, he learned lessons.

These first lessons in being a father were coming fast and furious, and in unexpected ways.

The tour of Far Hills he'd prodded her into giving would be abbreviated, she'd said, because she needed to pick up Matthew at Marti's.

That was one lesson—a parent's chauffeur duty wasn't only the stuff of stand-up comedians' one-liners.

He'd offered to drive his car.

Lesson number two. No car seat, no kid in the car.

His first purchase would be a car seat—and he'd install it carefully after hearing the statistics Kendra spouted about the dangers of car seats incorrectly installed.

She'd been so immersed in the topic that he hadn't gotten much more than general directions for getting around the ranch and a few identifiers. "That's Ridge House, where Ellyn and her kids live. Turn left here to go in the back way to the barn." Soon they were approaching the main house, what Kendra called the home ranch.

Home. That's what she'd called it in those hours during the hurricane when she'd thought he—or Paulo—didn't understand. But he had understood. And he'd recognized she'd reserved the word for the ranch, never the places she'd lived with her mother.

Seeing it now, he couldn't imagine anywhere more different from where he'd spent most of the past five years. Far Hills and Santa Estella both had mountains, but that was the only connection.

These mountains, unlike the lush peaks of Santa Estella so covered by vegetation that they were hard to see, stood out in stark relief, seeming unintimidated by a sky that could overwhelm the senses. Leading up to the peaks were folds of earth bleached by the dry autumn until they resembled immovable sand dunes.

Ahead, a line of trees allowed glimpses of buildings. They turned and drove parallel to the trees. A scattering of sheds backed along a pasture, then a corrugated metal structure, followed by an old building—well maintained, but the record of its repairs shown in varied states of the wood. A series of corrals connected it to a newer, bigger barn. If he hadn't already guessed, this confirmed Far Hills Ranch was no small operation.

The road passed through a loose ring of trees, and he saw the house.

He gave a soft whistle. "So that's where you stayed when you were here as a kid?"

Two full stories, with windows peeking out of the eaves of the third floor, and with substantial wings to either side of the central core, it was bigger than the public hospital on Santa Estella and considerably better tended.

The house was painted fresh white with sharp black shutters. Deep blue awnings shaded first-floor windows. The sweep of lawn, the plantings clustered around the house, the patches of fall flowers and even the big trees shading the whole thing showed signs they'd received more water than the arid areas along the road but not as much as they would have liked.

"Yeah. That's where we stayed," Kendra said.

They pulled beyond the house to a fenced side yard with children's playground equipment inside it and a trio of women standing outside it.

He scooped up a handful of fallen leaves as he got out of the passenger side. They crumbled like potato chips, leaving him with nothing but crumbs to wipe off his jeans.

Arriving brought his third lesson.

Other parents were a lot more interested in a "new" father than kids were, including his own. Of course, Matthew didn't know Daniel was his father.

And Kendra showed no inclination to tell him.

Daniel hadn't questioned that yesterday. He didn't have time to consider it now, either, not with three women staring at him with that half-abashed air and sudden silence of people who'd been discussing the person who'd just shown up.

One was Kendra's aunt, Marti Susland. He'd half remembered that from Kendra's confidings during Aretha; he'd confirmed it yesterday by getting the man at the gas station to gossip. The youngest of these three women, the one with the wounded eyes, had answered the door at Kendra's yesterday. The third woman had run the meeting at the church last night.

Beyond them, he saw two grade-school-age kids leading horses into the stable, followed by the man who'd volunteered to throw Daniel out yesterday.

Luke, that's what Kendra had called him. And that's what Matthew had called Daniel.

The man looked over his shoulder now toward Daniel, as if he didn't trust him. As if he might be hoping Kendra would give him the go-ahead to run off Daniel—to *try* to run off Daniel.

Kendra had said they were friends, she and this Luke. Was that feeling mutual?

Daniel waited for Kendra to introduce him to the three women, but she focused on Matthew, who in turn appeared intent on filling a bucket held by the dark-haired girl who'd been sleeping when Luke carried her out yesterday, Marti Susland's daughter.

"I understand you're Daniel Delligatti," said the woman from the meeting, stepping forward. He shook her extended hand, work-worn but neat. "I'm Fran Sinclair. Glad to see you signed up for duty at the baby-sitting co-op. We need some men."

Eyes wide, Kendra turned at Fran Sinclair's words, but

didn't have a chance to comment before the woman addressed him again.

"Sorry I've got to run off now, but stop by the co-op any time if you've got questions."

"Thank you, Fran."

With a general wave, she walked off to a dusty, mid-size car with a full decade under its hood.

Hardly noticing her friend's departure, Marti gave him a chillingly neutral up-and-down survey, then announced, "Kendra, I need to talk to you. Inside."

"Marti—"

"Go ahead, Kendra," he told her. "I'll watch Matthew."

Kendra opened her mouth as if to protest his ability to do that, then shot a look at the third woman, yesterday's door-opener, who responded with a nod.

Kendra pivoted and followed her aunt toward the house.

When the door closed behind them, he turned back and found the woman watching him. She smiled, genuine and warm.

"Hi, Daniel. I didn't get a chance to introduce myself yesterday. I'm Ellyn Sinclair. I'm Kendra's nearest neighbor."

The other people around yesterday had not been much more than blurs. But he recognized this curly-haired woman from last night at the church. She'd been the one to shepherd Marti and the woman he now knew as Fran Sinclair out of the room, leaving him alone with Kendra.

He also recognized an ally when he met one.

"Hi, Ellyn. Nice to meet you. Kendra pointed out where you live—Ridge House, right? And you have a couple kids." He tipped his head toward the barn, with a questioning lift of his eyebrows.

"Right. Meg and Ben are mine. The charmer with Matthew is Emily Susland. Marti adopted her nearly three years ago, right after a hurricane hit Santa Estella and killed her parents."

From her pointed tone, she clearly knew that he knew about Santa Estella and that particular hurricane.

"A lot of lives were changed by Aretha." His words were neutral, but a flicker in her eyes indicated she knew how they applied to Kendra and him. "Orphanages there had more kids than they could handle. Still do. Emily's lucky."

"Yes, she is. Marti has a great deal of love to give. She's very protective of those she loves."

He'd already seen that.

"So, did you grow up coming here for summers, too, Ellyn?"

"Not exactly. I grew up in town, but Marti let me come out here whenever I could get away, so I spent a lot of time with all of them." She hesitated, as if there might be more to her answer, then added a little stiffly. "We moved in about a year and a half ago."

He watched Matthew level off the top of the filled sand bucket. "I envy you that year and a half."

She rested her fingertips on his arm in a fleeting gesture of sympathy. "There are lots more memories to come, believe me. And there is a bright side—you missed a lot of dirty diapers."

She grinned, and he smiled back.

"Thanks for pointing out the bright side. But I'd have traded all those dirty diapers for the chance to have been around."

"Sometimes being around isn't all that counts." Her gaze wasn't judgmental, yet definitely assessing. "I lived here almost a year before Kendra started opening up. Even though—I'm even more certain of this after getting to know her—she needed a friend."

A friend? That wasn't what he had in mind. It sure as hell wasn't what his body had in mind.

He glanced at his companion, and she immediately gave him a nod, as if encouraging a tentative student. Maybe

Ellyn didn't mean friend literally. Maybe she had in mind that wall of Kendra's.

"Sometimes she just needs persuading. And you—" other than a glint in her eyes, her face was solemn "—look to me like a persuasive man."

Marti stopped inside the door to the mudroom.

"Kendra, is he bothering you? Because if he is—"

"I called him, Marti. Asked him to come out to talk."

"Are you sure…"

"I'm not sure of anything except that as long as he wants to be a father to Matthew, I'm not going to be the one who stops it."

"But—"

Kendra held up a hand. "I know, I know. The chances that he'll actually stick around and be a real father to Matthew are next to none, and I'm going to do everything in my power to see he doesn't hurt Matthew."

She sounded grim even to her own ears. She tried to lighten her tone as she continued.

"But I have to give him *some* chance. I don't know how I would explain it to Matthew when he's older if I didn't. Besides," Kendra admitted, "I'm not sure you, me and Luke combined could keep him away from Matthew right now."

"I suppose that's the way you have to approach it," Marti started to say rather doubtfully, "but—"

"Don't worry. I know better than most how much it hurts to have a father who's there one day and disappears the next. I'm not going to let Matthew count on Daniel just to have him disappear."

"I know you won't, Kendra. But I'm worried about you."

"Me?"

"About *your* getting hurt by this man. Again."

"Don't worry, Marti. I know what to expect now. If I'd had half a brain operating during that insanity on Santa Estella, I'd have known what to expect then, too. I *did* know. But now the lesson's ingrained even deeper. He'll realize that soon."

"So he *has* indicated he's not here solely to see Matthew."

"It doesn't matter," Kendra said firmly. "There's no danger of my falling for his lies again. Not even if we got caught in the middle of another hurricane. Besides—" she tried for a rueful grin "—to borrow from Eliza Doolittle, hurricanes hardly ever happen in Wyoming, so I should be safe."

At last Marti's frown lightened.

"You're saying he wants to pick things up between the two of you, and you've told him no, but he hasn't listened so far?"

"I'm saying none of that matters."

Marti appeared uncharacteristically willing to accept that judgment. Although, Kendra had the uneasy impression that the gears in her aunt's mind were whirring overtime as they headed out.

Ben and Meg had arrived after putting away their horses in the barn and were pushing Matthew and Emily in the safety swings, to the vocal delight of the younger kids. Ellyn and Luke stood by the barn, probably talking about Meg's and Ben's progress as riders.

That left Daniel alone, resting his forearms on the top rail of the side-yard fence, looking in.

He appeared unaware of anything except the playing, laughing quartet of children. The lines at the corners of his mouth dug deeper, his shoulders weighed down.

"Is something wrong?"

"No," he said slowly. "It's right."

Puzzled, she looked from him to the children and back. "They're awfully noisy," she ventured.

"Noisy, yes. But that's not awful."

Kendra's view of the children screeching with unrestrained laughter seemed to shift, as if she were seeing them through his eyes and, to a small extent, also seeing other children through his eyes, those children of Santa Estella who had so desperately needed his help.

Unexpected tears burned at her eyes.

An impulse to put her arms around him, to stroke her hands over his strong back, propelled her a step forward.

No!

She gripped the top rail of the fence, appalled.

Not three minutes ago she'd told Marti how the lessons learned about this man on Santa Estella and in the years since were deeply ingrained. Then, one sympathetic exchange with him—good heavens, she didn't even know if her suppositions were close to the mark—and she would throw her arms around him?

Maybe she needed to be more careful around him. Much more careful.

And maybe she better keep an eye on the weather forecast for hurricanes venturing into Wyoming.

"Now, Matthew, you stay put," Kendra ordered once she had him encased in his bib and safely in his high chair.

"'Unch!" he ordered.

"Please?"

"Pease."

"That's a good boy. I'll get it right away." Over her shoulder, she added to Daniel, "Keep an eye on him, will you? He's taken to thinking he gets to decide when and how to, uh, *dismount.*" She touched the faint remnants of a scratch beside Matthew's left eyebrow. "Sometimes the degree of difficulty gets away from him."

"Sure." Daniel took a seat beside the high chair.

As she sliced a pear and added cottage cheese, she thought of how closely Daniel had listened and watched as she'd put Matthew in his car seat. Nearly as closely as he watched him now, as Matthew played with his toy wooden car.

"Would you like to help?" she asked on impulse.

Another impulse. But at least this one didn't involve physical contact.

"Help?" His faint smile was crooked. "You need a plane landed on a dirt road? Want pointers on pulling together a disguise that would fool your best friend? Expertise in evading Santa Estellan government forces?"

She shook her head, trying not to smile. "I had preparing Matthew's lunch in mind, not taking over a small country."

"Can't say I've ever taken over a country, small or large. But if you insist on help with lunch… Need a jar opened?"

"Nothing that easy. You could give Matthew his milk while I finish."

"Or wait until he's old enough to pour his own," Daniel muttered.

Leaving the piece of leftover chicken breast half cut up, she turned and pointed the knife at him. "You said you wanted to be a father, Daniel. Didn't you mean that?"

He gazed at Matthew with such intensity Kendra half expected her son to react as he would to a touch. But Matthew was absorbed in running his wooden car around the tray top.

"I meant it."

He turned back to her and their gazes connected, but only for an instant before Daniel's slid away.

Last night he'd said he didn't know how to deal with Matthew, passing it off as the general ignorance many of his gender had of kids. But then he'd added a sentence that indicated it might be more specific than general.

I don't know how.

But was there more? Why was this man, so sure of himself in most arenas, intimidated by this two-and-a-half-foot-high dynamo?

"Then you might as well start with the milk."

He stood and took the duck cup she handed him with a quick lift of his eyebrows but no comment. She was aware of him passing behind her to get the milk from the refrigerator, but forced herself to not watch the process. Even when he returned to his chair and presented the cup of milk to Matthew she didn't turn.

"There you go. Milk. I'll hold—"

But not even the best of intentions could stop her from spinning around after a scuffling sound accompanied by the screech of a thwarted two-year-old.

"No! Mine! No!"

Apparently jolted by Matthew's scream, Daniel jerked back as if he'd given the child an electric jolt. At the same time, Matthew slung the newly captured cup around, as far away as his short reach could carry it from threatened recapture, spewing milk across himself, high chair, a corner of the table and the floor.

"Matthew!"

The cup came to rest on the milk-sodden tray with a splash, and her son emitted a rebellious, "Me do!"

"Matthew, you know better than that," she scolded as she gathered paper towels, sponge and damp cloth—the stalwarts of a toddler's mother's arsenal.

"Here—" She handed paper towels to Daniel. "Start mopping. It's good practice."

"Sorry, Kendra. It happened so quick—"

"It always does. That's part of the drill. No—start at the top and work down, otherwise it drips on where you've just mopped."

She unhooked the high chair's safety belt to wipe up around Matthew and the few drops beyond his megasize bib. They worked in silence for a moment, with Matthew an interested spectator.

"He's fast, isn't he," Daniel said with a rueful kind of pride.

"As a rattler."

He chuckled, and the atmosphere eased as they contained the milk spill.

"That should do it," she said after a while, heading to the sink. "I'll rinse out this sponge and do another pass."

"'Unch!" demanded Matthew.

"You have to wait a minute, Matthew. You made a mess and we have to finish cleaning—"

"Matthew!"

At Daniel's shout, she spun around in time to see her son, standing on the seat of his high chair—oh, God, she'd failed to belt him back in!—leap into the air as if reaching for a trapeze that wasn't there.

Chapter Six

Before a cry could reach Kendra's throat, Daniel snared Matthew with one arm and gathered him in close to his side.

For a second, all three of them remained frozen and silent.

She stared into Daniel's eyes and saw reflected there the same fears of what might have happened as she felt churning inside her. But something deeper and darker, too.

A gasp escaped Kendra's constricted throat—how much a reaction to her son's near miss and how much to what she saw in Daniel's eyes she didn't know.

She had no time to sort it out as Matthew began hollering in thwarted outrage, "Me do! Me do! Down! Down!"

Holding the toddler against his side in a cross between a sack of potatoes and a football, Daniel shifted for a more secure grip as the squirming boy arched his back and flailed his legs.

"Here, you better…"

It trailed off as he turned to give Kendra the opportunity to take Matthew off his hands. At the last second, and as much as she wanted to reassure herself her son was truly safe, she pulled her hands back.

"No. You should make sure he knows who's in charge."

"Isn't he?"

A chuckle escaping her efforts to stifle it, Kendra gave him a reassuring smile. "You're doing fine. Have you heard of the terrible twos? Matthew is a great believer in them."

Her laughter and their failure to pay attention to him had calmed Matthew. In fact, he apparently liked the novelty of his position and the new angle it gave him on the adults.

"Matthew," Kendra asked in an even voice, "what did I tell you?"

"'Tay put," he answered promptly. "Me di'n't"

"No, you didn't. You could get hurt, and Mommy doesn't want you to get hurt. So, this time, what are you going to do?"

"'Tay put."

"Good boy. Daniel, would you put Matthew back in his chair?"

Only a flicker of discomfort showed in his eyes before he said with a fair assumption of casualness, "Sure."

It was an awkward business. And accompanied by enough indignant squawks from Matthew that as much as Kendra tried to focus on finishing his lunch, she bounced from the temptation to laugh to the urge to do the job herself.

But in the end, Matthew was solidly seated in his high chair, facing forward, with a leg on each side of the divider and the belt around his waist. A sheen of sweat showed on Daniel's forehead.

Kendra fed a much subdued Matthew lunch, while Daniel watched and listened to her comments about their routine as if he were learning brain surgery.

"More milk, Matthew?" she asked.

He shook his head. "No. Down."

"Okay. Cleanup first." She wiped his hands and the moving target of his scrunched-up face, then unhooked him from the belt and pulled back the tray. She slanted a look at the man on the other side of the high chair. "You want to put him down?"

"Okay."

For a moment he and Matthew eyed each other warily, with such identical expressions on their similar faces that Kendra felt as if she were watching a time-lapse photo.

"Ready to get down, buddy?"

Matthew was torn—he wanted to get down but part of the two-year-old's creed was to say no as much as possible. He compromised by nodding.

Daniel wrapped his big hands around the child's chest, gingerly lifting him from the chair and setting him on the ground as if he were glass. Kendra thought she detected a faint sigh of relief from Daniel as Matthew headed off.

"Now what?"

Matthew's audible yawn made her smile as she answered, "There's your answer. It's nap time."

"Thank God," Daniel muttered under his breath.

Without her inviting or his asking, Daniel trailed behind as she gathered up Matthew and took him into his room. Daniel watched closely as she took off Matthew's corduroy overalls and laid him down on the changing table.

But when the diaper started to come off, Daniel developed a sudden interest in the row of pictures of Matthew at various ages atop the dresser.

"It's safe, I'm done," she said, letting a bit of a taunt into her tone.

She regretted that when he turned. His dark eyes looked haunted. What had he thought as he'd studied those pictures of his son? That he'd never know those days? Or had he thought of other children?

"You want to put him down?" she asked softly.

"No! Mommy do!" demanded Matthew. That surprised her, since his refrain for the past few months had been "No, Mommy! Me do!"

She was also surprised at the flash of relief in Daniel's eyes.

And she wanted to kick herself for that surprise, and the mist of disappointment that followed it. What had she expected?

She'd probably given him entirely too much credit a moment ago. Most likely what she'd interpreted as haunted was simply wondering what the hell he'd gotten himself into once he'd caught a whiff of a diaper.

She cuddled Matthew, as if her arms around him and his face against her neck could protect him from every possible hurt from all corners of the world. Including from his father.

"Okay, sweetheart. Time to go to sleep."

She nuzzled him a final time before laying him down. He grabbed the corner of his favorite blanket in a fist, and brought it to his mouth. Not quite sucking on it, but having it handy in case.

Matthew's long, dark lashes swept down over his beautiful eyes, dropping once, then lifted quickly before drifting down again, slowly, slowly. She would never tire of watching her son's slide into slumber.

Yet she was fully aware of Daniel beside her, of his shoulder not quite touching hers, of his hands resting lightly on the top of the crib's raised side, of his warmth and reality. And she felt a connection to him that she'd fought from the moment he'd said he'd come to find his son.

Our son.

She hadn't said the words aloud yet.

Her son, still, of course. Now, too, his son. But also *our son.*

She turned and walked out, aware he followed her, half wishing he wouldn't.

When they reached the hall, she heard him exhale.

"He's even fast falling asleep."

He sounded as if he were smiling.

"Some days that's the only thing that lets me keep my sanity. I guess it's because he expends so much energy."

"Is this a typical day?"

"Pretty much. He's active for his age from everything I hear and read. Marti says I walked late and talked early, so he must be taking after you in this."

Her probe hadn't been particularly subtle, and neither was his heavy and deliberate silence.

Halfway across the living room, she squared off to him. "You said I should ask my questions. You said you'd answer—"

"You're right. I did. But I can't help you with this one, because I have no idea when I walked or when I talked."

"You could ask your—"

He turned abruptly, heading toward the back door, with her following. "I've gotta go make a phone call before Washington closes up."

"Wait just a minute, Daniel Delligatti. You said—"

"I said I wanted a tour. But you can't do that with Matthew napping," he said, as if he didn't know perfectly well that was not the objection she'd started. "Can you get Marti or Ellyn to take care of him for a while tomorrow morning?"

"I'm working tomorrow morning, and that's not the point, anyway—"

"Okay, tomorrow afternoon. Tell you what—I'll bring lunch. Noon?"

"I won't be home till after one, but I don't—"

"See you then."

And he was gone as completely and inexplicably as he'd disappeared that night outside the consulate. Back into the shadows.

Except this time he didn't leave without a word. This time he'd promised to be back tomorrow. So, tomorrow she'd make sure she got answers.

* * *

Daniel drove beyond Far Hills land before pulling off the side of the road and putting his head back.

He wasn't going to sleep. It wasn't that kind of exhaustion. But no kind of exhaustion was an excuse for his bungling this afternoon.

Did he think his clumsy efforts to avoid Kendra's questions would hold her off indefinitely? Not damned likely. If anything, it would make her more determined. He'd known that even as he'd scrambled to get the hell away.

But by tomorrow, he'd have himself in hand. By tomorrow, he'd be prepared for Kendra's questions.

Would he ever be prepared to be a father?

He knew about stealing aid back from crooked officials without rattling a window. He knew about landing on mud ruts. He knew about giving desperate kids enough to keep them alive…at least for a little longer.

He didn't know about handling duck cups or little boys climbing out of high chairs or the Terrible Twos.

He didn't know any of the things to make a little boy with a smile as wide as the biggest sky feel safe and loved.

How *could* he know?

Kendra had expected him to be good with their son because of Taumaturgio. But Taumaturgio had all the advantages—a mysterious identity, arriving like magic, bringing supplies needed so badly that providing them seemed like love to those children.

And the biggest advantage of all—he wasn't Daniel Delligatti.

He lifted his head, opening his eyes. Listening.

Maybe this exhaustion was from five years of being someone else—several someone elses. From five years of seeing too many wrongs he couldn't right.

No…he had that wrong. Maybe the exhaustion came from being forced to take *off* the mask that had become so much a part of him. From losing the chance to fix the wrongs within his grasp.

Muffled by the closed windows of the rental car came a sound, familiar and welcome. Now he realized what had caught his attention.

He climbed out quickly. Tipping his head back, he spotted a small plane overhead. He shielded his eyes against the sun.

A Super Cub model. Descending. Like a bird heading home.

Home. A real home, like hers. A home where a little boy had all the food he could want, clean clothes, a comfortable bed, toys. And love.

He'd had none of those commodities until the Delligattis had found him. He'd be grateful to Robert Senior and Annette Delligatti for what they'd given him and what they'd saved him from for the rest of his life.

But none of that—his life with the Delligattis, what had come before, or the years as Taumaturgio—had prepared him for what he felt when he looked at Matthew.

Was he fooling himself thinking he could learn to be a real father? What did he know about being a father?

And did he think he had a hope of hiding his gaping ineptitude from Kendra?

At that moment, the plane slipped below a distant line of trees in a gentle, earth-bound angle.

Must be landing.

He started to drop back into the car, then halted abruptly, his right arm resting on the hood of the car.

He'd been an idiot.

The plane was landing. Just beyond that line of trees. So there had to be some sort of airport.

And, where there was an airport and planes, he was at home.

He was early. When Kendra drove up the next day, he was leaning against his car, pleased with his morning's work, absorbing the warm sun and the dry breeze while he scanned the sky.

When her car door opened, he forgot about the sky.

She had a skirt on. Dark blue with little splashes of color. Full enough to cover her knee when she swung her left leg out of the car. But then she reached for something on the far side of the passenger seat, leaning into the car, and the skirt molded to the curve of her thigh and hip.

In another instant she had both legs out, with only a discreet amount of calf visible under the skirt's hem—attractive, but eminently decent. Unlike the memories and desires churning through him, gathering like rain-ripe thunderclouds in his gut.

The sensation of those curved calves rubbing along his leg as slow and mesmerizing as a drum beat. Those thighs pressed against his, holding him to her, *in* her. Those hips under his hands as he brought her down to him, slowly, then faster and faster. Again and again and—

"Give me a minute to change, and then we can go."

By the time he'd adjusted his thinking enough to consider answering her, she'd breezed past him and the screen door had thudded closed. Leaving him to consider that even good memories sometimes carried pain.

She reemerged wearing jeans, boots, a battered cowboy hat and a roomy shirt the color of orange sherbet. She buttoned the cuffs as she walked past him without breaking stride.

"You want to drive, Daniel, or do you want me to?"

"I'll drive, but—"

No sense finishing his sentence because she'd disappeared into his car.

"Head for the home ranch," she instructed.

"Okay, but—"

"Can you ride?"

He turned to her. Her eyes held definite mischief, but

clearly not the kind that came to his mind at hearing her question.

"Ride?" he probed.

Apparently some of his thoughts came through in his tone. She cast him sideways glance, as if checking that the innuendo she'd heard really existed. Apparently his face confirmed it, because color started up her throat and her jaw firmed even before she faced away from him.

"Horses," she said shortly.

He knew he was treading a fine line. Push her too hard or too fast, and Kendra Jenner's wall would get another layer of quick-set concrete. But damn, it felt good to know that behind the wall, the woman from Santa Estella still existed.

"Why?"

"You wanted a tour, didn't you?"

"Yeah."

"Best way to see the ranch is on horseback. So, can you ride a horse?"

"I never fell off on the merry-go-round," he drawled.

"Okay, we'll see if we can fix you up with a wooden horse that goes up and down on a pole."

"I'd prefer something softer than wood," he murmured.

She clearly didn't catch the sexual connotation of that comment, because she chuckled easily.

"If you're not used to riding, after a few minutes in the saddle, the softest horse's back can feel as hard as a rock."

At the moment, he had more in common with a horse's back than was entirely comfortable. But he didn't let on.

After he'd followed her directions and parked by the main barn at the home ranch, he took a few minutes getting their lunch—a carton of fried chicken, potato salad and soft drinks—to give himself a cooling-off break before following her into the barn.

Kendra was at the far end, saddling a reddish-brown horse. The big doors at both ends of a central aisle had been swung open to catch the dry breeze. Luke Chandler settled a hefty saddle on the back of a dappled gray horse.

"Luke's getting Ghost ready for you," Kendra called out. *She's enjoying this.*

But what exactly was she enjoying? Taking control of this afternoon after he'd railroaded her into it? The hope of seeing him make a fool of himself on horseback? Or simply the prospect of riding on the ranch she loved on a bright Indian summer day?

"Can you ride?" Luke asked as he adjusted the girth straps.

"What I *can* do is fly. What I'm *going* to do is ride."

Luke glanced in Kendra's direction.

Daniel nodded, seeing no sense in denying the obvious. "That's right. Riding a horse is today's hoop to jump through."

Luke's expression didn't change and his capable hands didn't hesitate. "Don't know a lot of men who'd like jumping through hoops for a woman."

"I don't know *any* who'd like it," Daniel amended with enough feeling to draw a flicker of a grin from Luke. "But I figure the least I owe her are a few hoops."

Luke gave a noncommittal grunt.

The foreman found a plastic pouch to put the chicken and salad containers in, and stowed those in one saddle bag, the sodas in another, and strung on a canteen.

"Think you're going to have trouble staying in the saddle?" Luke's voice held mild curiosity, no more.

"I've been up a few times. Not what you'd count as riding, but unless you've given me a bucking bronco, I should be okay."

"Ghost's no bucking bronco." From Luke's deadpan delivery, Daniel guessed the horse was closer to the opposite.

The foreman held Ghost's head while Daniel mounted—he wouldn't get any style points, but he reached the saddle on the first try and that counted for something.

Kendra had brought her sidestepping horse nearby. Daniel couldn't take his eyes off her. The sun caught strands of loose hair beneath her hat, burnishing them to red. Her eyes sparkled almost pure green and her cheeks glowed with anticipation.

Luke checked the stirrups, slapped Ghost lightly on the butt, and they were on their way.

"This path used to be paved," Kendra said as they followed a trail away from the barn. "My grandfather's sister got polio as a child. She loved the ranch so much...they paved this path for her wheelchair." The trail abruptly changed, narrowing from a broad, defined, straight path to a narrow, meandering line through the brush. "This was as far as she could go."

Daniel thought he heard an ache of sympathy in Kendra's voice. If so, she regretted letting it show, because she immediately launched into a technical discussion of cattle ranching.

He followed most of it—despite her best efforts to leave him behind by rushing over complicated points—though some of the technical terms went by too fast. At least, he thought, she hadn't tried to lose him on the trail. So far.

He hadn't seen buildings for a good half hour. The only clues he had to their direction were the sun, beginning its slide toward the west, and the mountains. Otherwise range land rolled out to all horizons, with dips and creases that never repeated, yet weren't recognizable enough—at least to him—to form landmarks.

"You know an awful lot about it for only being back a couple years after some summers spent here as a kid."

"I'm a part owner. Marti runs it, of course, and she owns sixty percent, but my cousin Grif and I each have twenty percent. Grandfather's will set it up with twenty percent to each of his four daughters—Aunt Nancy, my mother, Marti and Amy—with twenty percent for whoever's actually running the ranch. Aunt Nancy's share went to Grif, and mother left hers to me. Marti inherited Amy's share, plus she has her own and the share for running Far Hills.''

She stopped her horse and scanned the horizon sweeping endlessly to the east. When she spoke again, he had the feeling she was saying aloud something she'd thought many times.

"And my share will go to Matthew some day."

"Unless…" He let it hang there until curiosity drew her eyes around to meet his. "You have more children."

Awareness flared across her eyes before she dropped her lids to shield them.

"You about ready for lunch? There's a spot over the next rise."

"I'm hungry," he confirmed, and was rewarded by the sight of a ribbon of red between her collar and the back of her hat.

He allowed himself a grim smile. Maybe he wasn't suffering entirely alone with this hunger that no amount of fried chicken would fill.

The creek where she halted her horse wasn't much more than a trickle. Down the creek bed, bare-branched trees mingled with the fading gold of a few aspen, parched brown cottonwoods and the occasional fir, which advertised the others' thirst by its own vibrant green. She shook her head over it as they dismounted.

"I sure hope we get some rain soon," she said. "It's been such a dry season, and with it staying warm so late, it's getting worse. I've never seen this creek so low. Or the brush so dry."

"You came here often?" He leaned back on one elbow, watching her face.

"Yeah. This was one of the spots where we used to have campfires when I was a kid."

"It meant so much to you…." He remembered her voice in the darkness of their refuge from Aretha, the peace that came into it when she spoke of her ranch. And he'd wondered what it must be like to have a place you loved so much. A place where you fit the way she fit at Far Hills Ranch.

"This was the only stable home I ever knew. From the time I could remember, we were moving from place to place. First, following my father to air force bases, though I don't remember that. Or him. Then he went missing. It was a year or so before they knew he'd died. Afterward, my mother kept taking us to new places, certain each one would magically solve all her problems as she would surely find the perfect man. A man just like my father."

"He must have been quite a man."

Apparently unaware of the thread of bitterness in her voice when she'd spoken of her father being perfect, she shrugged in a show of indifference. "I don't know. My memories of him are all from photographs. As for my mother, she thought he walked on water. Though from the examples of her men-picking skills I saw later, she wasn't much of a judge."

"But your father…" he prompted.

"Everyone says he was a fine man. You know I was named after him? Ken's baby daughter Kendra. If they'd had a second child, that one probably would have been named after him, too, like the boxer George Foreman naming all his kids George."

"There are worse things than having a mother who loved your father. Even if…"

"She loved not wisely but too well? Trouble was, she made a habit of loving too well and not at all wisely." She stared at the creek, and he suspected she was seeing it as it was two decades ago. "That's what made coming here each summer a blessing."

"But?"

"But what?"

"That's what I want to know. You said it was a blessing, like maybe it wasn't all a blessing."

She shrugged again, as if that would be all her answer. He waited, and eventually his patience was rewarded.

"I suppose, like most blessings, it was mixed. Don't get me wrong, I wouldn't trade those summers for anything. And later, having a place like this to come to when—" her eyes flickered as she broke off what she'd started to say, her gaze not quite reaching him "—when I needed it. I'm grateful for that, too. But as a kid, after a summer here, the reality of going back to wherever Mother had landed most recently seemed all the more difficult. Another interchangeable one-bedroom apartment with a sofa bed for me in the living room in another interchangeable town with another interchangeable 'uncle' hanging around."

She stood abruptly.

"We better start back."

For an instant there, she'd sounded almost as open with her words—and with herself—as she'd been during the hurricane. Now that was gone.

"Okay." But once they'd mounted, he tried the lure of memories to see if it would return her to that openness. "What was it like spending summers here? What did you do?"

"We did chores and rode and explored and went swimming and had cookouts. We had traditions. We slept out under the stars the last night here—no matter what the weather was. We went to the rodeo. And Marti always told us stories around the campfire, especially..."

"Especially what?"

"Oh, an old legend about the Susland ancestors. You probably have a slew of them about the Delligattis."

"Can't say I do."

Kendra turned in the saddle to get a better look at him.

Did he think she didn't realize what he'd been trying to do? Trying to get her to spill her guts the way she had on Santa Estella.

And she had...some. Despite her best intentions. Despite

knowing her confidences had been given the first time only because he'd deceived her and nature had threatened them both.

But now, did he truly think he could clam up on her this way? Shut the door, turn out the light and pretend nobody was home?

Oh, no you don't, Daniel Benton Delligatti. It's not going to work that way. Fair is fair. And, more important, I'm going to know enough about you to answer at least some of my son's questions when Matthew's old enough to ask them.

She waited until Ghost came up abreast of Rusty, the horses taking the familiar ground at an easy walk.

"You said I should go ahead and ask my questions."

"There you go, Kendra." Once again he'd used Paulo's pronunciation. It struck her that he used it to throw her off stride by reminding her of that other time, those other people, who'd been all too vulnerable—to nature and to each other. Or maybe to protect himself. Because he was vulnerable now?

"You said you'd answer—"

"You're right. I did. And I will. Just telling you, you're not going to like the answers." His voice had a new tension. He grinned, but she didn't buy it.

She'd intended to push him into talking about the past. She'd laid the groundwork, even bringing up some of her own past. More than she'd meant to. Now she had a right—a responsibility—to know these things for Matthew's sake. Besides, he *owed* her the truth.

But now she had the oddest impulse to tell him never mind. To change the subject. Steer away from the past—*his* past. To talk about something else, anything—

"I can't tell you whether Matthew's taking after me or not. I have no idea when I walked or when I talked. I have no idea who my parents were. Evidence points to them being South American. Maybe Argentines, maybe not."

She'd learned in reporting how silence could draw out more information than even the best question. Her silence now, though, was not the result of such calculation, but of not knowing what to ask. Or perhaps of how to ask all the hundreds of questions jumbling through her mind.

"First thing I remember—" his expressionless face was as unreadable as his voice "—was a woman who called herself *Tía*, aunt, slapping me across the face for messing up a con she was running. I learned real quick to play them her way. You could say the landmarks of my childhood were learning to beg, pick pockets and steal."

"Daniel…"

Something flickered across his face, quickly subdued. His tone remained matter-of-fact. "Don't waste any sympathy on me. I was lucky. I saw thousands like me, all trying to stay alive. A lot of them didn't make it. We hit so many towns and cities in South America, I can't remember which ones, or where we started."

He paused, clearly waiting for her to respond, while she tried to absorb not only what he said but all the things he hadn't said.

"I suppose that explains how you blended in so well in Santa Estella as Taumaturgio…and as Paulo."

Yes, she had to remember those aliases—two among how many? She shouldn't get too caught up in sympathy for the boy he was describing. How did she even know that was the truth?

Because it has the ring of truth.

Okay, it had the ring of truth, but she'd already learned that with this man her skepticism, even her instinct for self-preservation, could let her down.

"So you weren't born Daniel Benton Delligatti, and the name is another—"

"It's mine. It's real. It's legal." None of the calm of a moment ago, none of the gentleness of Paulo, none of the generosity of Taumaturgio remained in those words. So where did this cold-eyed, hard-jawed presence fit in?

In a way she understood it; she'd sat across from such presences in many an interview. It was familiar and would never slip past her guard the way Paulo Ayudor had.

"So, are you going to make me ask a question for each step of the way or are you going to tell me how a South American street kid came to be an American named Daniel Delligatti working in Santa Estella as a crusader going by the name Taumaturgio."

Her tart tone seemed to lighten the grooves around his mouth.

"I told you, I got lucky."

"That's all? You got lucky?"

"Damned lucky. I was adopted. Annette and Robert Delligatti. They named me Daniel Benton Delligatti." One side of his mouth lifted in a self-mocking half grin. "At first I was irked they'd given me such a long name to memorize. It took a long time to realize it was the last one I'd have to remember." The grin twisted. "At least until I became Taumaturgio."

"You were in an orphanage?"

"No, no orphanage. A market square, picking pockets. That's where I was. And I'm sure the last thing Annette and Robert Delligatti expected to find was a kid they'd adopt. Especially a kid who ended up with Robert's wallet." This grin was more genuine, though still thin. "Scared the hell out of me when I flipped it open and saw the American government ID. I was about seven by most estimates, but I knew that was trouble.

"When I felt the grip on my shoulder I thought I was dead. The *policía* had me, and they're not known for their tender care of street kids. They were getting ready to take me in, when Annette objected. They took me to the consulate instead. That's when they realized I had no family, no real name, no identity. They sent somebody to the shack where I'd been living, but *Tía* had seen me caught and she was long gone. Why the Delligattis didn't ditch me, I'll never know."

An image of a skinny, ragged boy, a blend that bridged the gap between the man he was now and the baby Matthew was, and yet was neither of them—came into her mind, and she thought she could understand very well why the Delligattis hadn't ditched him. They'd seen the intelligence, the character, the heart....

She forced that image out of her head, concentrating on questions, waiting for answers.

"So, you were adopted and had a normal family life?"

He laughed. A genuine laugh, she thought, with a tinge of underlying sadness. "I wouldn't say that. Not if you mean a typical 1950's TV show kind of family life."

"Wait a minute, if you spent your childhood on the streets of South America, how do you know about American television?"

"You never heard of reruns? Those old shows are in a lot of countries. Wherever the Delligattis were stationed, there'd be those old shows. That's how I learned a lot of English. Other than the swear words I knew from the streets."

"So you moved around a lot with your adoptive parents? Just them and you?"

"They had one son, Robert Junior, but he was in college when they picked me up. He made no secret of thinking they were crazy. Hell, they were nearly fifty, liked classical music, reading and quiet strolls in whatever country we were living in. I was a wild kid from the streets. They're good people, but I think they must have been ready to lock me up and throw away the key until..."

She was watching him as closely as she could with the movement of the horses. Otherwise she might not have caught the mixture of intensity and calm that came into his eyes. She'd seen that look during the hurricane. When they held each other…he'd leaned over her, his face close, his weight pressing against her body—

She jerked her mind away from the memory, unthinkingly twitching the reins, too. Rusty sidestepped in irritation at her rudeness, and the movement brought Daniel's attention back to her.

"Until?" she prodded abruptly. Of course he had no way of knowing where her thoughts had strayed, but she'd still preferred to keep the conversation focused on his childhood.

"Until I stowed away in a plane when I was twelve."

"Good Lord, why?"

"I was running away. I'd picked the Belgian ambassador's pocket at a party at the Chinese Embassy in Bangkok. The ambassador wasn't too irate—not after he got his wallet back—but the Chinese wanted to have me flogged, because I'd dishonored their hospitality. Robert Junior was visiting, fresh from finishing one of his litany of advanced degrees, and I overheard him saying, in his usual dispassionate way, that maybe turning me over to the Chinese would be the best thing for me. I didn't stick around to hear their answer. I lit out. Found my way to a nearby airfield and got into the first plane I found open."

"How on earth did your parents find you?"

"They didn't. The plane took off. I was lucky they didn't lock the hold area, because it got real cold. I went up front— it was like I couldn't help myself. I'd been in big jets when we moved to a new posting. but never anything like this, where you could *feel* the flying. Where there was no past, no future. Just now. Just you and the plane and the sky."

He'd been staring off to a patch of sky over the next rise. He glanced at her, then away, one shoulder lifting in a half shrug.

"Anyway—" the faintly self-mocking tone was back "—I had to see what was making this thing fly and what I'd see out the cockpit window. I was lucky there, too. The pilot wasn't a drug runner and he didn't have a heart attack when I popped up. He showed me how to fly. He showed *me*." Daniel shook his head in remembered wonderment. The gesture stood out starkly as his first completely unguarded moment since he'd started talking.

"It was like…like being given the sky, but not having to give up the earth. I never lived until I learned to fly."

A chill crossed Kendra's shoulders.

She could hear her mother's soft, wistful voice, *If he hadn't loved flying more than me, he'd still be here.*

Just like her father, Daniel Delligatti would probably keep flying until he didn't come back one day. But she wasn't her mother. She would never let herself rely so much on a man, let him count so much in her life that she'd fall apart if he didn't come back.

Never.

"He started showing me things right off, and I knew flying was what I was meant to do. By the time we got back to the local airport, I was ready to sell my soul to the devil if it meant I could fly." His mouth quirked. "It wasn't quite that bad—but I did have to toe the line—no flying if I didn't have decent grades. Besides, math helped with navigation. And geography—"

Kendra suddenly didn't want to hear any more about his flying.

"C'mon, let's ride." Without waiting for an answer, she tapped Rusty's sides, and he responded immediately. As she'd known he would, Ghost lumbered along behind, trying to keep up with Rusty's light canter.

Daniel didn't fall off.

She wasn't sure if she'd expected him to, but it wouldn't have surprised her, either. The canter was not Ghost's smoothest gait, unlike with most horses. Ghost was steady-footed at a walk, like a truck with bad shock absorbers in a trot, and the same thing but with a hairbreadth's worth of speed added in a canter.

She reined in Rusty for the last uphill to cool him down.

Daniel was no Grand Prix rider, but he wasn't even holding on to the saddlehorn. His toughly muscled thighs had a firm grip around the horse and he'd lowered his torso near to Ghost's neck, cutting the wind resistance.

Ghost did an even better job of cutting that wind resistance by dropping back to a walk as soon as he'd caught up with Rusty.

"Does this egg beater have a faster gear?"

She tried to stifle a chuckle, only half succeeding. She should have known he'd want speed. "You mean forward or up and down?"

He groaned. "I think I've had enough of the up and down. Okay, I've gone riding with you. Now, it's only fair—come flying with me. I guarantee you won't be as sore as I'm going to be. There's a little strip I found, and I can borrow a plane again—"

"You've been flying? Here?" Her chuckle dried up.

"This morning. Met a great guy out there. He had knee surgery so he can't take his planes up and he's feeling grounded. After we talked awhile, he had me take him up. He says I'm welcome to fly them anytime." His eyes lit with pleasure. "The air here is so crisp and dry, I really had a good feel for the machine. In Santa Estella the humidity made it like flying through gelatin. We could go up tomorrow—"

"No."

It was emphatic enough to halt his stream of enthusiasm. "Are you afraid of flying?"

"No. I have no trouble flying. I've flown a lot."

The look he slanted at her resembled a doctor checking a diagnosis. "Jets?"

"Yes, jets," she said defensively.

"Well, that's something." He sighed, then grinned. "But all jets can do is go fast and faster. Now, in small planes— you and a passenger or two or three—you can see all the details of the earth, but you're above it. Close enough to observe the constraints of the world, but not bound by them.''

And now she understood, with a chill that sank into her bones.

It wasn't speed he craved, but freedom and danger.

And no matter how much he said he wanted to stay, he'd keep chasing freedom by flying away, until someday, he would stop coming back. Whether because he didn't want to come back or because he couldn't—to a little boy like Matthew, the reason wouldn't make much difference.

She slid down from the saddle and took Rusty's reins.

"We need to walk the horses. Cool them down."

"Okay. But how about flying? Maybe—"

"No. I said no."

He studied her. "I can show you testimonials to my flying." He held his hand up like a Boy Scout. "No stunts, I promise."

"No thanks. I don't take unnecessary risks." She spun on him, unable to stop the words. "And you shouldn't. Not if you really intend to be in Matthew's life. I don't want my son to have a father who doesn't come back—no matter how noble the cause. I know how that feels."

Before he could answer, she walked ahead, putting space and two horses between them.

Chapter Seven

This time when the phone rang shortly after seven in the morning, Daniel wasn't surprised to hear the voice at the other end.

"Daniel? This is Robert. Your brother."

"Hello, Robert. Everything okay?"

"Yes, if you mean with Mother and Father. But...have you found your son?"

On one level he wasn't surprised, which was a little unsettling. "How do you know about that? Mother and Fa—"

"Know nothing. Though I am certain they would be most interested in their grandchild, especially since I have failed them in that regard."

Daniel tucked away that last phrase and the vulnerability it might reveal for consideration later. He wasn't going to be detoured now.

"How do you know?" he ground out.

"Between the circumstances of your determined search

for a certain reporter named Kendra Jenner who had been on Santa Estella, recent inquiries about your bona fides all tracing back to Ms. Jenner and the fact that she had a son nine months after being on Santa Estella, it did not seem an unwarranted chasm to jump to reach such a conclusion. Do you know for certain that the child is yours?''

"Yes."

"I see."

Did he? Daniel doubted it. Robert Delligatti had been born to stable, staid parents. Even if his childhood had included extensive periods living in far corners of the world, he had always known where he came from, who his parents were, that they loved each other, and that they loved him. He'd had a family.

Daniel hadn't had any of that for the first seven years of his life. Matthew hadn't had the full package, either. Not for his first two years. But he was going to. No matter what Daniel had to do to make sure of it.

"Do you love her?"

Robert's question was so unexpected the only sound that came out of Daniel's throat was a strangled grunt.

"The mother, I meant," Robert added.

"I know who you meant. I just don't know what business it is of yours or anybody else's."

"I can understand your viewpoint, Daniel. And in consideration of it, I won't pursue that line of inquiry, which would have proceeded to *Does she love you?* No—don't answer." Daniel had had no intention of answering, even if he'd had any hope of knowing the answer. "However, it is an important question, because it could have great impact on certain other considerations."

"Considerations?"

"I'm presuming that you want to be involved in the child's rearing and to be a presence in his life?"

"Yes."

"I thought you would," Robert said inexplicably. "So,

how the mother views you is germane to the scope of your involvement.''

"Kendra won't keep me from Matthew. She grew up without a father—he was a pilot in Vietnam, MIA for a while before they found his crash site—and she won't do that to her son.''

"That's her feeling now, and perhaps that will remain her feeling. But people's attitudes often undergo a transformation if their lives change drastically. Can you be certain of this attitude enduring if, for instance, she married another man who wanted to adopt Matthew?''

Daniel spit out a curse.

I don't want my son to have a father who doesn't come back—no matter how noble the cause. I know how that feels.

He'd tried to get her to talk about that, and she'd shut him off. She'd announced she had work to do, thanked him for lunch, reminded him of his scheduled stint at the baby-sitting co-op the next day, and exited his car practically before he'd come to a stop outside her back door.

Could that be what she'd meant—she was looking for another man to be Matthew's father?

But nothing she did would ever change that he was Matthew's father. Nothing.

Robert continued, his voice unruffled. "I have never met Kendra Jenner, so none of my observations are personal in any way. It is based on observation and my recent review of statistics from a study on family units ten years after the birth of a child out of wedlock. The study highlights an appalling number of fathers who do not attempt to remain in their children's lives. However, a father who is interested in maintaining a role in his children's lives should give careful consideration to safeguarding his legal rights.''

"Legal rights?'' Daniel repeated, even as he recognized that Robert's language became stiffer and more formal when he discussed a topic most people would consider emotional. Come to think of it, so did Robert Senior's.

"Indeed. Perhaps most important is that you be listed as the father on the birth certificate."

"I'm Matthew's father," he rasped out. "There's no question."

"Perhaps not between you and his mother, but the legal system can take an entirely different view."

"I've got to go, Robert. Somebody's at the door," he lied.

"Very well. If I can be of any assistance, be assured—"

"Yeah. Thanks. Goodbye."

He'd hung up before he heard the answering farewell. Robert Delligatti Jr. had given him some things to think about.

How long had their frenzy lasted? How long had they laid like this, still joined? Half-discarded clothes wrapped into uncomfortable wads that neither of them moved to shift. She didn't know how long. She didn't care. She considered it only in an unfocused wonder.

Then he shifted against her, inside her, and her wonder focused anew.

This time was slower—at first—with moments allowed to remove the last of the clothing that had kept them from touching fully. She clung to him, holding on as tightly as she had held on to her balance against the storm as it tried to sweep her away.

But this time she didn't fight the force that swept her away.

She heard the storm but it hardly seemed real.

Only he seemed real. Only...

"Daniel..."

Her own voice pulled Kendra out of the dream, yet she was not quite awake.

She blinked away the lingering images and saw the paint lines in the white ceiling. So different from their dingy refuge from the hurricane.

Turning on her side, she considered her dresser. Early morning light softened all the nicks and scratches, as if she saw her familiar room through a veil of chiffon. A huge, soft chiffon scarf drifting down across her naked body, covering her and Daniel—

Even as a shiver rippled across her skin, Kendra jerked her mind away from the image and into reality.

It was simply a hangover from the dream. It had happened before he arrived in Far Hills. There was no significance that it had happened now.

She saw no reason not to take advantage of Daniel's presence in Far Hills to free up more of her time to work on the special section. He'd said he wanted to be involved in Matthew's life. He'd said he didn't mind filling in for her shifts at the baby-sitting co-op. So why shouldn't she let him? Especially since it was in the midst of all the other kids and adults at the co-op. Daniel wouldn't be anyone special to Matthew.

She wasn't avoiding Daniel—no matter what Ellyn said.

It simply worked out better that he was with Matthew while she was working.

So for the past two weeks she'd seen him mostly in passing, when she dropped off Matthew and picked him up at the co-op.

The times they had overlapped, she'd observed what Ellyn and Fran never tired of telling her—how much more comfortable he was becoming with Matthew.

"If he'd relax a little more, he could be a natural," the usually down-to-earth Fran raved.

That was going a bit far, to Kendra's mind. But she would acknowledge Matthew had taken to him, even mastering a version of *Dan'l* in his first recognition that *Luke* was not a synonym for *man*.

She remembered her own first awkward hours, days and weeks trying to cope with the terror of having absolute responsibility for this child whom she loved more than she'd thought possible.

It should have been that hard for Daniel.

She rolled onto her other side.

Not that she didn't want him to be comfortable with Matthew. But he was the one who'd said he didn't know how. Who'd brought up that he'd had no parents until the Delligattis adopted him, and that they were older and set in their ways.

One day when they'd stood in the church basement watching Matthew play with another little boy, she'd tried to find out more about his relationship with the Delligattis.

"How about your parents? Do you get along with them now?"

He'd frowned, but answered readily enough. "Yeah, I get along with them."

"See them much?"

"They're retired, living in Florida. I see them when I can."

"Do you love them?"

"They've been very good to me," he'd said stiffly.

"But you're not willing to say you love them?"

"What's this about, Kendra?"

"I'm trying to get a feel for your relationships with your family. I think that could be important for Matthew—for how you deal with Matthew, don't you?"

"Are you complaining about how I deal with Matthew?"

"No, but your parents are the only grandparents Matthew has—it's natural for me to wonder about your relationship with them."

"I suppose," he granted, but then he'd changed the subject.

And she'd let him. Because Daniel was a pilot, a pilot with a government job with an unnamed agency that took him far away for unpredictable stretches of time—when he wasn't spending years at a time masquerading as a masked crusader and various supporting characters.

Once he left Far Hills and returned to his "regular" job, he would drop out of their lives. Oh, she supposed that for a while, there'd be occasional visits, probably cards and calls. But over time—long or short—he'd fade away from their landscape. As so many men her mother had hoped would be her next great love had done.

The chance of the Delligattis ever entering the small orbit of the life she and Matthew lived here in Far Hills, especially long enough to function like grandparents, was slim.

She simply had to get through these months while Daniel played at being father. She had to protect Matthew from getting overly attached and she had to keep her own head on straight. Then, eventually, everything would return to normal.

Normal. Just like today.

Time to get up. Time to get Matthew ready for another day. Time to get ready for work herself, then drive them into town—Matthew to the co-op and her to the *Banner*.

Time.

She swung her legs out of bed and sat up.

Only in the shower, scrubbing a body that seemed to tingle from caresses that occurred only in her dream—or maybe her memory—did she realize that this time the dream had not ended with her turning around to find Paulo gone, then shouting his name into an echoing silence.

This time the dream had ended while they were still wrapped in the fragile safety of their shelter and each other, as she'd whispered *Daniel*.

It was that kind of day.

First, she'd risked dressing Matthew before feeding him breakfast. Naturally, he had a particularly far-flung meal, requiring a complete change of clothes.

Then she decided she had time for a final sip of her nearly

cold coffee—and spilled it down the front of her navy slacks.

She changed into a red skirt in record speed, but had to put on stockings now instead of socks, and switch from her navy loafers to black flats. Then she exchanged the baby-blue blouse she'd started in for a white blouse, which was when she noticed a run in her stockings. So they were running late.

She dropped Matthew off at the co-op with barely a wave to Fran Sinclair and a kiss to the top of her son's dark head.

Daniel looked up from building a mountain out of blocks with some of the kids, but she pretended not to notice him.

After this morning's dream it seemed safer.

Not until she arrived at her desk at the *Banner* did she realize she had the tote with the boxes of animal crackers for her share of the day's snacks and not the tote with her notes for the special section.

That's why she was back at the church basement within twenty minutes of having left it.

As she opened the door, she heard her son's voice raised in his favorite chant: "No! No! No!"

Daniel was crouched down, eye to eye with the face so like his own, while a blond-haired boy named Jason stood nearby with tears sparkling on his lashes and his thumb stuck securely in his mouth.

Matthew defined *defiance,* from the tilt of his chin to his rigid stance to the truck clutched in a fist held behind his back.

"Matthew, give Jason back the truck."

"No! Mine!"

"It's *not* yours. It's to be shared, and Jason had it."

"Mine! *Mine!*"

"Matthew—"

But even as Kendra stepped forward to intervene, Daniel reached around and took the truck from his fist.

"No!" he shrieked. "Mine!"

At that moment Matthew spotted his mother and hurtled across the room. Automatically, she bent and opened her arms to him, feeling the wetness of his tears and the shudders of his sobs.

"Mommy" was the only totally coherent word she caught amid his sobs—that was enough. She straightened with her son in her arms, cuddling him close.

"You can't jerk things out of his hand like that, Daniel."

Part of her knew her tone had been too harsh, but the part of her holding her sobbing child—no matter what the cause—didn't care.

Still half crouched, Daniel regarded her with no expression and gave no answer.

"Kendra, I'd like to see you and Daniel in my office in five minutes," Fran ordered briskly. "For now, why don't you take Matthew outside until he's calmed down."

The words were framed as a suggestion; that didn't fool Kendra.

As she started out with Matthew, she caught a look between Fran and Marti that left her oddly uneasy about this impending meeting in Fran's office.

Matthew calmed down quickly. In fact, he soon requested a return to playing with "Ja'on," apparently his new best friend, truck or no truck. And that left her with no reason to delay going to Fran's office.

Daniel was already there, half slouched in a chair.

"Kendra, you know better," Fran said without preamble. "You can't undermine the authority of another co-op adult supervising play like that or we'll have bedlam. It's especially important for the parents of a child to provide a united front. Otherwise any child—and especially one as bright as Matthew—will start working one against the other. Turning to Mommy when Daddy gives an order and vice versa. That might not be so bad when he's little and cute, but believe me, you and Daniel don't want to be the parents of a thirteen-year-old doing that."

At one level Kendra had known Daniel's relationship to Matthew would become common knowledge. Someone considerably less astute than Fran Sinclair could spot the connection. Yet to hear it acknowledged so openly and so offhandedly disconcerted her.

Had all of Far Hills recognized the major points of her folly on Santa Estella?

"He's not used to me giving him orders," Daniel offered, filling in a growing silence.

"Then he better get used to it. He needs to obey his father as well as his mother." Fran accompanied those frank words with a stern look aimed at each of them in turn.

"Matthew doesn't know Daniel," Kendra said stiffly. "It's natural he'd be upset, so I—"

"That's easy enough to fix."

"—tried to calm— What?"

"I said, it's easy enough to fix. Let Matthew get to know Daniel better. Give the two of them time alone together. That'll do it."

"Alone?" she repeated numbly. How could she protect Matthew from getting too attached to Daniel if she left the two of them alone? How could she make sure Daniel didn't make promises he wouldn't keep? How could she make sure Matthew didn't get his heart broken?

"Sure, alone. Matthew will learn he can't use you as a court of appeals over what Daniel says."

"That's not a good idea."

"It's a fine idea. Daniel's really good with the boy— when you're not around," Fran added darkly. "And it's not like Matthew's not used to being with other people now, so it won't rattle his cage. How about some time next week."

"No. Fran, I—"

But the other woman didn't read her signals to drop this topic. Or, if she read them, she ignored them.

"Then the week after. Marti told me you're having trouble finding a baby-sitter for the night of the country club honors dinner. That's ideal!''

''But—''

''Is that okay with you, Daniel? That's a week from Saturday.''

From the corner of her eye, Kendra saw Daniel's nod.

''So, it's all set. Now, don't you need to get back to your office, Kendra?''

Kendra opened her mouth to deny anything was all set.

Then closed it.

To stop Fran's runaway train at this point would require going into issues of false identities, masquerades and lies that she had no intention of exposing. Whether she meant to protect Matthew or herself or even Daniel, she couldn't have said.

And so she found herself driving back to the *Banner,* with the animal cracker tote deposited where it belonged and the tote with the notes on the seat beside her. Leaving behind her son, his father, and a plan to leave the two of them entirely on their own less than two weeks in the future.

The day didn't improve.

None of the sources she called was available. She felt as if she'd left messages at phones machines from the Montana border to Casper. And none of them seemed in any hurry to call her back.

Her phone rang as she reached her desk. Instead of it being any of the return calls she'd hoped for, it was Marti.

''Are you okay?''

From the tone of those first words, Kendra knew Marti had reverted to ''aunt'' mode instead of ''equal'' mode.

''I'm fine.''

''You seemed upset when you left the co-op.''

She'd thought she'd seen Marti watching her from the side door, but she hadn't made eye contact because she hadn't wanted to talk then. She didn't particularly want to talk now, either.

"Just frazzled. It's a busy day."

"Kendra, Fran told me about her plan to have Matthew spend time alone with Daniel. She says Daniel's made great strides, and I must say, in fairness, he's quite good with the children."

Of course. Taumaturgio was always a favorite with kids.

"Fine. Let Fran arrange for him to take care of some of *those* kids alone."

"If it's good for Matthew—"

"It's not. It would be the *worst* thing for Matthew. He'd get used to having a father around, and when Daniel takes off it'll be all the harder for him. And I'll be left trying to patch up his heartache."

"Haven't you ever heard the expression that it's better to love and lose than never to love at all." Marti didn't quite pull off her attempted teasing tone.

"Yes, I've heard it, and I've always thought it incredibly stupid."

With no attempt at humor, Marti said, "Oh, I don't know. You came through it okay."

"Me?" It had hurt plenty when she'd discovered Paulo Ayudor didn't exist. Not that she'd really *loved* him. "It's Matthew we're talking about, not me. A child, and—"

"I know. A child who could get a lot out of spending time alone with his—or *her*—father. And even if that father can no longer be in the child's life for some reason, that time alone together remains special. Just like your time alone with your father was special."

"I don't remember my father, much less spending time alone with him."

"Don't you?"

"No, I don't. So apparently it wasn't as special as you and Fran think time alone for Matthew and Daniel would be—and I was four when my father left."

"I'm sorry you don't remember that time with your father, because you loved it so much as a little girl, but the fact you don't remember it argues that having Matthew and Daniel spend time alone together can't do any harm."

Kendra exhaled through her teeth. She wasn't going to leave her son's heart to something as paltry as logic. She *knew* Daniel would break his heart.

"I don't care what Fran says, or you say or anyone else says. I am not going to leave Matthew solely in Daniel's care. Not a week from Saturday night, not ever."

"I didn't—"

"Marti, I have to go. It's busy today."

"Okay, but I don't want you to think—"

"Bye, Marti."

She hung up, determined to concentrate completely on rewriting a news release into the required brief, leaving no attention to spare for anything else.

It took longer than it should have. She'd put the final touches on it and was storing the item into the editor's computer basket when the computer system burped over a power surge. When she called the item back up to check, it contained one line.

She had to start all over.

What else could go wrong today?

Kendra hadn't seen him angry before—not as Tompkins, not as Paulo and not as Daniel Benton Delligatti.

She had only a fraction of a second's doubt of his emotional state when she looked up from her computer at the *Banner* shortly after noon and saw him striding toward her.

Matthew.

That had been her first heart-in-her-mouth fear when she glimpsed Daniel, whose morning shift at the co-op should have ended shortly before. But as soon as she saw his face, she knew anger drove him, not worry or fear.

His face was grim, his posture tense, his mouth narrow, the glint that frequently lurked in his eyes nowhere in sight.

Even as her muscles prepared to bring her out of the chair, to meet him halfway, to ask him what was wrong, the whisper of memory echoed in her head.

What's wrong? Tell me what I did wrong? Please, just tell me— I'll do better. Please, don't leave. Please...

But her mother's pleas never worked. The men always left, one way or the other. And her mother always fell apart.

She left her young daughter to deal with the practicalities. Until, after a period that seemed to grow a little longer with each incident, Wendy Susland Jenner pulled together the pieces of herself that remained and went searching for the next man who would leave.

Kendra turned only her head toward Daniel as he came to a halt beside the desk.

''We have to talk, Kendra.''

''I'm working. It will have to wait. Tomorrow afternoon—''

''Now. Outside.''

''I can't leave in the middle of work, Daniel. And I don't appreciate this Neanderthal act. If you've got something to say to me, say it here or wait until tomorrow afternoon.''

''This isn't the place—''

''Then wait—''

''I'm not waiting, dammit.'' He didn't raise his voice, but his vehemence drew stares from Margo, taking classified ads, and the delivery guy who had stopped in for his check. ''Why the hell does it say 'father unknown' on Matthew's birth certificate?''

An odd prickling in her cheeks and throat might have been the blood draining from her face, but cold calm followed. Without a word, she rose and headed to the small back room employees used for breaks. She had no doubts about Daniel following.

Grateful to find the room empty, she closed the door and faced him.

"How do you know what's on Matthew's birth certificate?"

"I saw the copy at the co-op, the one in Fran's files."

"She shouldn't have shown you that. Even if she thinks—"

His flat words cut across hers. "She didn't show it to me."

"Ah, yes," she said with some bite, "I forgot your skills."

"Right," he said with a sneer, "when in doubt I revert to the thieving, scheming street kid the Delligattis picked up out of the gutter."

"That wasn't—" But she saw it wouldn't matter to him right now that she'd meant his government training and experiences at subterfuge as Taumaturgio, not his childhood.

She sat in the chair nearest the door, while he remained standing, so tense he seemed coiled.

"What would you have suggested I put on the birth certificate when Matthew was born? Paulo Ayudor? That would have been a lie, since I knew by then he didn't exist. *Father unknown* was the absolute truth."

Before he pivoted away, she glimpsed a raw pain she'd never seen on his face. Even when he'd spoken of his terrible childhood, the pain had been hidden behind a veneer of self-mockery, of practiced phrases lightly delivered. Maybe he hadn't had time to learn to hide this pain.

The rigidity drained from his stance as his shoulders slumped as if under a new weight. And his voice sounded heavy.

"All right. I deserve that. But now I want to make it right. I called the state offices, and there's some form we can get from the state—an affidavit of paternity. We both sign it and then they change the birth certificate."

After a moment he must have recognized the particular

quality of her silence, because he looked over his shoulder. Then he slowly turned.

"Kendra…?"

"I don't know."

"What do you mean, you don't know? I'm his father— you can't deny that."

"I don't intend to deny it. And I don't intend to keep you two apart as long as you're interested in acting as his father. But…"

A ripple seemed to pass over his tight face at her words, but his voice remained even. "But what?"

"I won't keep you apart, but I won't stop protecting Matthew, either."

"Protecting him? Protecting him from me?"

"Yes, from you. Don't sound so amazed. You're the one who can hurt him more than anyone else in the world. You show up, win his heart, make him learn to say Daddy, and then you fly off and never come back! How do you think he'll feel then?"

"*Then?* You're assuming that's what will happen."

"Look at your life, Daniel, and tell me you can promise it *won't* happen."

"You know I can't. No one—"

"We're not talking about anyone else. We're talking about *you*. Your job—with the 'government.'" She put sarcastic quotes around the word. "A job you can't even talk about."

"Kendra, I can swear to you right here and now that I would do my best to make every flight as safe as humanly possible while still doing my job, because that's exactly how I've *always* flown."

"That won't be any consolation to Matthew when he has to grow up without a father after you've gotten him to love you. I'll do whatever I have to do to protect Matthew."

He studied her. "Are you so sure this is all about Matthew?"

"Of course it's about Matthew."

"Or is it about you?" he continued.

"Wha…? It has nothing to do with me."

He didn't appear to hear her. "Is this about you not wanting to turn into your mother, the way you said on Santa Estella? You were hard enough on her, but I'm beginning to wonder. Hell, I wonder if it's even about me, and the chance I might not come back some day."

"I don't know what you're talking about."

"Or is it really about your father never coming back to you? Maybe you need to make peace with him for getting killed—and with your mother—before you can make peace with me being Matthew's father or with yourself."

Goaded, she fought back. "And what about you, Daniel? I don't see you having such a fine relationship with your family. Have you even told your parents—your adoptive parents—that you have a son?"

"Not yet. Because—"

"Because you haven't let them love you, much less let yourself love them. For all your fine talk about family, you know nothing about accepting love, Daniel. You hold yourself back."

"I don't want them to know about their grandson," he continued relentlessly, "unless I can also tell them they can see him and get to know him. And after this, I've got to wonder how much your fine promises that you'll never come between Matthew and me are worth."

She sat straight in the chair, her hands pressed together in her lap. "If you don't trust me, then maybe none of this will work."

"Trust? You're lecturing me about trust, when you've put every word I've said from day one to every test known to man? I'm not saying to take my words as gospel, but— *dammit!*"

He broke off with a string of muttered curses, pivoting away.

For the first time, something slipped past her determination to not be fooled by a man who might not be telling the truth. For the first time, she considered how her wary distrust might feel to a man who *was* telling the truth.

But before she could do more than glimpse that possibility, he faced her again.

"Dammit, Kendra, you're such an expert about growing up with your father gone. But, I'll tell you something—I know what it's like not knowing who your father *was*. Matthew deserves better than that. He needs better than 'father unknown.' I can't give him much. I can't guarantee nothing will ever happen to me—or to you, or anyone else in his life. But by God, I can give him the knowledge—the certainty—of who his father is."

She looked away. "It's more complicated than you're making it."

"Complicated? The state's sending me the forms. It's only complicated if I contest paternity—which I'm not. Or you took state aid—which you didn't. The woman said fill out the form, send it back in and sixty days later the birth certificate is amended. That doesn't sound complicated to me."

"It's an important document—a legal document—that Matthew will have his whole life." Defiantly, she added, "I'd have to consult a lawyer before I fill out any forms."

He went still. "I thought we weren't going to do that, Kendra. You said you wouldn't come between me and Matthew, wouldn't keep me from seeing him. And you said I should trust you on that."

"I *won't* keep you from seeing him, but this is so *permanent*."

The planes of his face shifted to something cold and expressionless. But not entirely unreadable.

"You thought I came here on a lark? That I'd see Matthew a few times, then disappear? Is that what you hoped, Kendra? Because if so, you better get over it. I'm here to stay in our son's life. *Permanent?* You're damned right it's permanent. That's exactly how it's going to be.''

He strode to the door and jerked it open, but his voice was deadly calm.

''You want to get a lawyer? Fine. I'll get one, too. Hell, I'll get a hundred if I have to. Because I'm his father, dammit. I'm his *father*. He has to know that. He has to be able to hold the proof of that in his hand!''

Chapter Eight

Three days later, Kendra called "Come in" to a perfunctory knock on her back door, and braced herself.

She'd seen the strange car pull up beside the pickup Luke had parked in her drive while he worked on the fence. She'd suspected, but she hadn't known for certain until he got out of the car, that the driver was Daniel.

She hadn't seen him or talked to him since their confrontation at the newspaper office, and now her heart gave a jolt at the sight of him, wearing old jeans, work boots and a flannel shirt.

"Hello, Daniel," she made herself say in a coolly neutral tone.

He stopped just inside the door.

"Kendra."

"Matthew's asleep."

"I figured he would be. I have some things to tell you."

"I'm working here."

"This won't take long. These are for you."

He pulled a sheaf of papers from the back pocket of his jeans and planted them on the counter near her hand. They were slightly curved, molded by his body.

She started to reach for them, then halted. Molded by his body—and warmed by it as well? She dropped her hand to her side.

When she didn't take the papers, he picked up the top one.

"I turned in my rental and bought a car. This is a copy of the certificate that a car seat has been properly installed."

He dropped that to the counter, starting a new pile beside the original one.

"I've left the motel and rented a place out on Kaycee Road. I moved in this morning. This is the address and my phone number."

That paper joined the first one.

He'd bought a car? Rented a place to live?

"But you're leaving in a few months."

"Actually, I'm leaving tomorrow morning, but only for a few days. And this—" he shifted another sheet from the original pile to the new one "—is a number where I can be reached at all times while I'm gone."

"I mean your leave of absence—to buy a car and move when your leave will be over, and then you'll go back to your job and your old life and—"

"The rental company wouldn't let me put the child seat in and I got tired of the motel." He tapped the third sheet again. "If I'm not there, leave a phone number and I'll be back to you in less than five minutes."

"But—"

"This is a college savings account I opened in Matthew's name, with you and me as guardians." Another paper joined the pile.

Because she was touched despite herself, her words came out stiffly. "I have a college fund for Matthew."

"Enough to cover four years? Any school he wants?"

"No, of course not. Not yet. He's only two—"

"Then more won't hurt. These are copies of my government benefits, with Matthew now named as beneficiary." He flipped several more sheets from the old pile to the new pile. "And I took out this life insurance policy with him as beneficiary, too."

"Daniel—" Her throat closed up without warning around the words she'd intended.

"Don't worry. I'm still not planning on doing anything reckless, but like I told you, anything can happen. If it does, call Robert Delligatti Jr., he'll get you through any and all red tape you encounter. My parents' address and phone number is here, too."

He didn't say it, but she suspected he meant this as another kind of insurance—insurance that his parents would be involved in Matthew's life as grandparents. Someday.

With him or without him.

The hollowed-out space in her gut at that thought echoed with the knowledge that she didn't like the implications of that.

"And these—" he slapped the final papers onto the new pile "—are the forms for amending Matthew's birth certificate."

She stiffened her spine and narrowed her eyes, ignoring all her earlier reactions.

"I told you—"

"And I told you," he interrupted, leaning forward, so his palm pressed down on the papers on the counter. "I'll give you some time, Kendra. But not much more of it. If I have to, I'll go to court to get my name on that birth certificate. I won't sue you over custody. And I won't push you to explain it to Matthew or tell other people, but my name is going to be on my son's birth certificate."

He was gone before she could form a response.

"Need some help?"

Luke Chandler looked up from the contraption he seemed

to be using to stretch the strands of barbed wire that reached from one wooden fence post to the next.

He didn't appear as surprised as Daniel felt that, instead of getting in his car and driving away, he'd strode over to volunteer his muscles to the task he'd noticed Luke performing as he'd headed for Kendra's door.

Then, he'd been prepared for battle—with her and with himself.

Now the leftover adrenaline and some other hormone that had been rioting against the discipline of his mind, demanding that he grab Kendra and kiss her until they both forgot everything except what they'd found during the hurricane, had him jumpy and on edge.

On second thought, Luke's expression not only didn't betray surprise, it didn't give *any* reaction away.

Luke Chandler would be hell to face across a poker table with a pot at stake. For some reason that thought cheered Daniel. He wouldn't mind the challenge.

"You know what you're doing when it comes to fixing fence?"

"Not a clue."

"You said you couldn't ride, either. Noticed you didn't fall off."

"Not while you were looking, anyhow."

"Would've known," Luke said with such offhand assurance that Daniel believed him. "You know that if Kendra had said she wanted you gone that first day, I would have tossed you out on your butt. And, if she changes her mind and says the word now or any time in the future, I'll still toss you out on your butt."

Daniel understood the other man was laying his cards on the table, and he appreciated that.

"You can try," he allowed equably. A small part of him almost wished the ranch foreman would try. It would give this pent-up energy somewhere to vent.

"Fair enough. There's another pair of gloves in that bag."

"Okay." As he walked back to Luke, pulling on the heavy gloves, Daniel surprised himself for the second time in these past five minutes, by offering, "I could take you up flying sometime, Luke."

"I might take you up on that." A slow smile spread across the other man's face. "I'd like to see what it is you *do* know how to do. Grab hold here while I use the stretcher."

Daniel grabbed hold, and for nearly three hours he tugged, held and yanked as ordered. Sweat soaked his shirt, then his chest, back and arms when he took off the shirt. Even his dark skin would feel the bite of the sun, especially across his shoulders.

It felt good, damned good to work his muscles, to sweat, to be physically tired.

But as a remedy to stop thinking about Matthew and Kendra, this little foray into fence-fixing was a total failure.

The first time she spotted Daniel out her back window, Kendra nearly spilled her fresh glass of water all over the keyboard of her laptop computer.

She'd gotten up and poured out the old water and replaced it in the hope that new water might somehow translate to a new train of thought when she sat in front of the laptop. Every stop on the old train of thought had been Daniel Benton Delligatti.

And now there he stood some thirty yards beyond her window.

Actually, if he'd simply stood it might not have been so bad. But he bent and twisted and squatted and stretched. When he took his shirt off, she'd considered for half a minute going out there and demanding that he leave.

Just as quickly, she'd realized what a mistake it would be to let him know how the sight of him affected her.

So, she stayed inside, stubbornly remaining at the table, telling herself she had the self-discipline to get her work done no matter who was outside the window.

When Matthew got up from his nap, she closed the lid of the laptop feeling like he'd brought her a reprieve from the governor. She'd written a grand total of four-and-a-half sentences in two hours.

At least she succeeded in keeping Matthew occupied so he didn't spot Luke and Daniel outside. There would have been no peace.

Maybe she'd actually get some peace with Daniel going away for a while. If she was lucky he'd stay away.

Even as the thought came, she had to acknowledge that contemplating the possibility of Daniel Delligatti never returning to Far Hills didn't make her feel the least bit lucky.

Kendra kept so busy over the next six days that she couldn't be expected to even notice Daniel's absence, much less come close to missing him.

She worked, did three shifts at the co-op and took care of Emily two afternoons. She also fed Ben and Meg dinner and oversaw their homework endeavors, leaving Ellyn free to have dinner in town with Fran before going to parent-teacher night at the grade school.

Yes, indeed, she was so busy, Daniel Delligatti never would have crossed her mind if other people didn't keep bringing him up.

Matthew's queries were direct and delivered each time he arrived at the co-op: "Dan'l?"

"No, Matthew, Daniel's gone away and he's not back yet."

People at the co-op were nearly as direct in asking when Daniel would be back. Not satisfied when she told them she had no idea, they went on to extol his good nature with the kids. Fran, too, followed that routine, then referred to Daniel caring for Matthew the night of the country club dinner as if it were a done deal.

Kendra ignored it.

Marti wasn't as easy to ignore when she came to pick up Emily six days before the country club dinner.

"About Daniel taking care of Matthew—"

"It isn't going to happen."

"When are you going to tell Daniel it isn't going to happen?"

"I can't very well tell him now, can I, since he's not around. Who knows if he'll even come back."

"You don't think he'll come back?"

"No—yes. I don't know."

Marti watched while Kendra took great care in folding Matthew's undershirt.

"No, I don't suppose you do know, do you? As you've said, he's a stranger. You don't *really* know him."

Kendra said nothing.

"Or don't you feel that way anymore?" Marti asked bluntly.

She prepared the words to deny that she'd changed her mind, the words that would reaffirm what an absolute stranger he remained. What came out was "I know pieces."

"Pieces?"

I'm all those men. They're part of me.

"Yes, pieces. Some pieces he's let me see, and other…fragments that have come out."

"You make him sound like a jigsaw puzzle," Marti protested with a half smile, as she watched Kendra's hands repeating the familiar, routine motions of folding Matthew's next undershirt.

Kendra shrugged. "If so, I'm a long way from putting that puzzle together. And I doubt I ever will, because he's not the kind to hand over all the pieces."

Marti's gaze traveled up to her face. Kendra found herself unable to read her aunt's expression.

"Ah, but you were always good at putting together puzzles, Kendra, even without the picture to go by."

That conversation rattled around in Kendra's head at odd moments, such as while rocking Matthew when he woke with a bad dream one night.

But a brief exchange with Luke as she arrived home Monday evening with Emily and Matthew from the co-op really got under her skin.

He pulled his pickup in next to where she'd just parked her car, and without any fanfare helped take the kids out, then carried two-thirds of the groceries into the house for her.

"Thanks for the help, Luke."

"Welcome. Expecting Daniel for dinner?"

Caught off guard, her voice skidded up. "No." She cleared her throat. "What on earth made you think that?"

He nodded toward two steaks showing at the top of one of the bags he'd carried in.

"I eat steak," she declared.

"Two at a time?"

"I often cook things two at a time and eat the second portion as leftovers," she said with great dignity.

"Uh-huh."

She started to protest that she was telling the absolute truth, when she caught the glint in his eyes and firmly shut her mouth.

"So, do you think he's coming back, or have you scared him off for good?"

Her resolve to ignore his prodding evaporated in a spurt of irritation. "Scared him off? I—"

"Yeah, you might be right," he interrupted with a solemn nod, as if her protest had been an answer. "You might have scared him off for good with your too-strong-and-too-smart-to-be-needing-anybody-anyway-anytime-anywhere act. It wasn't a bad act when we were kids, but you've got it down pat now," he said in spurious admiration.

"Luke Chandler, you—"

"'Course, I'm one who's hoping he comes back."

That surprised her enough to silence her sputtering.

"Yep," he said with a nod as he headed toward the door. "The man won't ever be much on horseback, but he's got potential for mending fence, as you saw for yourself last week."

Ellyn tapped the tip of her pen against one item on the yellow legal pad on the table between them.

"If you could break that out into a sidebar," she said, "I could package it with the line drawing of Fort Bighorn before the Indians burned it down."

"I could do that, but then— Oh, darn." Kendra gave Ellyn an exasperated shake of her head as she jumped up to get the phone. "How many times is this thing going to ring today? You'd think with Matthew at co-op— Hello?"

"Kendra? It's Luke."

"Hi, Luke. What can I do for you?" She let enough chill into her voice to remind him she was not amused by his comments the day before yesterday.

"Fran asked me to call. She thinks you better get down here, to the church."

Fear immediately overrode any other emotion. "Is it Matthew? Is he…?"

"He's fine. It's nothing like that. It's…well, I drove Marti in to pick up Emily because I had a stop in town, too, and… It's Daniel."

"Daniel?" Nothing in Luke's tone indicated he was kidding. Still… "He's back east."

"No, he's here, at the co-op. Got back this afternoon from what I hear. But…well, I think you better get down here."

"Luke, if you're—"

"Kendra. I'm telling you straight." His voice left no doubt. "You better get down here."

"Luke, you're scaring me. What's wrong?" she demanded, even while she stretched the phone cord to reach her jacket on the hook by the back door. She tended to slip her car keys into pockets—yes, there they were. Ellyn stood, looking worried. Kendra gave a small shake of her head to convey she didn't know what was going on. "Is he hurt? Is it—"

"No, I told you, nothing like that. The kids are mostly gone, and Daniel's just playing the piano, but..."

"But what?"

He paused so long that her lungs began to hurt with her held breath and half-thought worries.

"It's Chopin."

Air rushed out of her in surprise, and she gulped more in. "Chopin? I don't understand."

"You will when you get here." He sounded grim.

"I'm on my way."

Ellyn announced she was coming with her. "And," she added, taking the keys from Kendra's hand, "I'm driving."

On the way into town she insisted Kendra fill in the gaps of the conversation she'd half heard. Repeating it did nothing to ease Kendra's mind or to give order to her jumbled thoughts.

Luke waited in the hallway at the bottom of the stairs, outside the basement meeting room used for the baby-sitting co-op. Piano music seeped out of the closed door.

"What happened, Luke?"

"I don't know how it started. I'd dropped Marti off and swung 'round to the supply store for a mortar drill bit. When I came back, Fran and a couple of parents were here in the hallway and the kids were sitting on the floor inside, quiet as mice, everybody listening to that music." He tipped his head toward the door. "Fran asked me to call you, and she went in and started scooting kids out to their folks."

"She didn't think—" Kendra couldn't even voice the possibility that Daniel would hurt the children.

"Naw. She didn't want to disturb Daniel."

Through the door's glass insert, Kendra spotted Fran and Marti sitting to one side with Matthew and Emily in their laps, all four of them listening to the music coming from the old, vaguely out-of-tune upright more often used for "Happy Birthday" or "Old McDonald." Despite that—or maybe partly because of it—the music had a power and pathos that tightened her throat.

The piano blocked most of her view of Daniel, so she saw only the top of his dark head.

"You know the classics, Luke?" Ellyn asked.

"Can't say I know them. But Chopin…somebody once told me she figured Chopin wanted to make you hear pain in beautiful music."

Kendra looked around, but Luke didn't meet her eyes.

Ellyn laid a hand on her arm. "I'll take Matthew home with me, Kendra. You come by later if you want, or we'll keep him overnight, whatever you need, okay?"

"Okay. Thanks. Both of you."

Kendra inhaled, then eased the door open. The motion caught the attention of all four listeners. In a flash, Matthew slid off Fran's lap and trundled toward her with a big grin. The others followed more sedately.

"Dan'l," Matthew announced, pointing a chubby finger toward the piano.

She laid a finger across her lips, and wonder of wonders, Matthew obeyed as they all exited.

The music never faltered.

Letting the door swing silently closed again, Kendra scooched down to her son's level.

"Dan'l," he repeated emphatically.

"Yes, Daniel's back." That acknowledgment seemed to satisfy him. She concentrated on keeping her voice even and calm as she quickly told Matthew that he'd be going to the Sinclairs' for dinner and maybe overnight.

She had to admit this semblance of calm was for her own sake, not his. She probably could have sobbed out the news and it wouldn't have fazed her son. The prospect of going to the Sinclairs, where Meg and even Ben catered to his every whim, thrilled Matthew.

"I'll be in my office upstairs for another hour doing paperwork if you need anything, Kendra." Fran patted her on the shoulder before following Ellyn and Matthew down the hall.

"We'd best get going, too, Marti," Luke said to his employer, who still held her daughter's hand.

"Kendra—" She sounded worried.

"It's all right, Marti."

Marti nodded. "That boy's got a lot of pain in him, but you can help him, Kendra."

If she'd had time, the change in Marti's attitude might have astounded Kendra. Instead, she was too focused on the man at the piano to do more than file away the comment as something that needed mulling over.

In another minute the two adults and the little girl had disappeared up the stairs, and Kendra remained alone in the hallway with the haunting music seeping through the old walls.

She quietly opened the door and stepped inside.

Daniel sat on the battered wooden bench, slightly hunched, his eyes open but unfocused as his hands traveled the keyboard. Even from the distance she kept, the gaunt look his face had taken on shocked her. His jaw was darkened by stubble, the area under his eyes darkened by lack of sleep, and his eyes themselves darkened by the same kind of pain she heard flowing through the music.

He gave no sign of hearing her.

She stood motionless, except for tears that slipped down silently and relentlessly. Luke was right about the pain in this beautiful music. And Marti was right about the pain in Daniel.

But was Marti right that she could help ease it?

And then the music stopped.

"Kendra." He still hadn't looked around.

"Yes."

"I scared everyone else off, huh?"

"No."

"I started playing, and…"

"It was beautiful."

He half turned toward her, and she saw his attempt at a grin. It fell far short. "Madame Romaine would be pleased someone thought so. Or maybe she wouldn't. Not after all the times she gave me grief for not applying myself. She never thought I deserved to create anything beautiful, because I didn't practice. Didn't give it my all…like everything else in my life."

"Except flying."

He didn't look as surprised as she felt that she'd chosen that to remind him that he did give his all to some things.

"Except flying," he agreed without inflection.

"And Taumaturgio."

He said nothing. And before she could probe his silence, he positioned his fingers for a chord, then, instead of pressing all the keys together, he played each note separately.

"Being a father isn't flying. What if I let Matthew down, like I let Madame Romaine down and—" his fingers curled against the keys "—the others?"

"I don't know how you can talk like that, Daniel." She moved beside the bench, pressing her hand against her side to keep from stroking his hair as she would to console Matthew. As she had done to Paulo Ayudor during the storm, though the gesture had brought rather than given consolation then. "Think of all the people you helped in Santa Estella. All the children. That's not—"

"Helped? I let people down."

"How can you say—"

"I flew in, dropped a few miracles with a flourish—showtime!" Even in profile she recognized his grimace. "But how many didn't I help? Didn't get to. Couldn't get the right supplies. Didn't have the time. So many…I failed. Had to fight the system, try going for more, and lost it all. All those kids I can't help at all now. How about them?''

"Maybe it's somebody else's turn to help them," she said gently. "Maybe you can't do it all."

He shook his head. "It should be me."

He slid over on the bench, and she took the invitation to sit beside him. But he stared at his fingers spread on the piano keys.

"All those years, I used to wonder…. It didn't add up. But on Santa Estella, it finally made sense."

"What made sense, Daniel?"

"Why I got out. Why I didn't die on the streets like so many other kids. Why the Delligattis came into *my* life. Why my life was the one changed—saved. I wasn't any smarter or better than any of the rest of them. I stole the same things, told the same lies— It never made sense. But when I was helping those kids on Santa Estella… For the first time, I could see… Even the flying. Flying wasn't just a gift, it was a tool."

His voice dropped lower and harsher. "But now I'm not doing that—''

And now he couldn't see any reason for his luck in escaping a hell that no child should be in.

Don't waste any sympathy on me. I was lucky. I saw thousands like me, all trying to stay alive. A lot of them didn't make it.

"It makes sense that the Delligattis rescued you. It makes all the sense in the world, because you're you. You don't have to earn that, Daniel."

He said nothing. Still didn't look at her. He pressed two keys lightly, first one, then the other.

"Daniel…"

Before she had recognized the impulse, her fingers lightly skimmed the scar on his cheek. He went absolutely still as she traced the raised skin with the tip of her finger.

How many scars did he carry inside? From a childhood she couldn't even imagine. From years of trying almost single-handedly to right the wrongs of an entire country.

And from her?

Had she inflicted scars on him?

I know what it's like not knowing who your father was. Matthew deserves better than that. He needs better than "father unknown." I can't give him much...but by God, I can give him that.

She hadn't meant to add to Daniel's scars. She'd meant only to protect Matthew...and, yes, to protect herself.

Or had she?

Had she meant to punish him? To make him suffer as she had, first with the fear of not being able to find Paulo after the hurricane, then with the betrayal of realizing the name she'd called out in love belonged to a figment, and finally with the loneliness of having their child without him beside her.

She had barely begun to withdraw her hand, when he clasped her wrist. For a suspended moment they remained like that.

She could try to pull away. She *should* try to pull away.

Instead, she turned toward him, her knees against his right thigh, easing the stretch of her arm across her body.

He bent his head, his dark lashes partially lowered, and kissed her fingertips. Warmth flared from where his lips touched, down her arm, into her chest, then deeper.

His mouth dropped to her palm, a lingering contact that translated into a long, hot shiver down her backbone and pulses of sensation in her hardening nipples.

Thought had fled, evaporated by the heat and sensation of his touch, and her own longing.

He skimmed the heel of her hand, from under her little finger to the pad of her thumb. His own, callused thumbs dredged up the hem of her sleeve, exposing her forearm to her elbow. Again, he drew her arm up as he bent over it, kissing the tender skin there, then tracing a pattern with his tongue. The shivers deepened to shudders.

A nearly comatose instinct for self-preservation jerked her muscles into action, trying to capture her elbow from him and tuck it against her side.

But that solitary instinct hadn't figured on the way the back of his fingers, still wrapped around her arm, would brush against her breast, grazing her hardened nipple with a softness that sent a new jolt along all her nerve-endings.

And those muscles hadn't figured on the way he would follow her retreat, so his face came near enough to hers that a sway of motion by either one of them would bring their mouths together.

They held there an instant, so close she could see in his eyes, along with a reflection of herself, his memories of their kisses. Or were they her memories?

His grip on her arm eased—she'd been unaware how tight it was until he loosened it—and he backed away slightly.

It was enough.

She withdrew her hand, her arm and herself.

"I am sorry, Kendra, I didn't intend to make you sad. And I didn't intend—"

"It's all right, Daniel." She dredged up a smile. "No harm done."

Would there have been harm done if he had kissed her lips? If they had kissed each other? Harm to what? Or who?

She rushed past her own questions with words.

"And I'm the one who's sorry. Sorry I didn't understand three years ago what you were doing, didn't try to help instead of trying to hunt down Taumaturgio. Maybe if I'd known—if I'd understood—I could have done more, stayed in Santa Estella after the storm..."

"No. I'm glad you came here. I'm glad you brought Matthew here. Whenever I think of you leaving Santa Estella, I'm grateful."

"Daniel, now you have to leave Santa Estella behind, too."

"I don't have much choice." He seemed to make an effort to shake off his mood. "I can't got back to Santa Estella now without being as reckless as you're always accusing me of being."

"Good." She achieved a fair approximation of brisk approval. "You did so much, gave so much. Now someone else has to carry that burden for a while. For you, it's over."

His half smile disappeared.

"Sometimes a war's over, but not ended. Not inside."

Chapter Nine

She took him back to her house.

Even the next morning she couldn't quite believe that.

Not that anything happened.

The church custodian had clattered into the co-op room with buckets and vacuum, paying them no heed and breaking the spell of confidences. Before she could blink, Daniel's armor was in place and he'd disappeared behind a sardonic grin.

"I really know how to show a girl a good time, don't I?" He gave the piano keys a jazzy flourish, then stood.

It would have been a more effective gesture if he hadn't swayed.

"When did you last eat?"

"Eat?" he repeated distractedly. Apparently he was pouring most of his will into standing.

"Eat. Food. Did you have lunch?"

"No. Tight connection in Denver."

"Breakfast?"

"No time. Had to get to the airport."

"Dinner last night?"

He frowned, then gave her that twisted grin. "Wasn't much hungry then."

She clucked her tongue at him the way she would at Matthew. "C'mon. We're going to get you something to eat. And some rest."

"I'll take you to dinner."

"Not tonight you won't. I already have steaks out, and I'm not going to waste them."

Two steaks, which she'd defiantly vowed to cook at one time, to prove to Luke Chandler how wrong he'd been. And now he'd be right. Good thing he'd never know.

Daniel must have been weak because he didn't argue anymore. So she'd driven him to her house, leaving his car in the parking lot.

She'd cooked the steaks—meant to be her dinner and three days' lunches—added a green salad, beans and baked potato. He ate every bite on his plate and said little. She'd felt no need for conversation, either.

She'd suggested he go sit on the couch while she finished the minimal cleanup, and he complied. She discovered him with his head back against the top of the couch, sound asleep.

Just like his son. Feed him and he's out like a light.

Her smile faded as she remembered the day after his arrival, when he'd watched her put Matthew down for his nap. The haunted expression he hadn't been able to mask after looking at pictures of Matthew's babyhood had been back today. Now she understood more about the ghosts that populated that look.

He was a man haunted by his own expectations of himself. Expectations that he needed to rescue the world in order to deserve a place in it.

She could wake him and send him home—wherever he lived now that he'd left the motel. She'd purposefully not looked at the papers he'd given her, including the one with his new address and phone number, before storing them in a drawer.

Sending him home was probably the wisest thing to do. Safest.

Then she remembered that she'd driven him here. She'd have to drive him back to the church, and hope he could drive himself the rest of the way. And that was if she could wake him at all.

He'd needed food and sleep. She'd fed him. And now she could let him sleep.

She retrieved a pillow and blanket from the closet, took his shoes off, then tried to swing him around to stretch out on the length of the couch with his head on the pillow. It wasn't easy.

His shoulders were too broad for her to get a good grip from her angle as she bent over him across the couch. And tugging on one shoulder didn't work. He was solid—and heavy—muscle. She should have remembered that from the sensation of his weight above her, his strength beneath her when they—

Inhaling sharply, she stood straight, shutting off the memory.

But she couldn't shut off her senses. Her hands still tingled with the warmth of his shoulders. And she couldn't shut off her body's reaction to either the memory or her senses.

Heat pooled deep in her belly, leaving a shiver of awareness along her arms and a tightening in her breasts.

Thank God he's asleep.

The scrap of grateful prayer reminded her of how exhausted he was. How badly he *needed* sleep—her reason for leaving him on her couch in the first place.

She tugged again. Nothing.

"Daniel, you are as stubborn asleep as you are awake."

He stirred and murmured something. It might have been her name.

She couldn't manhandle him into a comfortable position, but maybe—just maybe—she could talk him into it.

She crouched, partly on the cushion, got as good a grip as she could with one arm on his shoulder and the other partly around his rib cage and put her mouth close to his ear.

"Daniel...Daniel, come this way."

He grunted and turned toward her.

"That's it. A little more. Lie down, Daniel. Right here. That's right," she encouraged as he started to tip toward her.

Then, before she could react, he had wrapped his arms securely around her and dropped down to the cushions, taking her with him.

"Daniel!"

He didn't stir and his breathing didn't change. Twisting her head at an awkward angle to see his face, she realized he was deeply asleep.

To consider the situation, she let her head drop to a more comfortable position, which happened to be where his neck met his shoulder.

She'd landed on her side, her front plastered against his side by his hold.

Even with the couch's narrowness, she was comfortable. An almost familiar comfort, but a comfort with an underlying *zing*. His scent surrounded her as thoroughly as his arms did. The imprint of his hard, muscled body made itself felt from her head to her toes. Unpremeditated, her lips opened against the skin of his neck and she tasted the faintly salty musk she'd never forgotten.

How strange. Her breathing and her heartbeat came faster, yet a strange lassitude affected her. She should be *thinking*, not lying in Daniel Delligatti's arms while he slept. And yet...it felt so...peaceful? No, there was too much physical awareness to call it peaceful.

Maybe for a little while she could stay like this—

No. No, she couldn't.

"Daniel. You have to let go," she said sternly, trying to pull away from him, not caring if she woke him. She had to break his hold on her *now.*

Using one hand to push against his torso, she picked up his arm from on top of her, then rolled free, ending on her knees on the floor.

She was still breathing heavily as she spread the blanket over him, then sat abruptly in the easy chair across from the couch.

She didn't know how long she watched the rhythmic rise and fall of his chest, with nothing as coherent as a thought emerging from the tumbling chaos in her mind.

Fragments of memories, of conversations, of people came to the surface, then disappeared again.

Three years ago she never would have hesitated over this situation. She'd have closed the door of her life on a man like him without a moment's hesitation.

But three years ago there hadn't been Matthew's future questions to consider. Three years ago she hadn't had the security of her life in Far Hills or the daily support of Marti and Ellyn. And three years ago she hadn't gone through a hurricane with the man now lying on her couch.

A man who'd saved her life, probably more than once. A man she'd trusted with her life.

A man in pain.

Maybe Marti was right. Maybe she could help him heal. Help protect him from the storm that pursued him as he'd once protected her from the hurricane.

She'd still have to be careful about Matthew, of course. Not let him get too attached to Daniel.

Because the very reason she could consider trying to help Daniel heal himself was the same reason he could hurt Matthew so desperately—because in the end Daniel Delligatti would leave.

He needed to be flying. He'd said that himself.

And flying would always take him away.

Yes, she was attracted to him—deeply attracted to him, as their history, ancient and more recent, proved. But as long as she kept her head on straight and remembered why this man was so impossible for her and dangerous to Matthew, it would be okay.

And she could do that. She *would* do that.

She'd keep Matthew safe. And she'd be safe.

She'd make sure of it.

Daniel was still asleep when Kendra got up the next morning.

It was strange waking up in a house that didn't have Matthew in it and *did* have Daniel in it.

She peeked at him from the hallway and saw he'd turned on his side, facing the room. He slept on.

By the time she'd showered and pulled on sweats, he seemed more restless. She left a clean towel and washcloth folded on the coffee table in silent invitation, then headed to the kitchen.

She was sipping from her first cup of coffee when she heard the shower start. She hadn't heard a single sound before that.

When the water went off, she started the eggs and toast. She'd planned on over-easy eggs until the first one hit the pan. Maybe *she* needed more sleep.

She didn't hear him come into the kitchen, either. Yet she knew exactly when he'd rounded the corner.

"I hope you like scrambled eggs. That's all Matthew will eat, and I seem to be out of practice at making any other kind."

He held his silence. She couldn't resist the almost palpable pull of his will. She looked up.

His hair was wet, slicked back the way Paulo had worn it, but already starting to dry enough to let the waves work free. The stubble on his cheeks had blossomed toward a beard and his clothes proclaimed they'd been slept in. But his skin didn't have the gray tinge of last night, his shoulders were straight and his eyes had shaken off some of the ghosts.

Or put them back behind closed doors.

"Scrambled's fine." He stepped to the edge of the counter that divided the working area from the eating area. "Kendra, I'm sorry about last night."

"There's nothing to be sorry about."

His mouth twisted. "How about for crying all over your shoulder?"

"You didn't." She turned back to the eggs. "If you want to be technical, I did the crying. You talked about some things. There's no crime in that."

He snorted. "Seems like talking's all I've been doing. They put me through more debriefing back in Washington." The toaster oven door clicked open. Without being asked, Daniel took the toast out, put it on the plate she'd left nearby, then started two more pieces. "You'd think they'd already have every thought that ever passed through my head down on paper by now, but they wanted more."

"And that's what got you thinking about Santa Estella again."

"Yeah, I guess. Butter or jelly?"

"Strawberry preserves for me." She spooned fluffy eggs onto two plates. "But you should feel proud of what you did, Daniel. You—"

"Those kids needed me to stick around—they need me here now. I let them down."

"Daniel, you gave years of your life—"

"I could still be there if I hadn't gotten so damned sure I could pull off anything."

They met at the kitchen table. She with the two plates

with eggs, he with the toast, plus a cup of coffee he'd poured himself.

He dug into the eggs, apparently still filling the hole created over several days of not eating. She nibbled at a piece of toast.

"You know, there are other ways to help kids, Daniel. Other kids—people—who need help. All around you. There might not be the headlines, but it's still important. It might not mean flying daredevil missions into dangerous spots. But it needs doing."

"Trouble is, I'm not sure I have those skills." His would-be wry grin stretched tight with pain. "I watch the parents with their kids at the co-op and especially I watch you with Matthew, and... I'm a hell of a lot better at flying in to some isolated spot in the dead of night. That's what I know. That's what I'm good at. That's what I should be doing."

"Did you ever think that if you were still doing that, you wouldn't be here for Matthew now, like you weren't here for him his first two years of life."

It was harsh, but it stopped him.

"You're right. I should have been there—for Matthew and you."

"What's important is *how* you'll be here for him now. As for me—" a memory of being wrapped in strong arms flashed through her, but she blinked it away "—I've done fine."

"If I'd been around, you wouldn't have had to give up your career."

"What do you mean give up my career?" she demanded in mock indignation. "I still have a career. I'm still a reporter."

The line of his mouth eased. "I meant network television—your chance to crack the big time, the way you dreamed of."

She'd thought that herself at first. Sometimes in anger

occasionally in self-pity. Now she felt only impatient at the thought. She busied herself with the dishes.

"I had a journalism professor who said that if you knew you were down to your last day of life and being on the air wasn't how you wanted to spend it, then network reporting probably wasn't for you. It takes the kind of dedication and single-mindedness that would make you *have* to get the big story, even if the big story is the end of the world."

"Are you saying you didn't have that kind of dedication?" Daniel asked skeptically. "I wish I'd known that when you were chasing Taumaturgio so hard."

"Oh, I wanted that story, all right. As a means to an end—the end being lifelong financial security." She remembered lying in the hospital bed, alone with her son for the first time, could almost feel the curve of his newborn cheek under her fingertip. "That didn't seem so important after Matthew came along. He changed my view. Don't get me wrong, I still want security. It's just that I've adjusted my view of what will make me secure."

She pulled up next to Daniel's car in the otherwise empty church parking lot. They had cleaned up the breakfast dishes in near silence. He'd said he could walk back to town, and she'd told him she had an errand in town anyhow. It wasn't the truth but it kept him from arguing.

"Listen, Kendra, I don't know how to say—"

"There's no need to say anything."

"I feel like—like I spilled my guts."

"Now you know how I felt after Santa Estella."

He stared at her a moment. "I suppose I do."

He got out of the car. Then, with the door still open, she called his name and he leaned back in.

She didn't stop to think about the words. "Are you still available for baby-sitting Saturday, Daniel?"

His eyebrows rose slowly.

"Yeah, I'm available."

He sounded almost as if he thought she meant to push him away somehow. But that made no sense when she'd offered what he and Fran had wanted—an opportunity for him and Matthew to be alone.

Trying to puzzle that out must have left a gap in the conversation and some doubts in Daniel's mind, because he asked, "Are you sure?"

"About Saturday? Yeah."

He gave her a long, considering look, and she knew he understood how unsure she was about so much else.

"Okay. Thank you."

"Don't thank me until you've survived the night."

His lips turned up—a faint smile, but a real one. No twists, no ironies to it.

He straightened, but he didn't move away from the open door. After a full minute he bent down, and she could see his face again.

"Kendra—"

"Don't start in again about saying you're sorry or saying thank you, Daniel."

"Okay, I won't. How about if I say I owe you a steak dinner."

She smiled. "*That* you can say."

"Daniel? This is Robert. Your brother."

"Hello, Robert. Everything okay?"

"The purpose of my call is to ascertain that information. Is everything okay with you?"

"Me? Fine." If you didn't count the fact that the mother of his son wouldn't open herself up to his being in their life permanently and that his doubts about being a parent kept dripping acid in his gut. "Just fine."

"Then why have you told your supervisors that you won't be returning after your leave?"

"The exact words were I'd go back when hell froze over."

"Yes. So, everything is not fine."

"Sure it is. Only I'm not going back."

"Why? All your evaluations were excellent. You were obviously very good at your job."

So, Robert was high enough up to see his job evaluations. A connection that high up might have been useful information for Taumaturgio. Now it didn't matter.

"But it wouldn't be good for my son, and maybe it wasn't good for me."

Robert's pause gave Daniel time to wonder why the hell he'd added that last part, and to Robert of all people.

"How so?"

"It doesn't matter. The only thing you and my *former* supervisors need to know is I'm off the payroll as soon as my leave time runs out. And, even if I hadn't earned every penny before, I earned it all over again by going through the grilling they gave me these last few days."

"A thorough exit interview is necessary."

Daniel snorted. "Hell, they'd already debriefed me from Santa Estella. This was for sport."

"They conducted the first debriefing with the expectation that they could call you in for further information. With your leaving the organization, we needed to be certain we had any potentially useful information you might possess."

"*We?*"

After a slight pause came, "The United States government."

"Yeah, right. Well, *you've* covered every possible question."

"Ah, but the realm of possibility is not a fixed site." He gave a discreet cough, as if changing subjects. "You know, Daniel, your decision to leave the organization need not be final."

I don't want my son to have a father who doesn't come back—no matter how noble the cause. I know how that feels.

"Yes, it does need to be final. If that's why you called—"

"I also wondered how the situation with your son stands."

"I'm working on it. I…" He rarely had trouble keeping a guard on his words, but more words came out before he'd considered them. "That's why my decision to leave is final. For Matthew."

"So you can be there for your son. I see."

And damned if Daniel didn't think Robert really did see.

Ellyn arrived with Matthew at ten. She looked around as if she half expected to see Daniel. After Matthew burbled on about his stay at the Sinclairs' he toddled off to inventory his toys.

Ellyn wasted no time. "So, what happened?"

"I gave him dinner."

"And?"

"No *and*."

"You're kidding."

"I'm not kidding. What makes you think anything would happen?"

Ellyn rolled her eyes. "History. Chemistry. My God—he looks at you and *my* temperature goes up."

"Those are all fine reasons to *not* let anything happen. Making lo—" she switched to the less emotional term "—sex just confuses things."

"How do you figure that?"

"Don't give me that dense act, Ellyn. Sex makes it difficult to think things through logically and come up with the most reasonable and practical approach."

Ellyn gave her a disbelieving look. "Kendra, honey, I hate to break it to you, but I don't think the human heart was designed for logic—"

The door opened after a short knock, admitting Marti and Emily.

Saved by the knock, Kendra thought. Nothing else would have stopped Ellyn from completing her lecture on the human heart.

Marti held her questions until the kids had settled in the den with a puzzle, blocks and a fleet of rubber trucks.

"So, what happened?" Marti demanded.

Ellyn started to laugh, and Kendra glared at her.

"As I've already told the other Ms. Nosy here, we talked, I fed him dinner and nothing else *happened.*"

Marti sat down with a sigh, shaking her head. "Most folks around here have a live-and-let-live attitude, but not one hundred percent. I've already had phone calls this morning from Helen Solsong and Barb Sandy reporting you drove away from the church with Daniel in your car and his car remained parked at the church all night. It means it's already being spread around town that you fed him breakfast as well as dinner, and they won't hesitate to speculate about what came in between."

"Oh, for heaven's sake," muttered Ellyn.

"What? Did they have Daniel's car staked out?"

"I wouldn't be at all surprised," Marti said. "They went on about how scandal has sullied the Susland name before and they were calling *out of friendship* so I would be prepared."

Anger burned through her, but Kendra touched Marti's arm. "I'm sorry you're getting fallout over my actions—"

Marti caught her hand. "I don't care about those two. I don't care about any of it except you."

Kendra had been accustomed for so long to carry things on her own. She'd had no close girlfriends growing up— even if she'd been of a confiding nature, her mother had moved them too often to let any of her acquaintances become friends. Only to Amy had she told her secrets. First during summers, and then through long letters. They had arranged to go to the same college and roomed together all four years, so she'd needed no other confidants.

Her nature and her career had kept her from forming close friendships after college. Since Amy's death, she'd grown closer to Marti, and Ellyn had become a true friend. But even with them she'd shared daily life rather than her thoughts or dreams or fears.

Only with a stranger in the middle of a hurricane had she opened that part of herself.

"We talked at the church about Santa Estella," she started slowly. "Then I brought him back here. You saw him, Marti—" She waited for her aunt's nod. "He was exhausted. I gave him dinner, and he fell asleep on the couch. When he woke up, I gave him breakfast and drove him back to his car."

Kendra drew a deep breath and took a plunge.

"I'll admit—" an admission to herself as well as them "—I'm very attracted to him. I don't suppose that's a big surprise considering what happened between us on Santa Estella."

"That feeling could have died," murmured Ellyn. "It happens."

Kendra remembered how she'd felt being held by Daniel—even asleep. "It hasn't died. But even if I had any thought of acting on that feeling—which I don't—it wouldn't have happened last night."

She searched for a way to make them understand.

"You're right, Marti, that he's got a lot of pain in him. He's carrying a lot of guilt that he didn't do more in Santa Estella—"

Ellyn's disbelieving tsking sound reminded Kendra why she liked the other woman so much.

"—but I think it started much earlier. He had a horrible childhood, until he was adopted when he was about seven. And—" she hesitated, knowing this would win their instant sympathy "—he's worried he doesn't know how to be a good father. He doesn't feel he knows much about families."

"But he wants to be a good father?" Marti asked.

"Oh, yes, he *wants* to be." With her elbows propped on the table on either side of her coffee cup, she dropped her chin to her palms. "I suppose that's part of why he proposed. I was so angry at him for sweeping in here like the masked crusader, that it didn't register at first that he thinks getting married will automatically make us a real family. He doesn't realize—"

"Wait a minute. Back up. What was that?"

"He proposed," Marti supplied. "You said he *proposed* to you."

Kendra straightened. She hadn't meant to let that out. "Ye-es."

"And you didn't bother to tell us?"

"It wasn't anything I seriously considered," she protested. Except for a few crazy seconds.

"Why not?"

She might have expected that from Ellyn, but Marti? Kendra gaped at her aunt. "Why *not?*" she repeated, dumbfounded.

"Kendra, you keep your heart under such close guard. Too close."

The surprise of those words carried a sting. Or maybe the words themselves held the sting.

"Professional hazard," she said shortly. "Can't let your emotions get involved with the story."

"How about letting your emotions get involved with your life? I do worry that you're overly cautious in emotional matters."

"You're basing this on the fact that I didn't jump at the chance to marry him as soon as he'd popped back into my life? That's—"

"I'm basing it on the way you've lived your life. It took such extraordinary circumstances—my God, you thought you were going to die!—to open yourself up to a man.

Maybe it took an extraordinary man, too,'' she added thoughtfully.

Marti laid her palm over Kendra's wrist. ''You were so busy showing how strong you were that nobody dared even mention that you walked around like a porcupine on constant alert.''

That came uncomfortably close to Luke's comments. Kendra glanced at Ellyn. Sympathy showed in her eyes but she nodded.

In a stiff voice she barely recognized as her own, Kendra began, ''I'm sorry I've been so difficult—''

Marti waved that off. ''Difficult is what you've made it for yourself. All your life I've watched you do it. So busy being strong and independent that you wouldn't let anybody in. Kendra, I know watching your mom bothered you a lot, but you must let that go.''

''The way she let my father go? Apparently not letting things go is one trait I inherited from her.''

Bitterness flowed from the words, a bitterness she couldn't remember expressing before…except during a hurricane to a man she'd thought didn't understand her words.

But he had understood. And now he was back in her life. And willing to hold those words up to her face.

Is this about you not wanting to turn into your mother, the way you said on Santa Estella? You were hard enough on her.

''There could be worse things to inherit. Tenacity didn't hurt you any in that network job.''

''Tenacity.'' Kendra tested the word. She'd never thought of her mother in that light. Foolish, silly, weak, but tenacious? ''I've always thought of you as tenacious, Marti. Not Mother.''

''Oh, yes, Wendy was tenacious. Especially in loving Ken. Your mother and father truly loved each other, you know. You might have been too young to see that, to remember it. They *glowed* with it. And when your father went missing…'' Clouded memories dimmed Marti's eyes. ''That was the absolutely worst thing that could have happened for Wendy.''

Kendra fought a tug of sympathy for her mother with sharp words. ''If loving my father hurt her so much, she would have been better off never letting herself love him at all.''

''That's the coward's way out. And Wendy never was a coward. Because she was tenacious in her hope, too. Even after she had to accept that he wouldn't come back… Wendy had experienced such wonderful love that she couldn't believe those few years with Ken were all she'd have. She became desperate to try to find another love like Ken.'' She shook her head. ''Instead, her heart was wounded again and again.''

''And she never learned her lesson.''

''No, she never did. When she lost your father, Wendy traded in the problem of her desperate loneliness for all those problems you saw growing up—the problems you vowed never to have. And you haven't. Only I worry that you've traded in the problems your mother had for the very loneliness she was running from.''

A silence stretched out as Kendra absorbed Marti's words.

Had she done that? Completed the circle her mother started? Run away from the troubles she'd seen in her mother's life, and in the process run right back to where her mother had started?

''Your blood will be alone.''

The words were so soft, Kendra might have imagined them.

''You turn away from your children, so your blood will be alone,'' Ellyn repeated. Then she spoke more forcefully. ''That's what the curse said—*You turn away from your children, so your blood will be alone*. That's what Marti is saying happened to your mother, and I've seen it happening to you, Kendra."

A soft gasp opened Marti's lips.

"That's absolute nonsense," Kendra snapped. "It's a stupid legend. It has nothing to do with me. Or Daniel. Or real life."

"It has to do with real love. I've wondered…" Marti said in a strange voice. *"Only when someone loves enough to undo your wrongs will the laughter of children live beyond its echo in Far Hills.* Charles Susland's first wrong was turning his back on his children. Daniel Delligatti sure isn't doing that. You said so yourself, Kendra—he wants to be a good father, he wants to make you and Matthew and himself a family. That sounds like real love to me. Maybe love enough to undo that wrong. If you let him."

"That's ridiculous. All of it. Listen to the two of you, carrying on about this legend. No more. We have work to do. It's—"

"But—"

"No!" The syllable might have crossed the line from emphatic to strident, but it silenced Marti. Kendra continued more calmly. "We're going to work on this supplement, and no one's going to say another word about legends or curses or any other nonsense."

And not another word was spoken about the Susland legend, or undoing wrongs with love, or Daniel Delligatti.

But Kendra could not regulate thoughts—not even her own.

The back door of Kendra's house was open when Daniel walked up to it at four o'clock Saturday afternoon.

He saw no one in the kitchen, so he knocked loudly.

"Hi. C'mon in." Ellyn smiled as she came around the corner. "I dropped by to lend Kendra a purse. She's about ready for you."

"No, Ellyn" came Kendra's voice from deeper in the house. "Daniel's not here for—"

"You must have misunderstood, Ellyn," he said, breaking into Kendra's explanations. "I'm here for Matthew, not Kendra. She—must have another date." He broke off as Kendra came around the corner into the kitchen area.

Her dress was a muted, rich red of some material that had no fancy touches at all, and didn't need them because it seemed to cling to her body. It had a plain V neck that allowed a glimpse of the creamy curves that lay below. He knew the taste and texture and scent of those curves, and his body immediately ached with the longing to know them again.

"It's not a…" Her words trailed off as she met his eyes. For a moment they just looked at each other. A flare of some sort of recognition crossed her eyes, recognition of the assumption he'd made, but also a recognition of something deeper. Maybe of the emotions that had pushed him to that assumption. Recognition of how he felt about her. At least of the part of how he felt about her that he understood.

She picked up her purse and keys from the end of the counter only to put them down again.

"I'm working. I'm covering the country club honors dinner—the cocktail reception, then the awards banquet."

Working.

She was going to this dinner as an assignment. Not on the arm of some sleek country club member who had a hell of a lot more to offer than a guy with a complicated past and uncertain future.

Trying hard to stifle a grin, Daniel informed Ellyn, "And I'm being trusted for the first time with Matthew on my own."

"Sorry. Guess I jumped to a conclusion," Ellyn said lightly. Then, with a look from her friend to him and back that might have been sly in someone less open, she added, "I'm also sorry you're working, Kendra. That's a definite waste of that dress. Guess I better get going. Hope the banquet's not too boring. And I hope you and Matthew fare okay, Daniel.''

"I'm sure we will. Thought I'd try taking him to his first movie. The library's showing *The Wizard of Oz* as a fundraiser.''

"Meg and I are going, too.''

"Don't let Matthew eat too much junk at the movie, Daniel, and he needs to be home in bed by eight-thirty. And don't let him get too excited or he'll never sleep. But—''

"I already signed in blood agreeing to all that, Kendra.'' He pulled out the typed instructions she'd handed him yesterday at the co-op. Two pages, single-spaced, with enough phone numbers to start a book. "Why don't you go on, and quit worrying.''

Chapter Ten

Kendra toed off her shoes as soon as she walked in the back door, and yawned as she hung her coat on the peg. The banquet had been pleasant, but hadn't held a single surprise.

Driving up to the house, she'd realized Daniel hadn't brought Matthew home yet, even though it was nearly nine-thirty. The only lights on were the living room lamp operated by a timer and the outside light by the back door. Besides, Daniel's car wasn't here.

Darn him. Matthew would be overtired—so tired he'd be difficult to get to sleep, and miserable tomorrow.

She should have expected Daniel to be this foolhardy, this unreliable.

She slipped her key ring in her dress pocket. That's when she noticed the light blinking on her answering machine. She punched it—fast—before her imagination could conjure more than the bare outlines of accidents, diseases or other traumas.

It was Marti. Excited. No trauma, but lots and lots of excitement about materials she'd found in an old trunk on the Susland ancestors. Expelling a pent-up breath, Kendra barely listened once she took in the fact that it wasn't about any of the phantom traumas she had feared for Matthew and Daniel.

As she started unbuttoning the back of her dress, working her way from the collar down to below the waist, she punched the button to repeat the message—this time listening closely enough that she wouldn't be lost when Marti mentioned it at their next session for the supplement.

She'd found a diary by Charles Susland's white wife. It told about his last meeting with Leaping Star. And it gave the details about the origins of the Susland legend—the Susland curse. She shivered slightly, hearing Ellyn's whisper once more.

You turn away from your children, so your blood will be alone.

Kendra shook her head at herself.

What had gotten into her lately? First imagining horrors had overtaken Matthew and Daniel all because of a blinking light on her answering machine. And then getting lost in the campfire-ghost-story atmosphere of that silly legend.

But where *were* Matthew and Daniel? If he'd lived up to his promise to have their son home and in bed by now, she wouldn't be worried about the two of them, no matter what was on that answering machine.

As she slipped the last button free, allowing the dress to fall forward, caught only by her arms still in the sleeves, her mind snagged on one phrase.

She'd feared for Matthew *and* Daniel.

Could she tell herself she felt simply the concern of one human being for another? Or for the father of her son?

Leaving the dim kitchen, she blinked against the light from the floor lamp by the sofa, unbuttoning the dress cuffs by feel, her movements dropping the already low neckline well past decent.

"You've been living alone too long, Kendra."

Daniel's low, slightly roughened voice came from the darkness beyond the lamp.

"Daniel! What on earth! I thought you weren't here. Matthew...?"

"Is in bed. Asleep. Like you instructed."

"But—your car? You're car isn't here."

"It wouldn't start at the library. I got it towed. Ellyn gave us a ride."

She squinted into the darkness. Car trouble could explain the tension in his voice.

"But how will you get home—I mean to your place? I can't drive you. If I wake Matthew up to take him with me I'll never get him down again, and I won't leave him here alone, so—"

He stood, coming toward her. "Maybe I won't want to leave. Not after this striptease."

"Striptease? Wha...?" She looked down at the dress's V dipping nearly to her waist, clasped the loose material as best she could to her throat and turned her back. "I...I didn't know anyone was here."

"As I said, you've been living alone too long." His warm voice, both teasing and tempting, came from right over her shoulder. "And if that's how you come in every night, it's a damned shame to waste it on a two-year-old who's already asleep."

The whisper of his touch against her back left a trail of shivers that expanded, deepened.

"Daniel... Don't."

But she didn't move when she felt his lips touch the back of her bare shoulder.

"Your skin was this soft three years ago, Kendra. But I could never see..."

She glanced over her shoulder and saw him rest against

the corner of the sofa arm. His hands at her hips were a gentle, persistent force that prompted one step back, then a second, so she stood between his knees. She felt his hands dip into the opening of her dress, then the heated touch against her skin as he ran his palms up to her shoulder blades, below the flare of her hips, and back again.

She should move away. She should leave. She should...

"Daniel, this isn't good—"

"It's good, Kendra. It's so good." His lips against her skin at the point of her shoulder blade added a new heat.

She clutched the material of her dress in both fists against her collar bone, while he made love to her back.

Each cell seemed to have a separate nerve ending, each communicating pleasure and urgency for more. The inside of his thighs pressing against the outside of hers, squeezed gently, encasing her. Snugly drawn against his crotch, she could feel the insistence of his reaction...and her own.

He unhooked her bra, the skin once covered by the strap soaked in the sensation as his unimpeded stroke started at her nape and slowly traveled down her backbone, lower and lower until his hands dipped inside the waist of her panties, his fingers gliding over the swell of her buttocks.

She gasped and nearly collapsed against him.

His hands rose again, sliding up either side of the valley of her spine, under the parted fabric of her bra. Then to each side, under her arms, his fingers light across the swell of her breasts, then farther.

"Daniel, I'm not...I've been pregnant, had a baby—oh!"

His hands covered her breasts, the touch possessive for all its gentleness. He cupped her, using his thumbs and forefingers to bring her nipples to aching, hardened awareness.

"I wish I could have touched you when you carried our son. To feel you rounding with our baby..." Where she pressed against his lap she felt the hot leap of his flesh, and couldn't stop her hips from rocking back against him. "I wish I could have made love to you then."

His mouth pressed hot and wet against the base of her neck. Her knees threatened to buckle.

If she was going to gather herself together—her wits and her body—this was the moment. Right now. This instant. Before it was too late. Much, much too late.

"I have to...Daniel, I have to ask you something. You promised...answers."

"Ask." His voice was muffled against her flesh.

"Why did you come after me?"

"I told you—Matthew—"

She cut him off. "I understand why after you knew about Matthew—your determination that he would have family, stability. But you didn't know about Matthew until you looked for me." His hands stilled. "Why did you *start?* Did you search out all Paulo's one-night stands?"

The withdrawal of his hands from her skin exposed its heated surface to a rush of chilled air.

"Don't dismiss it that way, Kendra." His voice was harsh.

"Why? I'm sure Paulo was no monk. And Taumaturgio surely wasn't. What was different?"

"I don't know."

He'd jerked out the words, with no attempt to make them believable. A lie. And not even a good lie.

She'd always heard about the power of truth. Now she knew the power of a lie. It had the strength she didn't have. The strength to make her straighten away from him. The strength to tug her dress up. The strength to turn and face him, now covered from throat to knees.

"You should leave, Daniel."

"It scares you, doesn't it, Kendra?"

"I'm not scared of you."

"Not me. At least not me alone. Us. What is happening between us. Because it reminds you of Santa Estella? Because it reminds you of when you let yourself really feel? Or because you don't want to feel that for me?"

It did scare her. At one level she understood that. But understanding didn't stop the fear, and it didn't stop the response.

"Which you? Which one of your characters do you think I'm feeling something for?"

He stood abruptly, jostling her.

"I'm taking your car. I'll return it in the morning."

The change in him, so fast, so complete, disoriented her. "My car? But—"

"Don't worry. I have the key." His mouth twisted as he held up the ring that she'd dropped into her pocket earlier. He kept one key and tossed the rest toward her. She caught them automatically, then had to grab at her dress again to keep it from falling. "Remember me? The pickpocket? I'm sure it doesn't surprise you that I haven't lost those skills."

Why had he done that?

Lying in bed, wishing sleep would stop the thinking, that's the question Kendra focused on. It was much better than thinking about what had happened between them. Or what *would* have happened if she'd let things continue.

Why had he picked her pocket?

To prove—to himself or her?—he didn't need to rely on her, the way he had the night he'd returned from back east?

Was that why he'd lied in answer to her question?

I don't know.

She'd known it as a lie immediately. So that meant he *did* know. But maybe he didn't *want* to know. Maybe he didn't lie well this time because he was lying to himself most of all.

Damn her questions.

She poked and probed until he felt like he'd been turned inside out. And, dammit, he had no answers. Not the neat kind she wanted.

Daniel leaned against the chain link fence that separated

the parking area from the pair of runways boasted by Far Hills Airport. If he'd had his own plane, he'd have gone up and been eye to eye with the huge, clear Wyoming sky. Instead, he had to settle for the familiar, lingering scents of fuel and flight.

Maybe Kendra had connected with Paulo during the hurricane because she couldn't hold Paulo at a distance with her battery of questions. Not speaking the same language had definite advantages.

Why had he come after her? Why three years after he'd left her at the consulate gate had finding her been his first thought when the door had been closed and locked behind his ever returning as Taumaturgio?

Damned if he knew.

And Kendra hadn't expected him to have an answer. She'd used the question to drive a wedge between them. To stop the feeling between them.

His body tightened in memory of that specific feeling.

She'd try to back away now. He'd bet every penny on that.

Go ahead and try, Kendra Jenner, he thought grimly.

He'd be damned if he'd let that happen. Not her backing away, not her trying to keep Matthew away from him, not even himself easing away.

Yeah, himself.

It had been a long time since he'd felt the nervousness he'd experienced tonight when he'd realized Matthew was completely and solely in his care. On second thought, he'd never felt the terror that hit him so unexpectedly when he'd glanced in the rearview mirror halfway into town and seen Matthew's expression of utter confidence that nothing could hurt him. Which meant he—Daniel Delligatti—was responsible that nothing *did* hurt Matthew.

The situation had gotten worse when they had passed by the Community Church and Matthew started fussing. It occurred to Daniel then that Matthew's equanimity had stemmed from a belief they were heading for the familiar baby-sitting co-op. It had a two-year-old kind of logic, since the co-op was where Matthew most often saw him. It also explained a couple of the words Daniel had understood in Matthew's prattling—Emily, Jason and Fran.

Not even a burger and fries—and the amazing mess they could make in the hands of a master—had ameliorated Matthew's cranky suspiciousness at not encountering those expected faces, though the cooing attentions of the teenage waitress had helped some. By the time they'd reached the library for the movie, Daniel had been sorely tempted to hand Matthew over to Ellyn Sinclair and bolt.

But the time with Ellyn and Meg Sinclair—and Matthew's fascination with Toto—seemed to restore some of his son's faith in the world, if not in Daniel. Matthew had some justification for his wariness. Not only couldn't Daniel get his car started, but transferring the damned child seat from his car to Ellyn's had been a fiasco.

Matthew's improved mood lasted until the moment Ellyn dropped them off at Kendra's house and he realized his mother wasn't there.

The military ought to check into distraught two-year-olds as a secret weapon. If the heart-rending pathos of flooding tears and pitiful cries for "Mommy, Mommy" didn't bring a man to his knees, the sheer volume would.

Kendra might have thought Daniel had been lying in wait for her, but in fact he'd collapsed on the sofa and fallen asleep.

Between mother and child, it had not been Daniel's finest hour, or evening.

He pushed off from the fence. That wasn't going to stop him. Not from spending time alone with his son. Not from pursuing his son's mother.

The next afternoon an assignment for the *Banner* took Kendra to Sheridan. She stopped in a drugstore for aspirin to fight a raging headache. She'd had it when she woke up. Finding her car keys on the counter and her car parked neatly by the back door hadn't helped.

He had to have been in her house to return the keys and he had to have been up before dawn to get her car back. On a Sunday morning, where'd he find a ride? Or had he walked back to wherever he lived now? What if he couldn't get his car fixed? Or—

No. None of that was her concern.

Aspirin in hand, she turned and came face-to-face with a display of condoms.

She would never need them. Certainly not with Daniel— that would be crazy. And, at the rate she was going, not with any man.

On the other hand, history showed that when she had needed them, she hadn't had them. From a practical standpoint...

Without regard for the finer points, she grabbed a packet.

If Daniel had had any thought of keeping where he and Matthew had spent Tuesday afternoon a secret from Kendra, their son's new word ended that idea immediately.

"Plane! Mommy, plane!"

Matthew started in as soon as Daniel freed him from the car seat and he came barreling toward where she stood outside the back door with the binoculars she'd been using to scan the mountainside.

"Yes, sweetheart. Planes are in the sky."

"No. *No.* Plane! Mat'ew—plane!"

"Plane? You saw a plane? Or—" Kendra spun around to Daniel, walking leisurely toward her. "You took him up in a plane! You had no right—"

"Don't be so fast to judge, convict and execute. We—"

"Pop'ler, Mommy. *Vrrrrm-vrrrrm-vrrrrm!*" Matthew tugged at Kendra's jeans. When she didn't respond immediately enough for him, he looked to Daniel. "Pop'ler? Dan'l, pop'ler?"

"That's right, Matthew. That's the noise a propeller makes."

"Daniel, how could you—"

"I know questions are your strong point, but how about if you hold off, Kendra? I think you've got someone right now who'd like to tell you what he discovered this afternoon."

Kendra glared at him long enough to convey she didn't appreciate the crack about her asking questions, or for being found lacking in paying attention to Matthew. Then she crouched to face her son.

"You heard a propeller, Matthew?"

He nodded emphatically, his dark eyes as warm and compelling as his father's, shining with excitement. "Pop'ler, Mommy!" Matthew prattled on with words tumbling over one another so rapidly that even she, who'd heard each of his words first—until today, she thought with a jolt—had difficulty making them out. Although *propeller, plane, sky* and *vrrrmm* reoccurred. Along with another word.

"Roof?" she repeated tentatively.

"Rufus Trent," Daniel explained. "He owns the airport and some planes. He showed us around and let Matthew sit in a cockpit."

And now she recognized another of her son's new words—pilot.

"Mat'ew pilot!"

He reached up toward Daniel, both arms raised.

Daniel reached into his light jacket and pulled something out. A couple of quick movements of his long fingers, and he handed over to Matthew a balsa wood plane.

"Me pilot!" Matthew exulted, running down the driveway making his version of engine noises.

Kendra glared at Daniel, hands on hips.

He shrugged but didn't sound the least apologetic. "He wanted a plane. He said he didn't have one."

She wouldn't be sidetracked. "Explain," she demanded as soon as Matthew was out of earshot.

"Explain? You make it sound like I've committed a crime." His frown matched his tone—irked. "I took him by Far Hills Airport. I wanted to introduce my son to something I love. That's no crime."

His expression shifted, allowing in a glint of joy. "He loved it. Rufus has a couple nice little planes. Matthew and I got inside, and he saw the instrument panel and even tried the throttle. But we never left the ground, Kendra."

"You told me before you two left that you wanted to show Matthew where you're staying."

"I said I wanted to show you both were I'm *living*." His emphasis disputed her less permanent word. "You said you had too much to do."

She did have work to do, but it had been the resemblance to a family outing that had kept her from saying yes when Daniel showed up at her door in his newly repaired car with sandwich makings and ready-made salad for lunch. When Daniel had said in that case he'd take Matthew, she hadn't been able to think of an excuse to say no, since Saturday night seemed to have gone well from what she could see and from Ellyn's breezily incomplete comments.

"You live at the airport?"

"Yeah. I told you I rented a place. I rented it from Rufus. The operation's run out of an old house—offices, a lounge and the radio room. There's living space upstairs. I've got a room, my own bathroom and run of the kitchen."

"And it happens to be at an airport."

He grinned. "Yeah, that's a bonus. So, with all the work you had to do, what are you doing out here with the binoculars?"

She ignored the gibe. "There are reports of forest fires in the Bighorns. I'm seeing if I could spot anything."

"Could you?"

"Smoke from the far side." She brushed that topic aside, coming back to the real issue. "I don't want Matthew around airplanes. Or airports."

"Flying is what I do, Kendra." He said it with deliberate emphasis. "I'm his father, and whether he knows that or not now, someday it'll be important to him to know about me, about my flying."

"You don't know what it would be like for him...if you don't come back."

He took her hand, she tried to pull away. He held on, clasping it between both of his. "Or if *you* don't come back."

"Me? I don't take risks."

"You live. That's the risk. You could—"

"You're going to say I could be hit by a truck, or struck by lightning. True. But I don't court risks, Daniel. I don't go meet them more than halfway. You fly into danger for a job."

"So did you."

"*I* did? How do you figure that?"

"You walked into a hurricane for your job. I remember you talking about taking calculated risks to get the story of Taumaturgio. You seemed to think *that* was reasonable." Before she could formulate an answer, he continued, "Kendra, you can't tell me you don't know how it feels. You wanted that Taumaturgio story so much—I could see it. Why do you think I followed you to La Baja?"

She gave him a look meant to be quelling, and tugged at her hand. He ignored the tug and grinned, obviously interpreting her expression to his own advantage. "Well, yes, that, too. I can't say that your appeal didn't figure into my following you."

"I didn't mean that." But her protest didn't stop the heat of certain memories from traveling through her body. "You followed me because you thought I'd be a danger to your plans.''

His grin evaporated. "You were *in* danger."

"All right, all right. I know. It was the stupidest thing I'd done in my life." She gave him a cutting look. "To that point."

He ignored that implication. "I hope you didn't do anything riskier. A storm like that—it's like a wolf on the hunt. It's going to tear into someone, you never know who or where. And yes, I worried about you. You were a stranger to hurricanes and a stranger to Santa Estella. I could also see the determination in you to find out all the secrets of Taumaturgio—and that worried me, too."

"So, you could have let the hurricane deal with me. That would have ended all your worries."

"Right." He used his self-mocking tone. "Wouldn't look good for Taumaturgio, defender of the weak, champion of the downtrodden, to let a gringa reporter drown because it was convenient."

"You talk as if Taumaturgio were a separate person."

He released her hand. "Still doing the story, Kendra?"

Body language, tone and words all screamed that she'd stepped into hidden territory. Into the realm of Daniel Delligatti. Not solely the facts he'd chosen to tell her to this point or the glimpses his lowered defenses had allowed her to see, but into other emotions he'd skirted away from.

"No. I'm not doing any story." Her words came out almost breathless, as if she'd stepped back from a precipice. "We're off the subject, anyhow. The subject is your job. And flying."

"My job... I don't know..."

Her heart jolted uncomfortably against her ribs. Something in his voice...almost as if returning to his job were in doubt. But he lived and breathed his job—the flying and the danger.

"You're trying to tell me this was such a great government job that you could afford to retire at thirty-two—'' His left eyebrow quirked. ''Yes, I got your age from my sources. You're going to be a full-time retiree?''

''No.''

She exhaled. Just as she'd thought. He'd go back to the job he'd had, and loved, before Taumaturgio. He'd be flying, but he wouldn't be doing his flying here. He'd be off somewhere far away, where she wouldn't be even tempted to cross into that other realm.

Kendra avoided any more direct contact with Daniel until Friday afternoon and the co-op's party to celebrate all the birthdays that fell in the month of October.

On that day, as many parents as possible were pressed into service to help with the cake, ice cream and games. As Fran said, kids, sugar and excitement were a highly combustible combination.

Kendra kept most of the room and the ever-flowing mass of kids between her and Daniel during the festivities.

She'd returned to the main room from attempting to clean up a four-year-old girl who tried to shower in juice, and spotted Matthew sitting on the floor beside his pal, Jason. Apparently they were playing a two-year-old's version of keeping up with the Joneses.

''My t'uck,'' announced Jason, waving a green toy in his fist.

''My t'uck.'' Matthew snatched up a red one from beside him.

''My mommy,'' Jason declared triumphantly, waving his arm in the vague direction of his mother, a petite blonde busy placing ice cream-sloppy paper plates carefully into a garbage bag.

Matthew levered himself to his knees, scanning the room. Honing in on her, he shouted with such glee that she couldn't stop an answering smile. ''My mommy!''

Jason pointed to the man holding the garbage bag for his mother. "My daddy!"

The next moment strung out like a series of still photographs, each etched into Kendra's heart.

Matthew's hesitation, followed by a kind of confusion. Jason clambering to his feet and trundling across the room, shouting, "Daddy, Daddy, Daddy," knowing somehow that he'd won, yet innocent of any malevolence. Matthew flopping back to sit on the floor, his face creasing into a pucker of uncertainty.

Kendra took a step toward him. But that brought Daniel into her line of sight and stopped her cold. His expression was so utterly shut down that she knew he had witnessed the episode. How could his face show no emotion and yet she feel such overwhelming blame?

She started toward Matthew again, but Daniel's curt gesture ordered her to stay still.

Movement from Matthew caught her attention. He'd put his thumb in his mouth. His left hand idly stroked the top of the truck by his side. Then he started to move it back and forth, gradually shifting his focus. In another minute, his thumb was out of his mouth and she heard his "Vroom-vroom."

She walked out of the room, not stopping until she'd reached the open side door, drawing in slow, calming breaths.

She wasn't surprised when Daniel spoke from behind her. "Don't you be the one to let him know it's a big deal, Kendra. He'll understand soon enough that it's a big deal that he doesn't have a daddy. If he doesn't, the other kids will let him know."

She squeezed her eyes tight against the pain buried so deep in his calm voice. He knew exactly how it felt to learn that, to understand what it meant not to have a daddy. Or a mommy.

"We've gone over this." It came out fairly steady.

"Yes, we have. You don't want Matthew to know he has a father on the chance that father might not come back someday."

She twisted around to find him leaning against the opposite doorjamb, arms crossed over his chest.

"Daniel—"

"I know, I know. Give you time." He uncrossed his arms, and pushed away. "At some point, Kendra, time's going to run out."

Chapter Eleven

A week later, Daniel sauntered in, bigger and more alive than anyone else in the basement room.

Kendra firmly reminded her accelerated heartbeat that was because most of the occupants of the room were under four feet tall and less than a decade old. It didn't help.

That had been happening more and more often.

She never should have let things get so carried away that night of the country club dinner. She knew the power of her attraction to him. She knew how it could shut down her brain and her common sense. She'd had proof of that not only in the middle of a hurricane, but in her own home. She had to be more careful.

"Dan'l!"

Matthew launched himself with no care or caution. Before Kendra could even gasp at the foolhardy leap, Daniel had caught Matthew in the air and swung him up to eye level, boy and man who looked so alike grinning at each other.

"Easy does it there, Matthew."

No one seeing the two of them now could doubt the relationship. Kendra thought she detected a couple of glances from parents dropping off children or preparing for a tour of duty at the baby-sitting co-op. Marti's look from across the room was more than a glance, though her expression gave no hint of what she was thinking.

Matthew was so young, surely that would protect him—from the gossip and from his own wondering about his father—until she'd figured out the best way to tell him. The best way to make sure he wouldn't be hurt.

Her son's delighted squeals brought her back to the moment—and Daniel spinning the boy around.

"Daniel, be careful! He could fall!"

Daniel slowed his circles to a stop. "I've got a good hold on him—he won't fall."

"Mo', Dan'l! Mo'!"

Daniel shook his head. "Sorry, fella. Your mom says no." As he put Matthew down, he softened the refusal with a smile that had Matthew mirroring the expression.

"I go play," the boy announced once he'd been sent on his feet.

"There you go, Matthew," Daniel approved. Then he repeated in a lower tone that reached only Kendra's ears, "There you go."

Three short words transported her to the middle of a hurricane, holding on to the only sane thing in a wild universe—him. She could feel his hands stroking her back, could almost reach out and touch his warmth, his reality.

And when he met her gaze, she knew he recognized her thoughts.

She bent her head, pretending great attention to straightening the straps of her tote bag she'd set on a chair.

"How are you, Kendra?"

"Fine. What brings you here?" She kept her inquiry briskly impersonal. "I thought you'd finished your co-op duty for the week."

"I did." He grinned, looking boyish and extremely pleased with himself. "I knew you'd signed up for today. That's why I came."

"Oh?"

"Yeah." He stuck his hands in his jeans' pockets. "I want to ask you something. Rufus is letting me use a plane this afternoon—"

Her throat constricted. "You are not taking Matthew in a plane."

"Kendra, I wouldn't even consider it if I hadn't checked it out myself. It's a solid plane. It's perfect flying weather, and that might not last—they're calling for rain by the end of the week. You have to know I'd never take chances with Matthew. I—"

"No. Absolutely not."

His dark eyes considered her. She broke the connection, only to discover the adults in the room were all watching them.

"Then you come, Kendra. Let me prove how safe it is."

She recrossed the straps. "I have too many things to do. After we leave here, I have to make calls for a story and I have errands."

"A couple hours. That's all. I can show you what Far Hills looks like from the air. Have you ever seen the ranch from an entirely different angle? Have you ever seen the *sky* from a new angle? Let me show you what it's like, Kendra. I'll prove to you it's not dangerous."

"No."

"Kendra—"

"I'm not going flying with you."

"I'll go."

All eyes turned to Marti Susland. But Kendra's gaze quickly shifted to Daniel. He was as stunned as she was.

"I'll go flying with you this afternoon, Daniel. If Kendra will take care of Emily. And if it's okay with you."

"Okay," he said slowly, then the corners of his mouth lifted. "This should be interesting."

Marti had watched Daniel's preflight check—first outside the plane, then inside—without comment, but with great attention. He'd heard one sharp drawn-in breath on takeoff, but otherwise, nothing.

Maybe discomfort about flying in small planes ran in the family. So why had Marti asked to come—

"This is...magical."

He felt his smile stretching across his face, and when she turned toward him, he saw an answering smile creasing her face.

He wondered about this change of attitude. She'd clearly mistrusted him at the start. Maybe his dealings with Matthew and Kendra had persuaded her he wasn't a threat to them. If so, that was more than he'd managed with Kendra.

"I hear you've been doing some volunteer spotting for the firefighters on the west slope."

"A little. Filling in for Rufus."

Marti didn't speak again until they'd landed, he'd shut down the engine and unbuckled his seatbelt.

"Did Kendra tell you about the founding of Far Hills Ranch?"

"Not that I remember." And he remembered it all.

"It happened right here, in 1878," Marti said in a dreamy voice. "The campfire burned for four days and four nights on that outcropping on Crooked Mountain."

Daniel listened to a story of Kendra's family five generations old. He didn't even know who his mother was. Was that Marti's point?

Marti ended with, "Kendra used to want to hear that story all the time when she came here for summers. I'm surprised she didn't tell you about Charles Susland. She seems to feel she told you everything there was to tell during that hurricane."

"She told me some."

"And you told her nothing. It's going to take some doing to get her to forgive that you know her so much better than she knows you—or so she thinks."

"Daniel?"

At the sound of Kendra's voice on the phone, Daniel pushed aside the sectional charts he'd been studying, acquainting himself with mountains he'd be flying over to spot the fires' progress.

"'Morning, Kendra."

"Daniel, I wondered—if you can't do it, it's all right—but I wondered if you'd be free to take care of Matthew for a couple hours today."

"Sure."

"I wouldn't ask you, but—"

"You can quit explaining, Kendra, I said yes. What time?"

"Oh. Twelve-thirty? It's the yearly meeting with the ranch accountant, and Marti likes me to be there. I'll be back by three. But you should know—Matthew was up all night with a sore throat and fever. That's why he can't go to the co-op. He's better, but..."

"I'll come now." He heard the beginnings of her protest and talked over it. "He was up all night, so you were up all night. You can get some sleep before your meeting."

"Daniel?"

"What?" He braced himself for more arguing.

"Thank you."

"I'm glad you called me," he said a little gruffly.

"So, Daniel's taking care of Matthew," said Marti, not for the first time. "Getting easier and easier to rely on him, isn't it?"

"I'd be a fool to get too deeply involved with him."

It was more a reminder to herself that she *was* a fool than an answer. Kendra did rely on him more and more, and that was a form of involvement.

As soon as he'd shown up, he'd hustled her off to her room with orders to sleep. And she had. Matthew's crying had awakened her once, but she'd recognized it as the sound of frustration rather than pain, and she'd fallen back asleep. Only when she was showering and dressing for the trip to Sheridan with Marti had she recognized that she'd trusted Daniel's ability to deal with their son.

She added aloud now, "He's going to be leaving soon."

"Maybe. Maybe not."

Kendra turned from watching storm clouds bubbling over the mountains. "What do you mean? Do you know something, Marti?"

"Can't say I know anything."

"Marti—" she warned.

"Look at that," Marti interrupted as she turned into the road to Kendra's house. "Somebody lost a hubcap."

Although Kendra spotted the shiny object in the ditch beside the road, she ignored the red herring. "You haven't said anything about going flying the other day. Did Daniel tell you something?"

"I decided you're right—I shouldn't be quizzing you about your young man, so I'm keeping my thoughts about the flying to myself."

Kendra had never said anything of the sort—thought it, yes, but hadn't said it. They'd reached her door, so there wasn't time to argue. Besides, arguing might sound as if she welcomed Marti's comments on her situation with Daniel or wanted to know what her aunt and he had talked about while they were encased in that tiny airplane.

Neither, of course, was true.

Marti pointed toward Daniel's parked car. "Must be his hubcap."

"I'll tell him. Thanks for the ride, Marti."

The only sound in the house was a faint murmur from

the back of the house. She hung up the red wool jacket she'd worn over a princess-seamed denim dress and followed the sound. She stopped in the doorway to Matthew's room.

Daniel sat in the rocking chair, with Matthew across his lap, the child's head cushioned against his father's arm and a blanket wrapped around him. In a low, soft voice, with his eyes closed, Daniel sang one of the soothing songs she remembered from Santa Estella. Matthew was sound asleep.

She'd thought so many times that for Matthew's sake she would never keep father and son apart. Now she saw it was also for Daniel's sake.

She stepped back, retracing her steps soundlessly, not sure if she meant to give Daniel privacy or protect herself from having to acknowledge what she'd seen—and felt.

In the kitchen, she clattered dishes in starting a pot of coffee. She was looking out the kitchen window at the patch of clouds now nearly on top of them when Daniel came around the corner.

"Hi. How'd the meeting go?"

"Fine. Marti would like to see my cousin Grif more involved, but..." She shrugged. "How's Matthew?"

"Fine now. I gave him more of that medicine at two like you said. That seemed to help. He's sleeping."

"Good. Thanks. Oh, you tossed a hubcap turning into the drive. Marti spotted it. One of the hazards of ranch roads. And you never know when you might need a hubcap to hold a fire."

If she could have snatched the words out of the air she would have. What was she thinking, reminding him of their refuge from Aretha? It gave him the perfect opening to bring up their past, when she'd been working so hard to avoid that.

But he said only, "I thought I heard something. I'll get it after a cup of that coffee you're making."

"You better go now. Storm's coming."

He looked toward the back door, which showed only blue sky in its window. "I've got time."

She raised her eyebrows, but didn't argue. He'd learn about Wyoming storms. She got out the last of the oatmeal raisin cookies Ellyn had brought over, and poured Daniel his coffee.

The conversation about her meeting was easy and casual. He'd finished his coffee and four cookies when he got up.

"Guess I'll get that hubcap now."

"Okay." She took the dishes to the sink to hide her smile.

As soon as he was out the door, though, she followed, watching him saunter down the driveway. Sure enough, he was about two yards from the hubcap when she heard the first, fat drops hit the roof. Daniel lifted his face to the sky as if he'd been hit, too, but picked up his speed only a little. He had bent over to retrieve the piece of metal when the skies opened.

She was laughing hard by the time he reached the door she held open to him. He was soaked—dripping, sopping wet. He swore in a mixture of English and Spanish as he dropped the freshly washed hubcap on the floor.

"I tried to tell you. No—stay there, I'll get a towel."

"You didn't try very hard," he called after her as she went around the corner to the laundry area. "And there's still blue sky."

"There's so much sky here, that most of it can look clear but if you're under the clouds, you'll get it."

She rounded the corner with the towel and stopped. One minute she was laughing, and then she wasn't. The storm had dimmed the small back hall. The rain had plastered his shirt and jeans to his body, and he'd combed back his wet hair with his fingers.

She would have liked to have been able to say the change in atmosphere started from him, but that wasn't the truth. He looked up, reaching for the towel, then stopped as their eyes met.

She took the final step forward.

His lips were cool and wet, then hot in an instant, as their mouths met and opened. She wanted to wrap herself in his scent and his taste. She felt him against her, his body solid and familiar, his arms around her bringing her a warmth she hadn't known since he had made her forget a hurricane.

Memories.

She jolted away from him. Pushing against his chest.

"I'm sorry. I'm sorry. I shouldn't—this was a mistake."

He backed off less than an arm's length, his hands cupping her shoulders. "Mistake."

"The rain…and… With your hair like that, you look like you did—*then.* Like Paulo."

She'd said the words deliberately. A weapon to make him back away before she no longer wanted him to back away.

And she could see from the way his skin thinned over his cheekbones that her weapon had struck home. She dropped her head and saw wet marks on her dress from where their bodies had met. She brushed at them, as if that would erase what had happened.

"You were kissing Paulo?"

She heard the anger in his voice, knew she'd pushed him toward some edge. But that was all right. Because it would pull her back from her own edge. The edge of forgetting what she couldn't feel, what she couldn't let happen.

"If that's what you want to call it. The rain, the smell. All those memories. It was Paulo. A memory—no, a figment. That's all."

Anger was in his eyes, too. But there was something else. Something not as easy to define—or withstand—as anger.

With deliberate movements he placed his hands to either side of her neck, resting against the wall behind her, then slowly he bent his elbows, leaning his body toward her.

"You're lying."

She tensed to keep from responding to the heat and damp surrounding her, to *him* surrounding her.

"Memories are powerful—"

"You're lying, Kendra. This isn't memory. This is now. This is *us*. You know who I am. You *know*."

"I don't."

"Who am I, Kendra?"

"It's the rain…you look—"

"Who am I, Kendra? Now."

"It's the rain—"

"Who am I?"

"Daniel, it's… You're—"

His kiss was relentless, demanding. She met it. Equaled it, deepened it. She felt the form of his body, under her hands, pressing against her tightening breasts, and lower, where the heat grew and spread. But she wanted more, she wanted to feel the texture of his skin again, the flow of his muscles.

Their mouths still joined, she struggled with the maddening buttons and wet cloth of his shirt. He grasped either side of her dress and pulled the snaps open down the front, his hands sliding over her body in hot, welcome strokes.

At last his shirt opened, and she spread her palms across his chest, the wet, curling hair clinging to her fingers. He'd opened her bra, freeing her breasts so they pressed against his bare skin as he drew her firmly against him, one hand spread across her back, the other across her buttocks. He stroked his tongue deep into her mouth, and she knew that rhythm immediately. Pulsed to it, strained to it. Until she thought she would explode with it.

He kissed down her throat, then lower. His tongue flicked over her hardened nipple, then his mouth covered it, as she felt his fingers tug at the waistband of her panties.

Longing and pleasure braided together so tightly that she moaned with it. As her hands stroked over his bent back, he gave a sound from deep in his throat that celebrated their heat.

And then another sound. A creaking—familiar, and yet

for an instant it didn't register in Kendra's desire-fogged mind.

"Hey! Anybody home?" Ellyn's voice.

Oh, God—the door! That was the sound.

"Good heavens, we had a real gully-washer for a while. I'm afraid it's already let up, though, and they're saying it won't be enough to break the—" A gasp, partially smothered, interrupted that flow. "Oh! I— Oh, I'm sorry."

Daniel shifted so his shoulder rested against the wall, his back to the door, shielding Kendra from sight.

"It's all right, Ellyn," Kendra got out. "We're just... It's all right." Her fingers couldn't manage the complex motion of hooking her bra in back with her dress still partially on. She gave that up and frantically pulled the sides of the dress together to start snapping it closed, and discovered the telltale wet blotches.

"I'll go," Ellyn volunteered, a laugh lurking.

"Don't be ridiculous. I'll...I'll be right back." And with that, she turned and fled, leaving Daniel to deal with Ellyn as best he could.

Daniel watched her go. It would take a couple days of fence-fixing to put a dent in this ache.

"Sorry, Ellyn," he said, still with his back to her.

"I'm the one who's sorry. I rushed in to get out of the rain—and now it's already stopped. Guess the drought will continue."

"Yeah." He didn't bother to button his wet shirt, but he adjusted his jeans before turning around. "No end for this drought."

He didn't see the other meaning for his words until he caught the glint in her eyes as she followed him out the back door.

"I might as well go, too. Somehow I don't think Kendra's going to be in the mood to talk about my great idea for the supplement's layout. But remember, Daniel—" She patted his arm. "The end of any drought starts with a drop."

* * *

She would have made love with him. Right there in her kitchen. She couldn't deny to herself, didn't even try, that in another few minutes, she would have joined with him with the same rush of rightness she'd experienced with Paulo on Santa Estella.

Only he wasn't Paulo.

There'd been no confusion in her mind. Or her heart. The man she would have made love with was Daniel Delligatti.

Daniel Benton Delligatti.

And who the hell is he?

He'd promised after he arrived at her door using a name she'd never heard that he would answer her questions, give her a chance to know him. She'd recognized what that cost him, a man accustomed to masking his emotions and burying himself. And she hadn't made it easy on him. Still, he'd kept his word.

Maybe more so than he'd intended. His emotions over Matthew's birth certificate and when he'd returned from his debriefing had been raw, uncensored, stripped of the self-protectiveness provided by the self-mocking delivery he'd used to reveal other hurtful elements of his past.

Was that when she'd started to fall in love with Daniel?

She covered her mouth, as if that could stop the words her mind had spoken.

Started? Oh, God, it *had* to be only started.

Because there remained that part of Daniel she couldn't reconcile with. The element in him that had given rise to Taumaturgio. The masked crusader. The risk-defying miracle worker. The man who would fly into the night to save the world, and never return to her or to their son.

Taumaturgio was as much a part of Daniel Delligatti as the street-hardened child or the confused adolescent or the rumpled Tompkins or the gentle Paulo. And Taumaturgio was the part of him that could break her heart, and Matthew's.

* * *

Daniel hadn't lost his skills. He knew someone had tracked him through the aisles of the Far Hills Market.

He stepped into the express lane with his coffee, crackers, apples and peanut butter, then turned to face his pursuer.

Marti Susland.

"Daniel. I'd like to talk to you."

"Okay," he agreed slowly. "Here?"

"No. I'll get us soft drinks from the machine—" she tipped her head toward the exit "—and meet you across the street on the bench by the post office."

She popped the top of her soda can as he arrived.

"Remember what I told you in the plane about the founding of Far Hills?" she asked as he took the can she held out. "About the legend?"

"Yeah, I remember."

"But I didn't tell you what happened after Leaping Star died up on that overlook." She gazed off to some distant point. "I'd always heard about the Suslands having a lot of tragedies, but I didn't know the details, not until I started doing research for the local history section we're working on. I didn't know a lot of things....

"Charles Susland and Annalee had five babies—one died at birth, another died of diphtheria. A daughter died in childbirth. A son died in an insane asylum. My grandfather was shot to death during a bank robbery in the thirties.

"The next generation didn't fare any better—World War II, polio and an uncle killed himself after he'd murdered his cousin. I was eight then—it's the first time I heard of the Susland curse."

She left another silence. When she finally turned, her face had an intensity that was far from dreamy.

"You see, Daniel? Our family's had generations of sorrow and tragedies. Kendra's mother lost her husband with Kendra still a baby, and was never the same. And my other sister died leaving an eleven-year-old son. And now Kendra..."

Uneasiness prickled at the back of Daniel's neck. "What about Kendra?"

"She's been alone a long time. Alone, like Leaping Star said. And now she's raising a son by herself."

"Not anymore. I'm going to be here to help raise Matthew. And—" He bit off the last words.

But Marti filled in. "And Kendra. You'll be with Kendra—if she'll let her defenses down enough to let you."

"That's between Kendra and me."

Her intensity eased into a glint of humor. "Of course, but an aunt can hope for her niece's happiness." And it couldn't have been any clearer if she'd shouted "I'm going to meddle."

"You weren't so impressed with me at the start," he said bluntly. "Why the sudden change?"

"I wouldn't say it's sudden. I was leery when you showed up—with good cause. All I knew was you'd gotten Kendra pregnant and disappeared. But I'm not one who sticks to an opinion when I see reason to change it. You might be what Kendra and Far Hills need."

He raised his brows. "I suspect Kendra would tell you that the last thing she needs is an out-of-work pilot."

She cut him a sharp look. "Out of work, huh? You intend to tell Kendra that?"

Hell, he hadn't intended to tell *her.* "Eventually. I'd like to say I have leads on jobs at the same time."

"What kind of job are you after?"

"What kind…?" He curbed his amusement enough to give her a straight answer. "Flying. Need a crop duster?"

"No. You don't want to do that, anyhow. Too tame." She tapped a blunt fingernail against the soda can. "You know, Kendra wrote an article a while back about a grant for a new position—regional instructor and coordinator for search and rescue volunteers."

"Search and rescue." He turned that over. "Around here?"

"Of course around here. So, what do you think?"

He looked from her to the mountains beyond the town's buildings. "Yeah, I might like that. But—why would you do anything for me?"

She'd wasted no time pulling paper and a pencil from her purse, and began writing. "I told you—I think you might be good for Kendra."

"You said Kendra and Far Hills. Why would having me around be any good for your ranch?"

"I wondered if you'd picked up on that." She seemed pleased he had. "I think you can be the solution to the Susland curse."

"Me? What do I have to do with some old curse?"

"You haven't turned your back on your son."

"Why the hell would I?"

"Why would any man? But some men do. Charles Susland did. That's why Leaping Star said his blood would be alone. Like Kendra's been."

She blinked rapidly before turning to him again. "You not only haven't turned your back on your son, you're staying around for him. And you certainly didn't turn your back on those children on Santa Estella. Besides, I figure maybe you and Kendra are meant for each other."

A jolt hit his gut. "She'd tell you different."

"Oh, she has. You ever wonder *why* she's so busy telling me, you, Ellyn, herself and probably anybody else she comes up against that you and she are wrong for each other?"

"Maybe because of what you said before, about her being the fifth generation here. Her roots are sunk deep. I have no roots."

"Of course you do. Everyone does."

She tore off the top sheet of paper and handed it to him. "Sheriff Johnson will expect your call in the morning. And don't be thinking I didn't notice how you didn't let me tell you why I think Kendra's trying so hard to convince everyone you're wrong for her.'' Shaking her head, she stood. ''Good heavens, for two brave people, you're acting like a couple of chicken-hearted rabbits.''

Daniel remained on the bench, the paper in his hand. He gave some thought to how he might approach this job possibility.

But mostly he thought about Marti's final words. Never before had he been called a coward, much less a chicken-hearted rabbit.

What bothered him was he suspected she had a point.

Daniel's hand shook.

Making a telephone call and his hand shook.

He'd felt nothing like this yesterday when he'd called Sheriff Johnson. And when he'd gone in to see the sheriff yesterday afternoon to talk over the operation, he'd been totally at ease. Partly because he'd immediately liked the no-nonsense sheriff. Mostly because the stakes weren't as high as they were in today's phone call.

But he didn't let himself hesitate as he punched in the long distance number. He'd promised himself a few weeks back—under the sting of an observation by Kendra—that when he settled his life a little he'd make this call. Thanks to Marti's lead on this job, he'd crossed one big hurdle to settling his life. It was time to make good on that promise.

The phone rang twice before a familiar female voice answered, ''Hello?''

''Hello. It's—''

''Daniel! How good to hear your voice. Wait a moment and let me get your father. Robert! It's Daniel. Here, I'm putting you on the speaker phone.'' Faint background noise came over the line.

''Daniel,'' said Robert Delligatti Sr. ''Where are you, boy? If you can tell us, that is.''

''I can tell you—Far Hills, Wyoming.''

''Wyoming? How did you come to be there?''

"More important, Daniel, tell us how you are," inserted Annette Delligatti.

"I'm fine. And I'll tell you what brought me to Wyoming and what's going to be keeping me here, but first I've…uh, I've got things to tell you both. There's something… Something I should have said a long time ago. I…" He rubbed his throat. "I love you. I love you both."

For an instant there was silence. No words, no sound of movement from the other end of the line. Then came a faint, wavery "Oh." And he couldn't be sure who'd said it.

"I mean, I've always been grateful, and I've respected you—"

"Oh, Daniel, we love you, too." That was definitely Annette. "We never wanted to push you, to make you feel obligated…"

The words faded into a sob. Daniel sat down abruptly. He couldn't ever remember seeing her more than faintly teary-eyed.

"You've made your mother and me very happy, Daniel. You'll never know." Robert's hoarse words were followed by the sound of a decisive nose-blowing.

He might never know what it was like to take in a street urchin, feed him, clothe him, educate him, discipline him, worry about him and—yes, he saw it now—love him for twenty-five years without ever having love expressed, but at least now he could imagine some of the complexity of their feelings. Now that he had a son who didn't know he was his son.

"I hope my news will make you happy, too." He was glad he had no witnesses to this call, because he feared he was grinning idiotically. "You might want to sit down—you're grandparents."

Chapter Twelve

"I've been doing a lot of thinking, Kendra. About things you've said. About the Delli—about my family. About the future."

Her heart hammered. He was leaving. All along she'd known he would. The pain still caught her unprepared.

When he'd called at the paper this morning gruffly asking to come over when she had time to talk, she'd figured her reprieve had ended. She'd had no need to explain away what happened that day it rained, because he'd made no effort to see her. He'd been at the co-op—Matthew talked about him nonstop. But she didn't see him, didn't hear from him, didn't even hear *of* him from Marti, Ellyn or Fran. She missed him with a continuous ache.

That ache deepened and widened when she opened the back door to him at two, as arranged. Matthew was already invited to spend the afternoon at Marti's. Kendra had planned to catch up on work for the paper. When Daniel called, she'd given up that hope.

He wasted no time, starting while they were still in the hall.

"I've made changes I—"

"Don't you want to sit down, have some coffee or—"

"No. There's a lot to tell you."

Not yet. Don't leave me yet.

That was the instant she knew she couldn't let him leave without loving him once more. She needed to hold him against her, inside her again. She needed that or she'd never be able to let him go forever.

"I talked to my parents, Kendra. I told them about Matthew, and you. I… I'm working at letting them in. They…they were touched."

Tears welled up before she had any chance of stopping them.

"Oh, Daniel, I'm so glad." She put her arms around his neck and kissed him on the cheek, below the scar.

His arms came around her and held her in place when she would have backed away.

"Why the tears? You're supposed to be happy."

"I am happy." She smiled up at him.

The answering smile in his eyes heated immediately, taking on an intent that stirred her blood. When his mouth came down on hers, she parted her lips and took him inside. The thick softness of his hair covered her fingers as she felt the shape of his skull under her palm. His arms wrapped around her, locking their bodies together, while their mouths feasted and explored.

At last, he lifted his head, touched her lips again, as if to be certain they were real, then said, "I have more to tell you, Kendra. About my job—"

"You could tell me later."

His narrowed eyes asked one question. She trailed her lips along his jaw, answering his need and her own.

"Later. Tell me later, Daniel."

She stretched up to take his bottom lip lightly between

her teeth, then slid her tongue over his lip, into his mouth. His tongue met hers, enticed her deeper. Matched her rhythm. *Their* rhythm.

"Kendra…" He turned them both, so her back was against the hall wall, his elbows locked to keep them arm's length apart. "Are you certain?"

That was the question. An echo of the doubt she'd heard in his demand after the rainstorm. *Who am I, Kendra? Who am I?*

"I'm certain, Daniel."

Dark eyes bore into hers. Then he bent his elbows and pressed against her, his lips tender against hers, his body fierce and taut.

"I swore the next time we made love, it would be in a bed."

She recognized the arrogance of his certainty that there would be a next time, when she'd been so adamant there would not. And she didn't care. Not now. Not when she needed this last time to get her through the rest of forever.

She was certain, desperate even, yet that first step away from the wall, toward her bedroom, her knees nearly gave way. Without a word, he wrapped her tightly against his side. She slipped her arm around his waist, and held on. To him. To the moment.

Streams of sunlight from corner windows stretched wide over her bed. Atop the forest-green comforter sat a pile of clean, folded laundry not yet put away. She scooped up the pile of clothes and deposited them on the floor.

The motion brought her eye to eye with her tote, hanging by its straps from the arm of the corner chair. And that brought her face-to-face with the realities of what they were going to do—what they had done before—and its consequences.

Not allowing herself to hesitate but also not facing Daniel, she fished out the packet of condoms she had bought in Sheridan.

"I...I told myself we'd never use these, that I'd never let... But as a practical matter, to have them on hand..."

He took the box from her hand, dropping it on the table beside her bed, and kissed her. Kissed her hard and gentle, hot and sweet, demanding and giving. Each kiss between them seemed not like a separate caress, but a continuation of the ones before and an introduction to the ones to follow.

Standing beside her bed, he lifted the hem of her sweater and she pulled it up. Before she'd freed her head, she felt his lips at the bared hollow in her throat, then lower, to the swell of her breast. She threw the sweater aside as his mouth closed over her nipple through the smooth fabric of her bra. The strong, pulsing pressure of his mouth echoed to her womb.

"I want to see you, Kendra...I want to see you."

She told herself the urgency of Santa Estella shouldn't drive them this time, there should be time and patience for exploration and leisure. But she had no patience. She wanted nothing between his mouth and her skin. Nothing between her hands and his flesh.

She pulled at her own clothes, his clothes. Met his fingers at the same tasks. Hurried them, exulted in their mutual success with kisses, caresses and moans.

"We can make it slow this time," Daniel said. She knew it wasn't true, she didn't want it to be true.

Both of them naked, he carried her down to the bed, pushing aside the comforter, skimming his hands over her as she reached for him. He was hot, smooth, hard. She tasted the salty musk of his skin, the taste she'd craved, the touch she'd dreamed of for three years.

A groan echoed through Daniel, and into her. He maneuvered away from her touch.

"Not yet—Slow..." He kissed her belly, then lower.

"No." Her head rocked from side to side. "No, Daniel... Inside...together. Please."

He held utterly still for a second, then he raised his head.

"Kendra..." His breath was another torment of pleasure across her sensitized skin.

She twisted to reach the box on the bedside table, tumbling out the packets. Both of them, together, sheathed him. Her hands shaking, his hands covering hers, slowing the torture, lengthening the pleasure. Finished at last, she gulped in air, while she watched him drop his head back, eyes closed, breathing through his mouth. She touched him, lightly, on the chest, and his muscles quivered.

"I want you, Daniel. Inside."

His eyes opened and his head came forward. Never releasing her look, he moved over her, between her legs, as she opened to him. He touched her once, and she gasped, her hips rising up, trying to meet him. He positioned himself, and plunged inside her.

A sob broke from her.

"Kendra...?"

"No—no. It's good. Oh...Daniel." She wrapped herself around him, kissing his rock-hard arm as he tried to hold himself off her. She drew him down. "So good."

The power and rhythm built fast and strong. She felt the strain in his muscles as he tried to slow what would not be held back.

"It's been—"

"—so long." She arched to meet his next stroke, and there was no holding back. The storm was inside. So was the peace. But the storm held sway now. Violent, awesome, powerful, unpredictable, life-changing. Climbing, howling, moaning, shuddering, crying. Conquering.

And as the storm ebbed, she held on to the peace and to Daniel.

He eased some of his weight off her, but they stayed joined. Just as such mundane matters as time began to assert themselves once more, he withdrew, rolling to the edge of the bed. He snagged a towel from the pile she'd placed on the floor, dealt with the practicalities, then pulled on another condom. And before she could muster the energy or desire to move, he had returned to her.

It was not the powerful stroke of earlier, but a slow, sweet glide. "Slow this time, Kendra. Building from the start."

He propped himself up on an elbow, his head resting against his hand as he studied her. She should guard her reactions, decide what she could let him see. Instead, she reveled in the sharp angles of his face, the curve of his lips, the depth of his eyes.

"Kendra?"

"Hmm."

"This is later."

She slid her hand down his chest, instructing her nerves to remember—always remember—these textures, these planes and hollows, this sensation. "Later later's even better."

He caught her hand as it ventured lower. His chuckle came out a little raspy. "That package had only three condoms in it, and we've used them all. Next time—" he dropped a kiss on her nose "—don't sell us short. In the meantime, it's time to tell you—"

Unfamiliar panic swept over her. "I can wait—"

"I'm staying in Wyoming—in Far Hills."

"What? But your job…"

"I quit."

"Quit," she repeated, trying to make sense of this. She'd had this all thought out, she'd known how to react, what to expect. Now he'd dropped a bomb into her order. She sat up, holding the covers to her chin. "Why? When?"

He frowned but answered readily enough. "'Why' is because of what you said about how could I be a good father to Matthew if I wasn't going to be around."

"But I didn't mean—"

"For me to quit," he said, filling in impatiently. "I know you didn't. You meant for me to give up and leave. But I don't give up that easily, Kendra. Not on things that count. And Matthew counts.

"You were right, though. I couldn't be a father to Matthew—not the kind I want to be—with that job. So I quit. I went back because I owed my boss a face-to-face."

"You *went back*—you quit when you went east? But that was weeks ago. My God, we've talked about your job! Why didn't you tell me?"

"I wanted to tell you at the same time that I had a new job—at least that's what I told myself." His voice turned grim. "I wonder if something told me I'd get this kind of response."

"I don't know what kind of response you expect when you tell me you've quit your job on a whim—"

"It wasn't a whim. And I also told you I'm staying in Far Hills. So I might have hoped for a response along the lines of your being glad it won't have to be the last time for this."

Her gaze followed the sweep of his hand to indicate the rumpled covers, and their nakedness. Then she met his eyes.

His face stiffened.

"I see. This was *meant* to be the last time. Sorry to disappoint you, Kendra." He climbed out of bed, yanking on his jeans. "I'm staying. I got word on my new job before I called you. I wanted to surprise you. Guess I did."

An insidious thread of hope wove into her confusion.

"What kind of new job?"

"Search and rescue. I'll be training volunteers and coordinating the regional efforts, ground and air."

The thread of hope snapped.

"It's just the same. Rescuing people."

"Once in a while, maybe."

"Like Taumaturgio."

"It's nothing like that. And it's nothing like my old job flying for the government. I would have been gone more than I was around with that job. This will mean some emergency calls, sure, but it'll be mostly milk runs. Routine. Scanning for a few lost campers.''

"Flying.''

"That's what I do.''

"It's what my father did, too.''

A whisper of words came into her mind.

You'll come back, won't you...?

Yes, I'll come back.

When had she heard those words? Who—?

Daniel reached for her. "Kendra—''

"No.'' She scooted to the far side of the bed so he couldn't touch her. She didn't want his sympathy. "I told you, I don't want Matthew to have to go through having his father take off one day and never return.''

"You can't guarantee that won't happen, Kendra, no matter what you do. You said my job with the government was the barrier to putting my name on his birth certificate, Kendra. The job's gone. So's your excuse. I'm not going anywhere.''

"Sheriff Johnson? This is Kendra Jenner at the *Banner*.''

"Hey, there Kendra. How're you doing? This seems to be my week for talking to folks from Far Hills Ranch. Had a call from Marti a few days ago. She's a sharp one, your aunt.''

"Yes, she is. Sheriff, I heard you might have found someone to fill that post you told me about—regional trainer and coordinator for search and rescue volunteers.''

He whistled. "You hear things fast. Thought I'd get Lucy to do a news release all neat and official before I heard from you.''

"You're that far along in the process?''

"Don't want to let this one get away. Not often we'd get someone with these kinds of skills. Damned impressive.''

"Hmm.'' She stretched the note of speculation before

asking, "So you've checked his credentials? Verified his résumé?"

A faint creak reached her over the phone line, as if the sheriff had shifted in his old-fashioned wooden desk chair.

"Can't say we've done that—yet. 'Course, we're not as formal as some places. We can go with our gut reaction, and my gut says this fella's the real McCoy."

"Of course, Sheriff Johnson. Although, with this person training volunteers, I'm sure your department would want to be certain you weren't dealing with anyone who had something to hide."

"S'pose not."

"So, should I tell my editor we're likely to have that news release in time for tomorrow's deadline, Sheriff?"

"Better hold off, Kendra. Let me do some checking."

"Of course, Sheriff."

Kendra hung up, trying to ignore the roiling in her stomach. She'd had no choice. For Matthew's sake. For hers. Maybe even for Daniel's. Now she had to do something much, much harder.

"Daniel?"

He turned from the map-strewn desk set into the window alcove with no attempt to hide his surprise.

The white-haired man who'd introduced himself as Rufus Trent had told her Daniel was in his room, and to go on up. Her heart beat much harder than the climb up the stairs could explain.

Some of it was dread. Some if it was simply seeing Daniel.

"Kendra." A frown chased the surprise. "Is everything okay? Matthew—"

"He's fine. It's—we need to talk."

"Okay." He surveyed the spare room. Besides the desk and chair, there was a double bed with the head pushed against an end wall, a wardrobe, dresser and two bookcases under the slope of the roof.

He gestured for her to sit on the end of the quilt-covered bed. When she hesitated, he gave her a knowing look, then picked up the desk chair, set it squarely facing her and sat there. His patient silence gave her the floor.

"Yesterday... Well, it caught me by surprise."

"What did, Kendra?"

"All of it," she said a little impatiently. "What I was feeling, what happened—well, maybe not what happened." She'd sworn to herself she would be totally honest. "But certainly the news about that search and rescue job. And I didn't say some things I need to say. Some things I've thought through."

"I'm listening."

"It's like what you said when I said the storm put me in an altered state. That drugs were one way to get people to reveal a truth that would come out no other way." She glanced up and he nodded. "You're right. I wouldn't have expressed my feelings without that storm. But you do it, too. You use the danger. That's your drug."

"That's—"

"Just like a drug, Daniel." She spoke over him, not letting him deny it. "It brings out the truth for you. Because that's the only time you feel you've earned the right to have survived."

He bent forward, his hands dropped between his knees, forearms resting across his thighs. He'd sat this way that first day he'd been in her house. Then he'd been watching Matthew with great intensity. Now his eyes seemed to be trained on his own hands. He didn't lift his head when he spoke.

"Remember what you told me your professor said—about what you would want to be doing on the last day of your life?"

"Yes."

"Well, this is it for me, Kendra. Flying and helping people. That's what I want to do."

"It's more important to you to save strangers than…"

He raised his head, and she couldn't finish.

"You're who I want to spend all my days with—you and Matthew. But this is what I need to do. It's not a means to an end. It's who I am. I'm not saying you're wrong about why that is—I don't know. And I'm not saying it might not change—some of it already has. It used to be I only knew about raising hell. Flying changed that. Then Taumaturgio taught me about helping people."

He took her hand, opening the clenched fingers and stroking it. "I love you, Kendra." Her heart jolted at the words. "I think you love me. And part of me is the need to do this."

"I know." A strange feeling washed over her. A mixture of sadness, empathy, perhaps even a little shame. But it did not erode her determination. "That's why you'll be leaving here soon."

His hands stilled. "What have you done, Kendra?"

"I asked pointed questions about the new search and rescue trainer's credentials. They'll check, and they'll hit the same dead ends my sources did. They'll wonder what you're hiding."

"So you think you've killed my chance at this job."

"Yes, I do."

"And my chance of helping people."

"Yes."

"I won't give up."

"I know that." Her voice trembled. She took in a steadying breath. "But you'll take your risks somewhere else. Matthew won't have to watch you. I won't have to watch you."

"I'm not a daredevil, Kendra. My defiance has been of regulations and red tape, not of the laws of nature. I have a healthy respect for nature, and for the limits of machinery and man. I don't push myself or my equipment beyond what it can do.''

"I wish I could believe that. Or that believing would be enough.''

"Do you fear for Matthew?''

"Of course I do. But I didn't have a choice whether to love Matthew or not. With you I have a choice.''

"Do you, Kendra? I didn't. I had no choice at all. Not from those first hours during Aretha, when you were so damned determined to be brave. When you feared for someone else's life and fought so hard to ease his pain. I had no choice at all about loving you.''

He leaned forward until his knees enclosed hers, then he took her face between his hands. She gave no resistance as he drew her forward so their mouths met. The kiss was soft and sad. With no warning, it shifted to hard and hungry.

It ended only when they parted enough to gulp in air.

"Dammit, I had no choice.'' He shifted around to sit beside her on the bed, and put his arms around her. She went into the embrace, resting her cheek against his shoulder.

"I'm sorry, Daniel.'' Her tears slipped down without check. "I know you wanted this job. I'm sorry I took that away from you.''

He kissed her hair. "I know you are.''

"I'd do it again.''

"I know that, too.''

She met his eyes, let her fingers trace the scar on his cheek. "The worst of it is, I still want you.''

His dark eyes held a million colors, each holding a different emotion, but the light in them was what she needed to see.

"That's the best of it, Kendra.''

They made love. Kendra couldn't explain it, couldn't rationalize it, but she accepted that in the long, hot kisses, in the slide of his skin against hers, in the building sensations, there was a certainty, a clarity that she had known only in making love with this man. Their joined bodies, like cupped hands, enclosed a space, a moment, where they could love.

Afterward, she lay wrapped in the quilt from his bed, listening to him in the bathroom, knowing that beyond them the problems remained. But content for now to allow only what was between them to exist.

He came back into the room. Naked and so *right* that her throat and eyes burned just looking at him. At the edge of the bed he stopped and looked down at her, his body changing, reacting.

"Do you have to go soon?"

"I have to pick Matthew up at the co-op at four-thirty, but I need to get something from the market for dinner before that."

He glanced at the clock, then grinned. "Tell you what, while you pick up Matthew, I'll get the fixings for that steak dinner I owe you. That gives us time..."

His knee on the mattress shifted her toward him. Using the damp cloth he'd brought from the bathroom, he slowly stroked from her throat down the center of her body, pushing away the quilt, until he reached the juncture of her thighs. Leaving his hand there, he settled onto the mattress beside her, each of them on their side, facing each other, looking into each other's eyes. He tossed the cloth aside and ran his palm across her buttocks, then down the back of her thigh, drawing her top leg up, over his hip.

"Daniel..."

"I know." He twisted around to the nightstand behind him, grabbing another condom and putting it on without changing their positions, the brushing movements of his hands and body against her vulnerable core producing a nearly unbearable tension.

Finished, he paused an instant. An eternity. And both threatened her—her resolve, her need, her belief, her desire.

''This doesn't change things,'' she said, because she had to.

He kissed under her chin, arching her head back, as he entered her, and she climaxed with that long, deep stroke.

''It doesn't need to.''

And then he began again.

This time, he'd had no idea he was being tracked, not until he came out of the Far Hills Market with a loaded bag of groceries tucked against his side, and heard ''Hello, Daniel.''

Daniel knew the voice. But it couldn't be. Here?

He turned slowly. Robert Delligatti Jr. In his three-piece suit, white shirt, discreet tie, regulation briefcase, thinning hair and thick glasses. As much as his bland appearance blended in in Washington, it stood out against the jeans, boots and cowboy tans of Far Hills. But Robert Delligatti's mild expression revealed no indication of feeling out of place or uncomfortable.

''Hello, Robert. This is a surprise.'' He let the full measure of his bemusement come through in that understatement. Robert in Far Hills was more than a surprise, it damned near reversed the laws of nature. Then he frowned. ''Mother and Father…?''

''Are in excellent health. I'm here—shall we sit?'' Robert took a seat on the bench in front of the Far Hills Market as if he'd done it every day of his life. Daniel followed, still holding the grocery bag. ''I'm here on your behalf.''

''On my behalf?''

Robert put his briefcase across his knees, twirled the combination lock, then flipped up the lid.

''Yes, I thought you would like to have a copy of these.''

He held out crisp official papers folded neatly in thirds.

''What are they?''

''They are copies of your work record, which indicates your expertise at search and rescue missions, as well as your experience in a training and supervisory role, and, of course, an official log of your extensive pilot experience. These should make you an ideal candidate for the search and rescue operation, and should satisfy those who were inquiring about your credentials and were turned away without answers. In future, these records will be available to anyone who should inquire about your suitability for such jobs.''

"But—''

"Oh, don't worry. It doesn't list your true experience. But neither would it mislead a prospective employer. Comparable experience, I would call it,'' he finished judiciously.

Daniel looked at the papers in his hand. "Why, Robert?"

"I felt an obligation. After your fine work in Santa Estella, and the sacrifice involved, especially the last years of Taumaturgio's existence, it seemed the least I could do.''

"What did you have to do with Santa Estella and Taumaturgio?"

"My office reviews certain reports from the various embassies and consulates.''

"Yeah?'' Daniel slid the papers into his shirt pocket. They'd do the trick, all right—Robert did thorough work. "What kind of reports?''

"The reports my section reviews are those that someone along the line has felt required a particular kind of attention.''

"Such as?''

"Such as getting aid to the children of Santa Estella.''

"The section where you work decided on that?''

"Ah, well, actually it's the section I head. I received the promotion because my superiors appreciated my particular brand of creativity. They felt it gives me an ability to find the unorthodox solution to unorthodox situations. As on Santa Estella.''

"Well, I'll be damned.'' Daniel wasn't sure which surprised him more—that Robert had been the one behind the operation, or he was considered unorthodox.

"So you felt a professional obligation because I was an operative on one of your missions."

"I would classify it as a personal obligation."

"Why?" he demanded baldly.

"I became aware that your assignment on Santa Estella had had a great impact on you. Your connection with Ms. Jenner, of course, but also your feeling about continuing your association with the—" his eyelid flickered, almost as if he'd winked "—government."

"So? Why would you... Good Lord, *you* recommended me to be Taumaturgio? You!"

"Why wouldn't I? I know some might see our relationship as a conflict, but I have confidence in my ability to separate my filial loyalty from my professional assessment."

"Filial loyalty," Daniel repeated, torn between laughing at the typically Robertian phrasing and an odd sensation in his throat.

"And from a strictly professional standpoint, you were perfect. Your appearance, your language skills, your ability to think on your feet. The name Taumaturgio, of course, wasn't part of the original conception. But I did think that added an appropriate touch when it was brought to my attention."

"Thank you."

"You're welcome. Well, with that settled—" he put the briefcase on the bench and started to rise "—I will be on my way."

"Wait." When his brother obeyed the order, Daniel wasn't sure how to follow it up. "I, uh...do you have to leave right away?"

"No. The next flight to Denver doesn't leave until 9:00 p.m."

"In that case, why don't you come to dinner. I'm grilling steaks at Kendra's. You can meet her and Matthew—" Daniel stood and met his brother's eyes "—your nephew."

A smile spread across Robert's unremarkable features, slowly and completely. "I'd like that."

As they walked toward their cars, for the first time he could remember, Daniel clapped a hand to his brother's shoulder.

Chapter Thirteen

It was unlike any evening Daniel had known.

Kendra reacted to his bringing Robert as if he'd bagged the biggest trophy ever created. Oddly, he felt the same way.

Robert had insisted on stopping for a bottle of wine, and Daniel had felt like a bumpkin for not having thought of that himself. He might have felt more that way as Robert and Kendra debated with relish the fine points of a political race that took place while he was in Santa Estella, except at one point Kendra met his eyes and totally lost her train of thought. After that, Daniel was satisfied to sit back and listen.

Matthew had clung to his mother. He'd called Robert first Luke, then Daniel. By the end of the evening, he had mastered a version of Robert that a close listener could understand. And Robert turned out to be a very close listener.

Somehow Robert maneuvered it so Daniel put Matthew to bed right before it was time to leave to get Robert to his flight. As he returned to the kitchen, Daniel heard the tail end of Robert's words to Kendra.

"...all extremely grateful for your influence in settling Daniel. You have been extraordinarily efficacious in bringing out the best in him. I have never seen him so happy. And with this new employment, he has an opportunity to settle permanently."

"New employ—"

Daniel hurried around the corner. "Robert brought along papers that should satisfy any questions on my credentials for the search and rescue job." He met Kendra's gaze and saw the realization sink in. "Thanks again for doing that, Robert. I'll fax them to the sheriff first thing in the morning."

"I do believe that will settle all these unresolved matters in your favor, Daniel."

"I hope so." But from Kendra's expression, it was a thin hope.

That didn't diminish her farewell to Robert, but she would have backed away when Daniel reached for her—if he'd let her. He held her face between his palms for an intended brief kiss. Her immediate response lengthened it.

"I'll call you after I get Robert on the plane," he promised when he released her.

Even as she waved them off, she didn't meet his eyes, and his half-dozen calls that night reached only her answering machine.

"Daniel, I think someone's here to see you," Rufus said from the other side of the single-engine four-seater they were checking out the next morning.

He came around the nose of the plane, and saw Kendra getting out of her car. He'd tried her phone again between faxing the sheriff and later receiving word that all was in order and the job was his. Still only Kendra's machine answered.

They met inside the main gate.

"Kendra—" He reached for her, she stepped away.

"No, Daniel. Let me say this. I've been up since you and Robert left, and I've thought this through. You would walk into the teeth of a hurricane to help someone. You fly into hell to help people.

"Those are choices you make, Daniel. Choices between staying home safe with your family or flying off to the rescue of strangers. No—don't say anything. I respect you for your choices. Respect you more than I can say. But I'm not as noble as you are." A tear slipped free and her lips trembled, but her chin firmed and she kept speaking. "I want you safe and by my side. And when you're not...I can't let myself love you. I can't take that pain."

"Anything you wanted to know about me, I've told you. I've followed all your rules with Matthew. I quit my job. And now you're asking me to give up flying?"

"No. I'm not asking that. I couldn't do that to you. I know you can't give it up. I do know that now, Daniel."

"Then what are you...? *Matthew?*"

"No, I'm not saying to give up Matthew, either. I don't have that right to take that away—not from either of you. But the only way I can...if something happens to you, I have to know that I won't be so lost in grieving that I can't help him."

"And you think not loving me will do that?" The misery in her eyes was the only answer. "Kendra— Dammit." He rubbed his hand across his eyes, trying to erase an ache behind them. He stared away a moment before facing her. "I won't give up on what's between us."

"I...I'm sorry, Daniel." Her fingertips brushed his arm, then were quickly withdrawn. "Please try to understand."

She backed away a few steps, then turned and walked toward the parking lot. At her car, she looked back and saw him watching her. He thought he detected a moment of weakness in her resolve. Then she slid into the car and drove away.

Understand?

Hell no, he didn't understand. Nobody could who wasn't convinced he was going to crash every time he took a plane up.

But she'd come to her senses.

She had to.

Marti had browbeaten Kendra into coming up to the home ranch to watch old home movies of her youthful summers at Far Hills.

She hadn't been in the mood for company, not even after a week of being a virtual hermit, but Matthew had a fine time forming a chorus of "Who dat's" with Emily before they both drifted off to sleep. Meg and Ben, on the other hand, said little, but avidly watched the movies of their parents as youngsters—especially their father.

Ellyn had been totally silent until another reel started. "I don't remember seeing these before."

"You might not have. You remember them, don't you, Kendra?"

Yes, she remembered them. She remembered her mother watching them hour after hour, night after night. "Mother had copies."

"Not copies. These are your mother's."

"No. I threw those out when we cleaned out after mother died."

"You put them in the trash, I took them out."

A solidly built young man in immaculate uniform, with a crewcut the same color as her hair strode into the frame. He put an arm around her mother's waist and said something that made her grin. Then the two of them waved to someone still off camera. A girl in a frilly green dress ran into view and was scooped up in one motion by Ken Jenner. Her. Her father holding her the way Daniel often held Matthew, with the casual strength of power. And with the same almost fierce expression of adoration. He tightened his hold on his wife, and the three of them smiled into the camera.

Kendra's focus shifted from the dashing young man to that youthful, happy version of the mother she remembered.

I understand why you loved him.

She'd blamed her mother for falling in love with a man who didn't take the safe route. She'd blamed her mother for giving her a father who was the kind of man who didn't come back. Now she understood. And forgave.

Something Ellyn had said that day Daniel came drifted into her mind. About why she'd chased the Taumaturgio story.

To find a man who showed up against all odds—in an airplane, by the way—to help children in need of rescuing. Haven't you ever wondered about that?

She never had. Now she saw it. She'd been a child who'd needed rescuing from an unhappy reality, a rescue that could only be accomplished by a father who had gone off in an airplane and never returned. And chasing the story—some might say searching for her lost father—she'd found Daniel. Had she blamed him for being like her father? Or for not being her father? For not bringing him back?

She made hurried excuses to leave that neither Ellyn nor Marti questioned. Home once more, Kendra tucked Matthew into bed and went to the drawer where she kept important papers. She found the sheaf Daniel had given her weeks ago, and filled out the certificate to amend their son's birth certificate.

Daniel smoothed the paper and stared at it.

He hadn't believed first Ellyn, then Marti, when they'd told him about how Kendra had spent this week he'd left her alone. He'd meant for her to stew. Instead, they'd said, she'd spent it convincing herself that defining her relationship to him strictly as Matthew's father was the only *prac-tical* decision. Now he wasn't so sure.

What kept ringing in his head was Marti's question "What are you going to do about it?"

One minute she was answering a knock to find Daniel or her back doorstep with the sun barely up. The next, she was in a small airplane, belted in.

"I'll be right back," Daniel announced, then disappeared

It was her first real opportunity to think. Her first chance to consider her options, not just his orders.

He'd barged into her house, declaring, "The least you owe me is a chance to prove you're wrong."

"But—"

"No buts. Every but's covered. Ellyn's here to take care of Matthew. Your boss knows you won't be in. And here— put this on."

"What is this about, Daniel?"

"It's not time to talk about that yet. We have all day."

And he hadn't budged from that stance as he'd bullied her into putting on the jacket, then whisked her off to the airfield and into an airplane. But now that the power of his will was absent...

She had her hand on the seat-belt buckle when the door opened.

"Just checking if you're belted in safely," announced Rufus.

He pushed aside her hand from the buckle and tugged it snugly.

"That's good. Daniel's in checking the weather—up-dates, since he'd called the Flight Service Station before he picked you up. Wouldn't have gone up if there'd been any-thing. He's real careful."

"Rufus, I—"

"Here." He shoved a paper into her hand. "Thought you

could follow along on the preflight checklist. Daniel's a stickler. It's a pleasure to watch him.''

She stared at the list, some items recognizable, others more like a foreign language. Before she could react, Rufus closed the door and gave it a thunk, the way people patted a horse's rump.

Through the cockpit window she saw Daniel striding toward the plane, his movements controlled yet easy. A breeze riffled the dark waves of his hair. Determination showed in his jaw, anticipation in the up-slanting corners of his mouth. A man in his element.

He didn't enter the plane, though. Instead, his voice drifted through the open door on his side, the phrases unfamiliar, the tone businesslike.

Then, the voice seemed to shift timbre somehow, no longer Daniel's, but another's. A voice she hadn't known she remembered. Yet, this voice resided in her heart—or maybe her blood and bone and sinew—the same way Daniel's did.

Now, Daddy? Are we going to fly now?

Not yet, angel. Have to make sure everything's ready to go on this bird.

So we can fly?

That's right, so my angel can fly and then come back to earth safe and sound.

"Kendra?"

She started. She hadn't noticed Daniel get in the plane.

"You okay? You're pale."

Like she'd seen a ghost? Or heard one?

"I'm fine. Other than wondering why I've been kidnapped." The words should have cut, but she couldn't pull it off.

Her father... Was it a memory or a hallucination?

"It's not time to talk about that yet. I won't keep you up long, but you are going to try this."

He closed his door and concentrated on the instruments

before him. Absolutely matter-of-fact, he explained each move. His words—or maybe his voice—so absorbed her that she barely noticed until the plane lifted off the ground.

Panic jolted her back against the seat, hands clenched.

So my angel can fly and then come back to earth safe and sound.

Her eyes popped open. The voice had been so close....

A trailer of cloud drifted in front of them. Closer, closer—the propeller would shred it. But it didn't. The cloud flowed around them, uninhibited by form or space.

"When I took Marti up," Daniel began, "she said flying in a plane like this lets the hills look curvy. That's why I don't like jets. They flatten everything out. Make it look like a two-dimensional jigsaw puzzle, instead of some place people live and breathe and work."

"Daniel, I—"

"When you go up in a jet, you're detached from the earth. You're above the clouds. Where the skies are always blue. I like this kind of flying because I'm on top of the world, but still part of it. With birds as next-door neighbors."

Is this what the birds see, Daddy?

It's exactly what birds see.

She shut her eyes, not in panic, but to hear the voice better.

It's so blue! Like the ocean. Like we're on top of the waves.

A chuckle rumbled in her memory.

Exactly like being on top of the waves. That's one of the reasons I love it up here, angel.

Better than you love Mommy and me?

Not better, sweetheart. Different. I miss you and Mommy when I'm away from you. But flying's my job. And it's my duty to go when they tell me to.

You could get another job.

I suppose I could. But it wouldn't be a job I loved. You see, just like I miss you and Mommy when I'm away, I miss flying when I'm away from it. I hate leaving you and Mommy, but I love doing my job. I hope someday you'll understand, angel. That's why I brought you up today, so you could see what flying's like and so you'd think of me doing something I love while I'm away.

But you'll come back, won't you, Daddy?

Yes, I'll come back.

Only he hadn't.

And all these years she'd forgotten about the first time she'd gone flying. The only time her father had taken her flying.

Or *had* she forgotten?

Did it explain her aversion to small planes and tolerance of jets, even though her father had gone down in a jet? It made sense if her five-year-old self had connected that single small-plane trip with her father with his failure to return. At least she knew now that he *had* loved them, her and her mother. And he'd loved flying.

Just like Daniel, he'd taken every precaution to make what he loved safe. But he hadn't come back.

She opened her eyes to Daniel's profile, the straight, strong nose, the solid chin, the defined cheekbones. A swell of love as strong as any of Aretha's blasts swept through her, leaving her shaken.

"So, what do you think?"

"Daniel, I—"

"About flying—just flying. We won't stay up much longer. But it's not time to talk about the rest of it yet."

The rest of it was the big part. *The rest of it* was them.

"But there's one thing… Kendra, I admired your courage during the hurricane. But the courage you have every day in raising Matthew—raising him alone for so long." Their eyes met, and she saw his regret. "That's a special courage."

"Daniel—"

"Not yet. After I land, then we'll talk." He sounded grim.

"You can say all you want about how impractical it is to think we can be a family. But before you start, I want to say a couple things."

"Okay, Daniel."

Her calm agreement earned a sharp glance, but he was all business as he communicated with Rufus over the radio, then maneuvered the plane into a pattern around the runway that led into a descent to earth accomplished with barely a bump. Off the runway, he stopped and turned off the engine.

The silence roared around her head as he helped her from the plane.

"After all your questions, Kendra, it's my turn. And I want you to answer with the truth—not what you *think* is the truth, but what you *feel* is the truth."

With each beat, Kendra's heart lunged against her chest painfully. Her breath came short and sharp. "Okay."

"If you knew this was the last day of your life, if you knew you were walking into another hurricane tomorrow and this time you knew—you *knew* you weren't going to walk out—who would you want to be spending today with?"

The answer came—immediate, clear and simple.

Daniel and Matthew.

Her heart lunged again but it didn't hurt.

The two people she loved most if this were the last day of her life, or the most ordinary day of her life.

Daniel and Matthew.

Every day.

"Taking this long, you're thinking instead of—"

"With you and Matthew," she said. It felt like a shout in her throat, but it came out a whisper. "Oh, Daniel, with the two people I love more than life."

The dark depths of his eyes lit, but the rest of his face remained stern. "With Matthew and—"

"Daniel! Hey, Daniel!" Rufus's shout carried across to them.

Around Daniel's shoulder, Kendra saw Rufus standing outside the open door, with a telephone receiver in one hand and waving the other one imperiously.

"Damn it," Daniel muttered, then set his jaw and kept talking. "With Matthew *and* me. Including everything I am and…?"

"Daniel! Daniel!!"

"Maybe you should see what he wants."

Daniel ignored her suggestion as well as Rufus's shouts. "Even with the flying, and—"

"Daniel!"

"Dammit to hell, Rufus, in a minute!"

"Don't have a minute! It's an emergency!"

"It sounds urgent, Daniel."

"We're going to finish this," he vowed grimly.

"Yes. We'll finish it."

He frowned at her words, but she'd already started toward the building, and in another second Daniel followed her.

Rufus had retreated into the office and was talking into the phone when they walked in. Spotting Daniel, he gestured him closer.

"He just walked in, Sheriff. I'll put you on speaker phone."

"Daniel?"

"I'm here," he said, none too cheerfully.

"I know you're not on the payroll yet, but we've got a situation."

Daniel's posture didn't change, but Kendra sensed his shift from irritated to intense as he sat on the edge of the desk.

"Couple of hikers missing. Lady called and said her husband and son hadn't returned from a hike in the Bighorns as scheduled last night. She said they're experienced, didn't have equipment to stay out overnight and they're regular as clockwork about checking in."

"Any sign of their vehicle?"

"We're trying to spring somebody to check their PLS—place last seen—but our manpower's tied up with the fires, including our search and rescue volunteers. It'll take at least a couple hours to shift around enough resources for a ground search. Rufus says he's got a plane fueled, ready to go. If you can spot 'em, we can send the ground team right to them. That could be important time when daylight starts fading." The sheriff paused. "If you're willing."

Without taking his eyes off Kendra, Daniel said, "Give me a minute, Sheriff Johnson. Rufus, take us off speaker phone."

Rufus complied but made no secret of watching and listening as Daniel walked over to where she'd stopped inside the door.

"You heard. It's not my job yet, and I promised you the day. If you say not to go, I won't."

She knew what his going—now and always—might do to her. But she could see what not going would do to him. If she ever intended to test her fear against his courage, it might as well be now.

"Go."

A flame seemed to go on inside him. Not only for what he was going to do, but for her. He kissed her, hard and fast.

"It's routine, Kendra. When I land, we'll talk more. I want the rest of my answer."

"I'll be at the paper." Working would be better than going home and trying not to think, and far better than staying here and waiting.

Chapter Fourteen

"Got 'em," Daniel said in a satisfied mumble as he sighted two figures in a clearing after some two hours of searching.

Now he understood why they'd failed to return on time. One of the figures was stretched flat on the ground, with a leg wrapped in what appeared to be a makeshift splint.

Into the radio, he said, "Far Hills, this is Cessna One Four Six One. I have visual on the two hikers. Repeat, visual on two hikers. One appears to be injured, Far Hills."

He gave the location coordinates. The standing hiker had spotted the plane and waved to him. Daniel gently tipped first one wing then the other, to let the hikers know they'd been sighted.

Not bad for his first mission with Kendra's blessing. Well, *blessing* might be too strong. At least she hadn't given him an ultimatum. That was something to pin his hopes to. Along with the fact that she'd come to the conclusion he'd been banking on with that "last day" question—*You and Matthew.* If he could be sure—

"Cessna One Four Six One, good going" came Rufus's voice, distorted by the radio yet as capable of interrupting thoughts as his shouts had been of interrupting Daniel's crucial conversation with Kendra. "We'll get the ground crew headed that way."

But as he circled, Daniel saw trouble.

Big trouble.

The hikers were in a large area bare of trees but with low, dry brush scattered across it. That underbrush would turn to tinder when the fire hit. He wouldn't want to be down there trying to dodge burning bushes. Especially not with an injured leg. The whole area sloped gently upward until it fell off as a sheer rock wall on three sides. The fourth side—the route they'd come in—was forested. And between them and where any ground crew would have to come writhed a snake of fire.

"Far Hills, this is Cessna One Four Six One. Ground crew cannot reach their position. Unless you know another route." He described the setup.

The pause before Rufus answered confirmed Daniel's conclusion that there was no other route. "We'll have to wait for the Forest Service to get a chopper in there."

"How long, Far Hills?"

"A few hours, most likely."

Daniel took a closer look at the advancing fire, then checked his fuel gauge.

"Far Hills, I'm going in. After I land and pick them up, I won't have fuel to get to Sheridan or Casper. Arrange for another plane or helicopter to meet me at Far Hills to get the injured to a hospital."

"Negative," Rufus said. "Daniel, I know that patch. You might be able to land, but you can't take off. It's not big enough."

"I'll make it big enough. Listen, Rufus, one thing—let Kendra know I'll be late."

"Daniel, you've got to wait—"

"Negative. No time. I'm going in."

"Kendra, something's breaking." Larry Orrin, editor of the *Banner,* looked even more harried than usual.

She automatically stored the story she'd been working on and grabbed her notebook. "The fires? Are you sending a photographer?"

Larry took her arm. "I'm not sending you—not to report."

"Why? I've got plenty of time to finish the food-drive story."

"I know. It's—Rufus Trent called and asked me to tell you. It's Daniel Delligatti's plane. He landed to pick up some hikers trapped up top by the fire and they've lost radio contact."

Kendra knew she held her breath, but for an instant it felt as if she'd held her heartbeat, too. Then she turned quickly and grabbed her purse. "I'm going."

Rufus was talking into the radio, informing the pilot of the medical plane from Billings about ground conditions, when Kendra and Larry joined the crowd packed into the office.

"Have they heard from Delligatti?" Larry asked.

A gray-haired man Kendra thought she recognized as a part-time mechanic for Rufus slowly shook his head. "Not a word."

"Quiet," barked Rufus, fiddling with the radio.

Then came the sound his ears had already picked up. A crackling on the airwaves that seemed to be broken into short segments.

"Is that him?"

"That's him—it's got to be."

"Quiet!" Rufus roared. "Far Hills, requesting repeat on transmission. Repeat."

"Far Hills, this is Cessna One Four Six One. Do you read?"

Kendra dragged in air, along with the sound of Daniel's voice.

"Yes, Daniel, we read you. And we're damned glad to hear you."

"Feeling's mutual, Far Hills. Fire line must have interfered with the radio signal."

"What's your status?"

Kendra stared at Rufus's lined face as she concentrated on Daniel's voice—trying to read unspoken messages beyond their words.

"I have both hikers. One's injured. Compound fracture of the left leg. I can't tell about internal. I had to take off west and circle south because of the fire, so fuel's tight. Do you have medical transport at Far Hills?"

"Plane from Billings is in its landing pattern here right now."

"Good." Daniel's calm voice gave his location, some twenty minutes southwest of the airport.

"Roger. How'd the landing go up there, Daniel?"

"Not bad. The takeoff had rough spots, though."

Rufus frowned. "Is that going to affect your landing here?"

"It wouldn't hurt to have a fire truck. Gear might be messed up."

"Roger."

Rufus released the button that had allowed his words to go up to the airplane, and glanced at Kendra.

"Why is Daniel worried, Rufus?"

"Sounds like trouble with the retractable landing gear. Where he had to land up there... It's awful rough."

"We couldn't get a fire truck here in time—even if there

was any to spare. Everything but the bare essentials is fighting forest fires." Larry looked at Rufus. "You know that."

"So does Daniel. He's giving us a heads up."

Rufus barked orders to bystanders about finding fire extinguishers and where to position themselves. Kendra watched half a dozen men take off running toward the hangar and a nearby shed.

The landing gear had to drop down. It had to. Her prayers should reach up and wrap around the tires and yank them down. "Can't Daniel do something, Rufus?"

"There's a backup, but if the hydraulics are gone..."

"What then?"

"He lands on the belly of the plane. And tries like hell to keep the wings level.

"Why?" She had to know.

"That'll keep the plane balanced—less likely to spin or pinwheel. And—" Rufus studied her from under his brows, adding gruffly "—because if the tip of one wing or the other drags against the runway it'll spark, and even with him low on fuel it could start a fire—the kind of fire we'd have a damned hard time putting out."

"Can't you foam the runway?" Larry asked.

"Sure, if this were O'Hare or Kennedy. Not Far Hills. We can do a little. But it's mostly up to Daniel."

Kendra nodded her thanks for telling her the harsh truth, then dredged up a smile. "If anyone can do it, Daniel can."

A grin lit his sun-lined face. "Damn right. He's a hell of a pilot."

Rufus stepped outside to watch the medical plane from Billings land, and Kendra followed as if he were her lifeline to Daniel. The plane eased in, then rolled somewhat cumbersomely off the runway. The pilot and a medic hopped out and jogged over to Rufus, shaking hands.

"I heard your transmissions. I spotted him up top. He should be in sight any minute."

"Kendra!" Marti hurried from the parking area toward the knot of people.

"Marti, how did you—"

"Fran heard, she called me. What's happening?"

Larry and Rufus filled her in with a few brief phrases.

"But he was going to take you up today," Marti protested.

"He did. We'd landed when this call came in."

"And he went, anyway? Just left you here?"

"She told him to," Rufus said. "Not that the boy didn't want to go."

Marti turned to Kendra, perhaps waiting for her to refute that.

"Daniel said he wouldn't go if I asked him not to. I...I couldn't make the words come out, Marti. I couldn't have lived with myself if I'd told him not to go."

"Oh, honey." For a moment Kendra thought her aunt was going to take her into her arms. Then, as if the older woman saw how fragile her control was, she instead wrapped both hands around her upper arm. "This is going to work out. This is all going to work out."

"There he is!" shouted someone.

All among the growing crowd, hands went up to shield eyes as they peered at a dot coming from the southwest. To Kendra's eyes, the dot had barely resolved into an airplane when the medical plane pilot and Rufus Trent dropped their hands and exchanged a look.

The medical pilot said, "I'm going to get my machine started, and out of the way. If there's a fire—"

"Yeah, go on," Rufus interrupted in a quelling voice.

The pilot shot Kendra a look, then sprinted back to his plane.

Daniel's voice came from the radio inside. "Far Hills, this is Cessna One Four Six One."

Rufus reached the radio in three strides. "Go ahead, Daniel."

"Instruments indicate landing gear has not deployed. Do you require a flyover for visual confirmation, Far Hills?"

"No flyover needed. Visual confirmation, Daniel—gear has not—repeat *not* deployed."

"Understood, Far Hills."

"Daniel, there's a fairly flat pasture north of town—landing on grass could be softer—"

"Negative. The plane waiting to take this passenger to a hospital is here. Besides, the fuel won't stretch. I'm coming in."

"It's all yours, Daniel."

Oh, God, what if not even Daniel could pull this off?

An answer came that she hadn't known was inside her until Daniel had found it—then she would be forever grateful that she had spent this morning with him. Hours she would have forfeited if not for his stubbornness.

As if by silent order, the crowd edged closer to the open gate that led to the runway. She became aware of Marti holding her hand and Rufus at her other side, his big hand cupping her shoulder.

"Don't worry, Daniel'll bring 'em to earth safe and sound."

My angel can fly and then come back to earth safe and sound.

"About to land, Far Hills" came Daniel's voice over the radio, as calm as ever. "See you in a minute."

Please, Daddy, watch over Daniel.

And then, just before the radio transmission cut off came the bleat of a siren from inside the plane.

"Oh, my God…!"

"No. That's okay. It's the stall horn. He cut the engine on purpose, so when it hits it's not as likely to explode."

Explode.

Silence again. All breath held. All the world suspended. The propeller still circling, but slowing slightly, changing the texture of the blur made by its passing blades. The plane carrying Daniel and two people she'd never met seemed to float, as if it rode on a cushion of air. As if her prayers and hope alone could hold it up.

And then it dropped those final inches, squealing metal against groaning tarmac.

The back connected first. Screeching, howling, ripping metal.

The left wing dipped, then leveled. The plane skidded slightly sideways, all the while protesting the harsh brake of friction. The propeller broke its teeth trying to bite into the solid surface.

It seemed the sound would go on forever.

And then it stopped.

For a second no one moved, echoes of metal screams crashing in their ears, while their eyes tried to absorb the stillness of the crumpled tube before them.

"Hot damn! Let's go!" shouted the medic. He sprinted to the medical plane, already taxiing closer, while Rufus and the others closed in on the maimed plane that held Daniel.

Kendra was aware of all the action around her and its purpose, was even aware of what the voices said—Marti announcing she had phone calls to make, some assuring her everything was okay, others extolling Daniel's bravery and his flying skill.

She remained rooted to the same spot, just outside the gate.

Never taking her eyes off the plane.

Watching as the workers on the ground yanked open the stuck door under the plane's high wing. Watching as they awkwardly scrambled to unload the injured hiker from the angled fuselage and started the gurney toward the awaiting plane.

The second hiker emerged, a teenage version of the injured man. Father and son looked as much alike as Daniel and Matthew did. The boy started after the gurney, then reached back into the plane, shaking hands with the man still inside, the man who had rescued him and his father.

The boy jogged across the pavement to catch up with the gurney, coming alongside it a few yards beyond where Kendra stood, and clasping his father's hand.

Kendra felt an amazing connection herself in that instant—to a woman she'd never met and probably never would. The mother and wife of these two strangers Daniel had rescued.

The woman who could have lost so much if it hadn't been for Daniel Delligatti.

As if it were her own emotion, Kendra felt the unknown woman's never-ending flow of gratitude that there had been a man like Daniel to rescue the man and boy she loved.

I couldn't have lived with myself if I'd told him not to go.

And maybe she couldn't have loved Daniel Delligatti as much as she did if he hadn't been the kind of man who wanted to go.

A man like Daniel…

A man who was so much more than the sum of the parts he'd played. A man who wasn't yet convinced of that himself. But she was.

She had been from those first hours sheltering from Hurricane Aretha.

She had loved him in those hours—*him*, the person beyond the names or the history. Not with the depth and complexity she now felt, but with a clarity and simplicity she no longer denied.

Daniel appeared, framed in the elevated doorway.

He jumped lightly down. A familiar slash of white split his face as he grinned at Rufus and shook the older man's hand.

She had a sudden, clear memory of Daniel's hand on the piano the day he'd come back to Far Hills. Fingers positioned to play a chord, instead hitting the keys one by one.

That's what she'd been doing to him—looking at each

part of him individually, when they really formed a chord. If any note was missing, it would not be the same sweet sound—and he would not be the same man.

The others crowded around Daniel, and she could see him dampening their hyperbole. He and Rufus walked side by side around the plane, with their admiring entourage following. Daniel looked as if nothing had happened, as if nothing had changed.

Until he spotted her.

Daniel never took his eyes off her as, first, Rufus said something to him, then as he started toward her. She never took her eyes off him as he stopped half a foot away, not touching her.

"I heard you said that if anyone could land that plane safely, I could."

"I did."

He waited, but she said no more. She couldn't. There were too many emotions to try to fit into words that couldn't hold them.

"But that's not enough? Dammit, Kendra!" He rubbed his hand across his eyes, then reached across the space between them to grasp her upper arms. "Listen, I was wrong, charging in here demanding you marry me, thinking that would make a family. You've taught me. About family. About loving day to day, and letting other people love me. But *you're* wrong now.

"What happens if I give up trying to change your mind. And then I keep coming back every day. Like I've always done. Like Rufus. Like Joe, who taught me to fly—he kept coming back through a war and more bad flying conditions than I'd see in two lifetimes, right up until he died in his sleep at ninety-two.

"Would you deny us all—you, me and Matthew—a life together on the *chance* something bad might happen? That's crazy."

She'd been wrong about a lot of things, including thinking she'd ever had a choice about loving him. Loving him was too deep in her, embedded in her soul by hurricane winds, then cultivated with the clumsy caresses of an uncertain father, the painful integrity of an honest man and the determination of an unrelenting lover.

"I have a question for you, Daniel."

He eyed her with wary intensity. "Yeah?"

"You said this was routine. Did you mean that? All your search and rescue missions are going to be like this?"

One side of his mouth lifted a fraction. "No, I wouldn't call this routine."

"Good. Because even though I want to be with you when it's the last day of my life—or the last day of your life—I truly don't think I could take watching my husband do this on a regular basis."

"Your husband."

"Yes. If that's all right with you."

"I'm not going to ask you if you are sure." His voice was low and rough with warning. He'd hold her to this. Give no quarter. Allow no backing out.

"I'm sure."

He looked into her eyes for a long moment, then kissed her until they both had to gasp for air.

"There you go, Kendra."

Wrapping one arm around her shoulders, he started toward the door that led to the stairs to his room, and his bed. And then he let her know exactly how all right it was.

Epilogue

"Tell us the story, Marti."

The drought was long over. Snow had broken the dry season, finally blanketing the fires on the mountainside. Here on the overlook, the snow was fine enough to be stirred by the horses' hooves, as the people of Far Hills Ranch gazed down on their home.

Two days ago, Marti had announced her resolve to go up to the overlook on the November day her research had shown Leaping Star died. Luke had been just as adamant that she wasn't going alone. If only in the name of research, Ellyn and Kendra wanted to visit the spot. Daniel expressed an interest, too. After that, Meg and Ben Sinclair insisted on coming. With a warm day, gentle pace and layers of protective clothing, Matthew and Emily had been allowed to complete the group.

Now even the little ones seemed to feel a sense of solemnity.

Marti silently laid a spray of dried flowers in a protected area between two rocks, then stepped back to the group.

That's when Kendra urged her to tell the Susland legend.

"It happened right here, in 1878. The campfire burned for four days and four nights…"

As the familiar words flowed from her aunt, Kendra felt Daniel's arm tighten around her waist, and she leaned into him. His other arm balanced Matthew, perched on his jacketed shoulders.

He'd been right from the start. They *had* known each other during those days in the hurricane. Known each other in a way neither had been known before. Stripped of the identities that had been her protection and his burden. Those days sheltering from the hurricane had been like the pencil sketch of their love. Now they were beginning the oil painting.

They were going to spend the week after next in Florida with the Delligattis—Daniel's family, Matthew's grandparents and her soon-to-be in-laws.

The wedding was set for January, at the Far Hills home ranch, because she couldn't imagine being married anywhere else.

Marti's voice lightened, and she smiled faintly at Daniel, Kendra and Matthew. "'You turn away from your children, so your blood will be alone.'"

Kendra wasn't alone anymore.

She knew Marti thought it had something to do with Daniel's refusal to turn away from his child, releasing part of Leaping Star's curse by righting Charles Susland's old wrong. But Kendra knew it was because he'd never given up on her. Now she would never give up on making him see how much she loved him.

She smiled to herself, remembering his expression the first time Matthew called him *Daddy*.

The silence when Marti finished the tale didn't last long.

"Wow, five generations, so time's running out or the

ranch will be cursed *forever,*" said Ben Sinclair with ghoulish delight.

"You missed the point." His sister's disgust was complete. "It has to be true love."

"You're both right." Ellyn put an arm around each set of shoulders. "'Only when someone loves enough to undo your wrongs will the laughter of children live beyond its echo in Far Hills.'"

"The laughter of children sounds pretty good," Daniel said, close to Kendra's ear. "How long after the wedding until we start working on giving Matthew a little brother or sister?"

His tongue flicked against her earlobe. She stretched up to kiss him, parting her lips, and his tongue slid in, then out as a tempting promise of more.

"Who says we have to wait until after the wedding?"

The fire in his eyes was an immediate and unmistakable answer. Without another word, they started toward their horses, as Daniel hoisted Matthew down from his shoulders.

"You two leaving?" Luke asked.

"We thought we'd get a head start," Kendra said. "We've, uh, got a project we want to work on back at the house."

From the adults' smiles, they knew exactly how she and Daniel intended to contribute to the laughter of children at Far Hills.

* * * * *

Watch for Ellyn Sinclair's story in

AT THE HEART'S COMMAND

the second book in Patricia McLinn's
exciting miniseries

A PLACE CALLED HOME

On sale in September from
Silhouette Special Edition.

And now for a sneak preview of
AT THE HEART'S COMMAND,
please turn the page.

Chapter One

"What the hell is this, Grif?"

Colonel John Griffin Junior looked up just in time to see the bearlike figure of Brigadier General William Pulaski slap a sheaf of papers on the desk of his Pentagon office.

"That appears to be my request to take my accumulated leave, starting as soon as possible, sir."

"You're damned right that's what it is! What I want to know is *why?* Why in Sam Hill would an officer who's pegged to join the White House liaison team next month up and request this leave?"

A rumbling bass would have fit Pulaski's build. Instead, nature had doled out a high, light voice. He made up for the lack of lower notes with volume.

"And not just a regular leave—an *extended* leave, since we both know you've been storing up time like a squirrel expectin' winter!"

Grif could try to tell the general his reasons, but he hadn't reached the rank of colonel by being suicidal.

"I have the time, sir," he said without emotion. "I'd like to take it now."

General Pulaski gave him a long look that Grif returned. The older man broke the stare, sighed, then dragged the visitor's chair close, so the desk seemed as much his as Grif's, and spoke in—for him—a softer voice.

"As long as I've known you, Grif, you've taken tough assignments, but *smart* tough assignments. Always advancing. No ties, no entanglements. Just like your father."

Grif's hold tightened on the pen he'd been using to sign letters. He said nothing.

"You have a promising future—hell, more than promising." The general rubbed both hands across his bald skull. "But with this leave... What about after you've used up this time? White House liaison isn't going to stay open waiting for you, you know."

Grif met the dark eyes boring into him. "Then I'll take the next tough assignment available."

"If time to think this over might make you change your mind..."

"I'm not going to change my mind, sir."

Grif accepted that this might not be the right decision—certainly it wasn't for his army career, but it also might not be right for reasons that had nothing to do with the army—but he was sticking to it.

Pulaski glared. "Take your damned leave, then. I hope there's plenty of wine, women and song every damned night, because you might as well have a good time before you put your career in the—"

"Thank you, sir."

The general abruptly rose and strode out, followed by a fading trail of profanities.

Grif wondered idly how many degrees hotter those profanities would have turned if the general had known that instead of wine, women and song, there would be an eight-

year-old boy, a ten-year-old girl and one woman named Ellyn Sinclair.

None of whom could ever be his.

Ellyn Sinclair straightened the final pillowcase, took a
clothespin out of her mouth, clipped it over fabric and line,
then bent for the emptied basket. The Wyoming breeze
would dry this laundry fast and for free. And up here behind
Ridge House the breeze didn't stir dust; that made the climb
worthwhile. She scanned the sheets flapping peacefully.

Even if her dryer fund wasn't needed to fix the car, she
wouldn't have used a dryer on such a perfect day, an oasis
of warmth in Wyoming's unpredictable April. Although it
would be nice to have the option. Of course it would be
nice to have a number of other things, too.

Ellyn raised her free hand and let the breeze float clean,
crisp cloth against her palm. That was one worry she didn't
have—

MONTANA MAVERICKS

WED IN WHITEHORN
The legend lives on...as bold as before!

MM

Coming in September...

THE MARRIAGE BARGAIN
by
VICTORIA PADE

Corporate raider Adam Benson vowed to bring
down the man he blamed for his family's ruin.
And what better way to start than by marrying
his enemy's daughter? But he hadn't planned
on falling for his own prisoner....

MONTANA MAVERICKS:
WED IN WHITEHORN continues with
BIG SKY LAWMAN by **Marilyn Pappano**,
available in October from Silhouette Books.

Available at your favorite retail outlet.

Silhouette®
Where love comes alive™

Visit Silhouette at www.eHarlequin.com   PSMM4

USA Today Bestselling Author

SHARON SALA

has won readers' hearts with thrilling tales
of romantic suspense. Now Silhouette Books
is proud to present five passionate stories from
this beloved author.

Available in August 2000:
ALWAYS A LADY
A beauty queen whose dreams have been dashed in a
tragic twist of fate seeks shelter for her wounded spirit
in the arms of a rough-edged cowboy....

Available in September 2000:
GENTLE PERSUASION
A brooding detective risks everything to protect the
woman he once let walk away from him....

Available in October 2000:
SARA'S ANGEL
A woman on the run searches desperately for a reclusive
Native American secret agent—the only man who can save
her from the danger that stalks her!

Available in November 2000:
HONOR'S PROMISE
A struggling waitress discovers she is really a rich heiress—
and must enter a powerful new world of wealth and
privilege on the arm of a handsome stranger....

Available in December 2000:
KING'S RANSOM
A lone woman returns home to the ranch where she was
raised, and discovers danger—as well as the man she once
loved with all her heart....

PSSALA

**Don't miss
an exciting opportunity
to save on the purchase of
Harlequin and Silhouette books!**

Buy any two Harlequin or
Silhouette books and save
$10.00 off future Harlequin
and Silhouette purchases

OR

buy any three
Harlequin or Silhouette books
and save **$20.00 off** future
Harlequin and Silhouette purchases.

**Watch for details
coming in October 2000!**

PHQ400

Silhouette®

SPECIAL EDITION™

COMING NEXT MONTH

#1345 THE M.D. SHE *HAD* TO MARRY—Christine Rimmer
Conveniently Yours

Lacey Bravo wasn't marrying a man just because she was in the family way.... She was holding out for true love. And that meant Dr. Logan Severance had to do more than propose. He had to prove he was offering the real thing—his heart!

#1346 FATHER MOST WANTED—Marie Ferrarella

Being in the witness protection program meant not letting anyone get too close. And that had been fine with Tyler Breckinridge—until his three little girls led him to Brooke Carmichael, a woman whose sweet temptations were breaking down his barriers and driving him to distraction....

#1347 GRAY WOLF'S WOMAN—Peggy Webb

Lucas Gray Wolf wasn't about to let Mandy Belinda walk out of his life. For she was carrying something that belonged to him—*his twins*. But the red-hot passion this handsome loner felt for Mandy made him want to claim more than his babies. He wanted to claim his woman!

#1348 FOR HIS LITTLE GIRL—Lucy Gordon

An unexpected turn of events had the beleaguered Pippa Davis returning to Luke Danton—the man she'd loved but left behind. He was the only one she'd trust to raise their daughter. Was his undeniable connection to this beloved woman and child enough to turn a bachelor into a devoted daddy?

#1349 A CHILD ON THE WAY—Janis Reams Hudson
Wilders of Wyatt County

Who was the delicate and pregnant beauty Jack Wilder rescued from the blizzard? Lisa Hampton was a mystery to him—a mystery he desperately wanted to solve. But would helping her recover the past mean sacrificing his hope for their future?

#1350 AT THE HEART'S COMMAND—Patricia McLinn
A Place Called Home

With one sudden—*steamy*—kiss, Colonel John Griffin's pent-up desire for Ellyn Sinclair came flooding back. His steely self-restraint melted away whenever he was in Ellyn's irresistible presence. But could a life-hardened Grif obey his heart's command?